Just a Poor Country Girl

Just a Poor Country Girl
Based on the life of Charley Louise Dorsey, written by Rose L.
Hammond

1.   Just a Poor Country Girl - Interviews
2.   Just a Poor Country Girl - Portaits
3.   Just a Poor Country Girl - Menus

Non-fiction publication

ISBN 978-0-615-75834-3

Book cover design: Rose L. Hammond

The author gratefully acknowledge permission from Charley Louise
Dorsey (Hammond) for use of photos.

For information contact: Run With It, P.O. Box 1419, Grand Rapids,
MI 49501-1419. rdarlene22@hotmail.com

Just a Poor Country Girl

Based on the life of Charley Louise Dorsey

Acknowledgements

In preparing for this book "Just a Poor Country Girl" the author had a chance to interview Charley Louise Dorsey, the family's matriarch, before she passed away on April 22, 2006. The two had been working on this book on and off since 1992, and was unable to complete the publishing. Charley Louise Dorsey, who married Melvin Hammond, told the author, "Life tells us that we are a product of someone, and I am a product of the Dorsey family. I would like to have my history written."

Rose, the author, acknowledges a special appreciation to the children of Charley Louise Dorsey (Hammond), aunts, uncles, cousins, nephews, nieces and the Melvin Hammond family.

The author acknowledges the Michigan State University Archives and Historical Collections for research on locating the "Hospital Food Service Supervisors course that was offered jointly by the College of Home Economics and Continuing Education Service beginning in the mid 1950s at Michigan State University and one of the brochures marketing the course. As well the 1968 class graduation photo.

The author acknowledges the Fremont Area District Library for research on the July 4, 1963 Fremont Times-Indicator Newspaper photo of Charley Louise Dorsey (Hammond) and Governor Romney inside the dedication of the Medical Care Facility in Fremont, Michigan.

Introduction

"My feet are worn and tired from the years of walking back and forth on the concrete floor. I slide through my house from room to room, grunting and moaning from the pain. I am no longer able to make the numerous trips to the various food warehouses at 5:00 a.m., lifting the heavy boxes of food and preparing the many meals throughout the day.

My hands don't have the same strength they used to decorating the thousands of cakes and cooking the hundreds of catering meals over the years.

I'm starting to realize it's time to let the catering business go. What will I do with the rest of my life? What will fill the day's void when all I have known to do all of my life is work? I had come to the realization that I'm part of the senior citizen generation. I'm just a poor country girl."

Charley Louise Dorsey

Chapter One

Sloppy joe, bun, potato chips w/dip,
relish tray w/dip, dessert … $4.25

First thing in the morning, Mama would get up and open the drawer where she kept her aprons. The loud sound of what was called "popping the aprons" was heard and the day started.

####

Rose Dorsey was my mama and a housewife. She stood 5'10", heavyset with a round face.

When one walked past the Dorsey house, it always smelled like a restaurant—a soul food restaurant.

In the morning for breakfast we usually had eggs, bacon, homemade pancakes, and milk, all fresh from the market. Lunch was a sandwich with juice.

But, dinner "wow".

The dinner preparation started in the morning, right after the breakfast table was cleared and the dishes washed.

I'd watch Mama's fingers knead the dough for the bread like she was playing a piano in the orchestra.

She'd shape and knead, shape and knead until the dough was round and smooth. Then she'd cover the uncooked dough with white cloth.

It was mysterious to me how the dough rose into a bread form. I'd sit at the kitchen table waiting for each loaf to rise.

Most of the time, I'd fall asleep, feeling defeated when I woke up only to catch one loaf forming in this round, smooth shape and ready to go into the oven.

The meal would be completed with fried chicken, collard greens, potato salad, corn on the cob and Kool-Aid. My favorite was grape Kool-Aid. Dinner would be topped off with Mama's infamous sweet potato pie with homemade vanilla ice cream.

I helped in the kitchen as much as I could. In the morning I'd go to my own apron drawer, pick out an apron, and perform the "popping of the aprons."

I held the apron with both hands and flung it up in the air until I heard the sound of a "pop," and that banana boat smile came across my face. I wasn't as good as Mama with the popping, but I wrapped the apron around my tiny waist, double-tying the strings, and headed to the kitchen.

In the kitchen, inside the bottom cupboard drawer was my personal cooking set that Mama had given me for Christmas.

With my imaginary food, I'd copy Mama's every step and followed her cooking direction. If she stirred, I stirred. If she poured something into a pan, I acted like I was pouring something into my pan.

"How does this look?" I asked.

"From that flour-covered face, seems like it helped you more than you helped it," Mama said.

My favorite part of baking, besides eating the cake, was licking leftover cake batter from the beaters.

After licking the beaters, I'd say, "See, you don't have to wash them."

"I see, young lady," she said with a smile.

There was always enough for my belly's enjoyment, but like a recording, each time after Mama baked, I'd remind her by saying, "Now don't forget."

"I know, Charley Louise. Can you lick the beaters?"

####

On March 1, 1927 in Natchez, Mississippi, a baby girl was born. Me. They named me Charley Louise Dorsey. I was an only child. Having no sisters or brothers to talk to or play with, I created imaginary friends.

When I told them my name, they were just as surprised as I was. I said, "Yep, you got it right. C-H-A-R-L-E-Y, named after Daddy and Aunt Louise."

Charley Dorsey was a petite man. He stood 5'8", skinny with a gentle appearance to his face. He worked for the railroad and provided the only money coming into the house. Our family relied on Daddy to take care of us, and he did.

There were times he'd go off to work early in the morning and come back late at night. And there were times that he'd stay on the train for a few days at a time.

When he walked through the door after coming home from work, I ran and jumped into his arms before he could put down his lunch pail, yelling, "Daddy! Daddy! How was your day? Were there many people on the train? Can we play?"

Mama would tell me, "Let your Daddy get inside the door and rest for a while before you jump all over him." Mama wasn't the playing type. She was more serious and took care of the house.

Daddy and I had many games, but we loved surprising one another. That was our favorite.

I'd catch him or he'd catch me.

"Let's take a break for a minute for me to catch my breath," he'd say.

He'd give me piggyback rides or I'd sit on his foot and wrap my arms around his leg. He walked me around the house for a few minutes and we'd have our private conversations. This became a daily ritual.

When we played, it seemed like heaven.

Most days when Daddy headed for the door to go to work, I'd hurry up and hop onto his foot. He'd stiff-legged walk me around the living room. I'd hop off his foot just before he got to the door to leave.

"I'm leaving for work now," he'd yell to Mama.

Right before the door closed behind him, he turned around, quickly peeping his head around the corner and there was always that banana boat smile.

"See you later, alligator," he said.

"After while, crocodile," I said.

####

Except for Grandpa, Grandma and Aunt Louise, Unk lived a few doors down from Mama in what was called the Colony. Daddy had found a new plat of land on the other side of Natchez and away from Mama's family. Mama wasn't happy about this, but decided to move. Unk moved because the family felt that Mama shouldn't be left alone. Aunt Louise stayed with Grandma and Grandpa.

There were small homemade stores in the Colony, but for the most part our family had to go into town to buy our food and household items.

One day I asked Mama why we lived so far away from town. That's when she told me colored people weren't allowed to live in town. To avoid any problems, coloreds started buying land in the surrounding rural areas and built communities called colonies. She said, "Living next to each other provided a sense of pride and protection."

I was confused and not quite sure what Mama was talking about until later that day. A day I'll never forget.

It was an early Saturday afternoon because that's when my family would go shopping in town. Usually when the family went to shop I was left with Grandpa and Grandma or Unk and Aunt Louise, but this time they took me with them.

I sat in the back seat and rolled the window down so that I could feel whatever air I could. But, as we got closer to town, Mama told me to roll my window up.

"It's hot outside. Why can't I keep it down?" Just before I started to roll the window up, I saw people staring. It was like their eyes were going right through me.

"Roll up that window," Mama yelled.

"Yes ma'am," I said.

Our family parked away from the stores and walked the rest of the way.

When we got to the first store, I looked up and saw signs that said, "Whites Only" and "Coloreds Only."

I was already holding Mama's hand, and when my eyes saw the signs and stares, I squeezed her hand tighter.

Mama whispered, "Don't be scared. Just stay close to us and don't run off no matter who or what you see."

I whispered, "Okay."

The store owners took our money but never smiled or said, "Thank you ma'am" or "Thank you, sir." At every store our family went to, we'd get in and out making little, if any, eye contact.

As we walked through the town, it seemed like the "white only" and "coloreds only" signs were everywhere.

When we walked out of the store, I noticed two things. One was my white friend, and on the other side of the street a colored man being bothered by white men.

"Honey, isn't that Mr. ..."

"Wait right here," Daddy said.

Daddy started walking over to help, but as he got closer, one of the men said, "If you don't want the same, I suggest that you walk away and take your family with you, Charley."

I hid behind Mama, hugging her waist, and peeked around her body to look at Daddy.

He looked back at Mama and me. Then he looked up toward the white men and said, "He ain't causing any harm. Why don't you let him go his way, sir?"

One of the men walked closer to Daddy and whispered something to him. Daddy turned around and walked toward us. Mama asked what happened, but he kept walking, telling us to get into the car.

Mama kept telling Daddy to do something. That's when my soft-spoken Daddy with the banana boat smile yelled, "Do like I said and get in the car."

I looked up at Daddy, startled. I had never heard him yell like that before.

"Let's go."

Daddy opened the car door, but not before looking back to see what was happening. I sat in the backseat and saw Daddy looking in the rearview mirror, watching to see what they were going to do as we drove off.

I turned around to look out the back window and saw the white men shoving the man around before letting him go.

When I turned around, Daddy's eyes and mine seemed to catch each other at the same time in the rearview mirror, and there was that banana boat smile, but this time it seemed expressionless.

Once again, we had one of our private conversations. This would be a day I'd never forget.

After that experience, living in the Colony and family meant more to me because in the Colony, families helped each other.

We grew our own crops, shared pots and pans, learned how to fix our own things, shared home remedies, and fellowshipped together.

####

I was waking up when I heard footsteps coming up the stairs. I leapt out of bed, slid into my slippers, reached out to grab my robe at the end of my bed, and tied it around my waist. That's when the doorknob turned. I opened the door and said, "Good morning."

She moved back from the door, startled, her eyes wide and said, "Why Charley Louise."

"Yes, ma'am," I answered.

"You're up and getting ready for school on your own?"

"Yes, ma'am."

"What's the hurry?"

"I'm excited."

This was no ordinary day. This was the last day of school.

After I cleaned up and got dressed for school, I quickly ate my breakfast and grabbed my raggedy, knotted up jump rope. I don't think that I could had run out the door any faster to meet my friends.

We had been walking to school the whole year, but that day we were all on time and didn't have to wait for anyone. Usually, my friends stood outside of my door yelling, "Charley Louise," extending each letter of my name.

Mama would open the door and calm the girls down, saying, "Do you have to yell every morning? She'll be right out."

This time, I ran past mama for the door and said, "See you later, Mama."

We all giggled because it was a half day of school and the last day of school. Summer vacation was about to start.

When the school bell rang, I never saw kids run so fast. Even the slow ones ran fast and made a mad dash out the school doors toward home.

My friends and I caught our breath by walking slow. There was no need to hurry because no one had homework to do.

Like normal, I came home, threw my school bags on the chair next to the door, and called for Mama. This time, there was no answer.

I was about to call out her name again when I heard her and Aunt Louise's voices on the back porch. I leaned closer to the screen door and the floor made a crackling sound.

Before I could move again, Mama looked through the screen door and said, "When did you get home?"

I said, "Right now?"

Mama and Aunt Louise looked at each other. I didn't know if the look was because they thought I was lying or because they were wondering how long I'd been at the screen door.

Daddy worked long hours at the railroad, and that's when Mama and I spent most of our time visiting Aunt Louise and Unk, her sister and brother. This made Daddy mad.

One Day when we got home and opened the screen door, there he was.

I walked in first and Mama walked in behind me letting the screen door slam.

Daddy asked in a disgusted voice, "Why are you always over at your sister's house eating? I leave enough money for food. There's no need to go over to your family's house to eat."

"I'm just visiting and there's nothing wrong with that," Mama said.

This would usually start the arguments.

I was playing with my dolls, acting like nothing was happening, when out of the corner of my eyes, I saw Daddy wiggling his finger at Mama and then looked at me. The room was silent and he walked away.

Later that same day, Daddy and I were sitting on the front porch when I asked, "Are you happy?"

At first, he kept staring out toward the road. In a soft, distant voice, he said, "Yes, I'm happy."

He rubbed his hands, looking straight ahead.

With a soft, stuttering voice, I asked, "Do you love Mama and me?"

He reached over and put his arm around my shoulder. With a gentle hug, he said, "Yes."

"Then why are you and Mama always arguing?"

Looking down at me Daddy said, "Don't worry your pretty little head with such stuff. Families argue all the time. It's nothing to worry about."

He changed the subject and we started playing our who can see the farthest game. Most times I won, but today I let him win.

Still, I wondered how this soft-spoken, man sitting next to me could be so gentle with me but constantly arguing with Mama.

Was it because of Mama's close relationship with her family or the fact that his family wasn't close?

Daddy's family, the Dorsey's, lived in Natchez, Mississippi, but on the other side of town. Daddy didn't speak much about his family and they seldom visited.

Passing my parents' bedroom, I saw the oddest thing, Mama putting money away.

What made it odd wasn't the fact that she was putting the money away. We, like all of the coloreds in the Colony, didn't use the bank in town. We didn't trust them. What was odd was where she was putting the money.

I wasn't going to say anything, but as she closed the drawer, she turned around and saw me.

I had to say something, but what? All I could think of was, "Why are you putting money there?"

Mama grimaced and wrinkles formed in her forehead. With a stern voice she said, "Don't tend to grown-up business. Go to your bedroom and play."

I turned around and ran to my room as fast as I could, but still wondering.

####

I remember it was a sunny day and kids were playing outside. Daddy was about to head out the door for work, but not before we had our usual ritual of me hopping on his foot and wrapping my arms around his leg.

As we walked closer to the door, I climbed off and moved back from the doorway. I thought he was going to leave without saying the alligator rhyme. I started walking away when the door opened.

He stuck in his head and caught me off-guard. With the biggest banana boat smile, he said, "See you later, alligator."

I smiled back and said, "After while crocodile." I ran to the window and watched him walk away to the train station.

Later that afternoon, when I was sitting in the chair playing with my dolls, Mama came running down the stairs. "Hurry up," she said. "We have to go to your Uncle's house."

"Why?"

"Just come along, young lady, and don't forget your coat."

"It's hot outside. Why do I need my coat?"

"Just come on."

Mama and I got into the car and headed up the road to Unk's house. When we arrived, Mama stepped on the brakes and parked the car. She got out of the car but told me, "Stay put. I'll be right back."

Next thing I know, Mama, Aunt Louise, and Unk came running out of the house. Aunt Louise had some luggage and Unk was carrying the rest.

"Where are we going?" I asked, but I didn't get an answer.

All I knew was that Daddy left the house going in one direction. And when Unk drove us to the train station, we boarded a train leaving in the opposite direction.

I sat staring out of the train window, confused and sad. The train ride was to take us to my grandpa and grandma's house, Mama's family.

Suddenly I yelled, "What's going on?"

"Stop yelling. Everything will be all right," Mama said. "This is for the best."

For me, this was not the best. We were leaving Daddy behind. How could this be for the best?

"I'll be going North to look for work, and for the time being you'll stay with Grandma Emma. Once I find work and a place to stay, I'll be back to pick you up."

I started crying.

Mama said, "We'll have a better life if we move up North."

"We have a better life right here with Daddy."

"Please calm down. It's for the best. You'll see." The train ride to Grandma's house wasn't that long, but long enough. Although there were a lot of people on the train, I noticed a little boy and girl with a note attached to their shirts. We introduced ourselves and said, "Hi" but not much else. I mostly stared out the window, wondering what Daddy was going to think when he came home and found his family gone.

Grandma Emma was very tall and seldom raised her voice unless you decided to test your courage by talking back or mumbling at her when she turned her back.

When that happened, you might as well have signed your fate over to the Lord. She would look at you with squinting eyes. The frowns in her forehead would start to build their own family.

Then her finger wagged and pointed at the same time while her other hand rested on her hip. All you could do was to pray you didn't get a whipping when the word slinging stopped.

Everyone told Mama that she and Grandma looked like twins. When she looked into a mirror, it was like looking into the eyes of Grandma. I could also see where Mama learned her feistiness in the way she was raising me.

I had visited Grandpa and Grandma many times, taking the same train and looking at much of the same scenery. This was the first time I would not be leaving.

Mama and Aunt Louise spent two days at Grandma's house preparing for their trip up North. Before they left, Mama and I hugged, holding each other tightly for a long time. I whispered, "What about Daddy?"

"Just remember we all love you. Your daddy loves you too. Remember that, okay?" Tears ran down my face. I tried to rub them away and nodded.

Mama and Aunt Louise got on the train and went on their journey to what they said would be a better place.

Grandma Emma and I hugged each other, waving good-bye as thousands of thoughts were going through my head, none greater than *what will Daddy think when he comes home and sees that his family has left him? I know I'm a child, but my God, did anyone think about me?*

Charley Louise Dorsey

Chapter Two

Assorted meat w/cheese, potato salad,
relish tray w/dip, assorted bread,
dessert w/condiments ... $5.00

After the move to Grandma Emma's house, I'd dream about Daddy a lot. In those dreams, I'd be walking near the railroad tracks kicking rocks. He'd step down from the train hollering, "Where you been? I've been looking all over for you."

I'd wake up calling his name and sit up in bed with sweat rolling down my forehead like I'd just taken a shower or something, using the neck of my nightgown to wipe the sweat off my face.

Maybe the nightmares came because every night before I went to bed I'd say my prayers. Right before I'd get up off my knees, stepping on the hem of my nightgown, I'd whisper Daddy saying, "See you later, alligator." And then I'd say, "After while crocodile."

Maybe it was because those were the last words that Daddy and I had said to each other while he walked out the door to work, waiting underneath that willow tree to catch his train.

Even though Mama and Aunt Louise took me away from him, Daddy will always be my best friend. I went to my bedroom dresser, looking for paper and pencil, and whispering, "If Daddy can't be with me for our private conversations, I'll pretend and write to him." That's how the journal writing started.

Day 1, Journal Entry 1 ... Mama and Aunt Louise took me with suitcases in hand, leaving our home, friends, and Daddy on our way to Grandma Emma's house. They told me that I'd be staying here for a while until Mama could find work up North. I didn't have a chance to say good-bye ... to let my friends know where they could write to me. This is indeed a sad time in my life. Charley Louise

####

My bedroom at Grandma Emma's house was next to the graveled pathway, what we called the "bypass" because people would walk through it, drunks spent the night and men sat on wooden crates playing cards. The bypass separated our house and the neighbors. The drunks didn't wake me up, but the loud clacking sounds and laughing right outside my window did.

It was Saturday and I didn't feel like getting up, so I lay in bed with my eyes closed, hoping to go back to sleep. There it was again. I looked at the clock and saw that it was 9:00 in the morning. I slipped into my house shoes and looked through the window but didn't see anything. Opening the window, I leaned out, looking left and right. Some boys were playing with marbles against our house.

I wrapped my housecoat around me and tiptoed downstairs to see where Grandma and Grandpa were.

Grandma was in the kitchen, and I didn't see Grandpa. I snuck out the front door and around the side of the house. The clacking marbles got louder and louder.

I put my hands on my hips, frowning. "Excuse me! Why do you have to be so loud? It is Saturday morning, and you are disturbing my sleep."

"Trying to get your beauty rest?" One of them said.

"No, I'm naturally beautiful."

"Did you forget to look in the mirror?"

I stood there with my arms across my chest, frowning and tapping my foot.

They waved their hands up in the air at me and laughed saying, "Why don't you go and play with your dolls?"

My first thought was to turn around and walk away. But, I told myself, Charley Louise Dorsey never walks away. 'I'll be back.

I snuck back into the house and went upstairs to my bedroom.

Unless you were sick or something, stayin' in the house all day wasn't heard of.

Grandma Emma felt bad that I didn't have any friends and instead of sitting on the top stoop by myself a couple of days later, she took me a few doors up the road and introduced me to some of the girls who were my age, Sylvia and Gloria.

It was dead silent until Sylvia asked, "Do you know how to jump rope?"

I leaped up and said, "Are you kiddin'? I'm the jump rope queen."

We jumped single rope and then double dutch until our legs were tired. Every now and then I heard, "What?" or "Neighborhood rules." I couldn't help but walk two houses up and peek around the corner.

"Why do you keep looking at the boys?" Sylvia asked.

I paused before answering and then told them how I was awoken by an annoying noise on Saturday and couldn't get back to sleep. When I got out of bed and peeked out the window, those boys were playing a game of marbles. All I heard was the constant clacking of marbles and them yelling.

"They're probably cheating anyway," Gloria said.

Most weekends I heard the clanking of marbles and arguing. While the boys were playing, I leaned out of my window and yelled, "Where can I buy a bag of marbles?"

The boys looked up at me, surprised. One said, "Why? So we can beat your butt?"

They all laughed.

"You won't laugh so hard when I beat your butts."

The only money I had was the allowance Grandma gave me on Fridays, but I was saving that money for when Mama came back to get me.

I came up with two plans. The first plan was with every allowance I'd save some money for when Mama came back and the rest would be for a bag of marbles. The second plan was to do what most kids do—ask someone for the money.

I ran downstairs, calling for Grandma. She was in the kitchen cooking.

I walked into the kitchen, hesitant. I told myself, *What's the worse that she can say ... No?* I walked closer to her. *Okay, go for it. Ask her.*

Words blurted out of my mouth. "Grandma, I saw these pretty colored marbles in the store and was wondering if you would please buy them for me." My body froze.

"What do you want marbles for?" She asked.

"Just to play with."

"How much do they cost?"

"I think 10 cents a bag."

Grandma's expression didn't look like I was going to hear, "Here, baby, take this money and get your bag of marbles."

No, it didn't look like that at all. She said, "Let me think about it."

"But Grandma ..."

She turned around with a stern face.

"I said that I'd think about it. If you keep mouthing back at me I won't even do that."

I turned around, wondering how to get a bag of marbles, and saw Grandpa, sitting in his favorite chair.

The cushions were worn and crocheted dollies covered each arm to hide the torn fabric.

Just as my mouth formed the word "Grandpa," Grandma said loudly, "And don't ask your grandpa either."

Darn it. How did she know?

Two days passed and I still had no marbles. But, I kept watching the boys play. "Charley Louise?" Grandma said in a high pitched voice.

Oh, no, I told myself. Grandma just said my full name.

It's not that she didn't call me by my full name anyway, but when anyone called your full name with a sense of seriousness in their high-pitched voice, it was like putting the fear of God in you. You might as well get the belt.

I turned around the corner and started running up the stairs. There was Grandma, hanging onto the screen door. "Where have you been?" She asked.

With a stutter in my voice, I said, "Just looking for my friends."

"How many times have I told you not to leave the stoop unless you ask me?"

"I'm Sorry. I won't do it again."

We went to the kitchen, where she was cookin' a dessert. "Are you getting an allowance every week?" She asked.

"Yes."

"Couldn't you use some of that money to buy the marbles?"

That's not what I wanted to hear. "I'm saving money for when Mama comes to pick me up ... to help out with our trip."

She put the pies she was making into the oven, picked up something, and smiled.

I turned away for a moment, and when I turned back around, her arms were behind her back. I tried to peek, but when I moved in one direction, she moved the other way.

I figured that it had to be a letter from Mama or a bag of marbles.

Excitement was running through my body like it was Christmas. Slowly she pulled one arm from behind her back. It wasn't the bag of marbles, but a letter from Mama.

I walked away opening the envelope when Grandma said, "You don't want these?"

Jumping up and down, I yelled, "Are you kiddin'?"

I couldn't turn around and put one foot on the floor when I heard, "Just one minute, young lady. There are some rules."

"Rules," I asked.

"Don't let me catch you playing in that bypass between the houses where I can't see you with the boys, and don't go near the men who gambled there." Wagging her finger up and down she said, "You hear me?"

"Yes ma'am," I said.

Heck. How much fun will it be playing by myself? So I came up with an idea. Every time the boys were playing marbles, I leaned out my bedroom window and watched them play.

When they hit the marble, I'd try to do the same shot against my bedroom wall. The marbles would clank and I'd bounce up, hitting my head on the window, making sure Grandma didn't hear.

The day came when I decided to play against someone. There was another group of kids that played but not as good.

Between watching the boys from the window and playing against the other kids, I gained courage to challenge the better players—the boys, Jimmy, Don, Mike, Lewis and Joe.

If you wanted to play with them, you had to walk with courage and determination. You couldn't look scared.

Holding my shoulders back, I said, "Can I play?"

"No," they hollered. "Go and play with the girls. You ain't good enough."

I stomped of my feet and said, "Oh, yes, I am."

"Well, let's see."

They got closer to each other and started whispering and chuckling.

I looked around the circle, and they had the weirdest looks on their faces. Joe said, "Sure. You can play."

Something was up, but I didn't know what.

We started playing the game. Within a short time, I lost most of my marbles.

It was my turn and I had to decide to play or quit. I looked around at their faces and saw their smirky smiles. Then, I looked down at my marbles to see how they were positioned. I wasn't going to win and leave with more marbles than I came with.

Holding my head down, breathing in and out I said, "I quit."

"What was that you said? We didn't hear you."

Jimmy leaned in closer. "What did you say?"

"I quit."

The boys' laughter got louder, "That's what you get. Go play house or dolls with the girls."

I turned around and stomped my feet when all I heard was laughter from Jimmy and his friends.

Today I lost because I didn't know the neighborhood rules to play the game. They must have known I was watching them from my bedroom window.

"This will not happen again," I mumbled.

The next day, me, Sylvia and Gloria were sitting on the top stoop of my house. I was telling them how Jimmy and his friends won just about all of my marbles.

"Why don't you ask your grandpa to help?" Gloria asked.

"Grandpa," I said in a questioning tone.

They told me that everyone knows he was one of the best marble players in the neighborhood.

I jumped up and ran into the house, yelling back at my friends that I'd see them later.

"Grandpa," I yelled as I ran into the living room. "Can you teach me the game of marbles? You know the real game. I heard that you used to be the best marble player in the neighborhood."

Grandpa leaned to the side of his favorite chair. He put his finger up to his mouth and said, "Shhhh. Don't want your Grandma to hear you."

He then asked me what I knew about the game of marbles.

I said, "Nothing much because the boys just whipped my butt."

"You promise not to tell your grandma?"

I promised and told him that I wanted to know everything.

He told me that he had seen me in the bypass playing with the boys. "Nobody should get beat that bad," he said. "And for that reason I'll help you."

It was the perfect time because Grandma had gone to the grocery store. To make sure she wouldn't catch us, we played in front of the big picture window in the living room.

Bent on one knee, he taught me how to position the marbles and about bumping. Bump is when you hit the other person's marble just enough to put your marble in a better spot to win or to knock their marble out of the way not to win.

He said the main thing I needed to have was patience. He taught me the real way to play marbles and the neighborhood rules.

He told me to put my marbles next to the wall.

"Now, slowly roll one marble. Pretend that the other marble belongs to one of the boys in the bypass."

"This is too hard," I said.

"Stop being so impatient," He said. "You'll have to practice every day."

"Grandpa, tell me what the colors mean. I thought I knew."

"All of the marbles have unique colors and designs."

He took one striped marble out of my hand and rolled it on the floor toward the wall. "This is called cat's eye."

Next he rolled a solid colored marble.

"We call this one solids or colored."

I looked up at him, and he told me to open my hand. He dropped a marble in it and said, "What you have in your hand is a very important marble ... the infamous black marble. We called this one mother of pearl or blackie."

"What is so great about black ... I mean mother of pearl?" I asked.

"That's the big money one. You earn more points," Grandpa said.

He told me to be very careful when playing someone using the mother of pearl because this is when they'd usually use the neighborhood rules.

"What are the neighborhood rules?" I asked.

He looked down at me as if to say, "do you really want to know?"

Grimacing, he said, "The neighborhood rules are made up by the people playing the game. If the mother of pearl was to be used for their advantage, right before you took your shot, they'd yell, neighborhood rules."

"That's cheating," I said.

He told me I was probably right, but those were the neighborhood rules.

"Hi Emma, how you doing?" A neighbor said.

We looked out the window. There was Grandma walking down the road.

"Hurry, Grandpa. Help me pick up the marbles."

I picked up the last marble and Grandpa had sat back in his

favorite chair when Grandma opened the door, holding a bag of groceries, looking at both of us like we had stuck our hands in the cookie jar.

"Is everything all right?"

"Yeah, everything's all right," Grandpa said.

"Charley Louise, come help me with the groceries.

"Yes, ma'am."

As I walked away, I turned around and caught Grandpa winking at me.

I smiled and winked back.

####

Grandpa showed me how to play the game of marbles, but at first I played with the kids who weren't that good.

I knew I would have to play against Jimmy and the other boys who had laughed at me, so I walked up to them with my chest stuck out, trying to look confident, and said, "Let's play!"

They looked at me and laughed, holding their stomachs. Jimmy asked, "Are you kiddin'? Do you really want to play us?"

This time I laughed. "Are you scared?"

Frowns came on all of their faces when one said, "Do you have any marbles?"

I had one hand on my hip and the other behind my back. I pulled the one hand from behind my back, dangling the bag of marbles and said, "I hope you have enough."

"Let the whippin' begin." Jimmy said.

The boys were beating me pretty badly until I looked up at the window. There was Grandpa. He winked, and that's when I remembered what he had taught me.

At a critical time in the game, sweat came down my forehead, and the boys noticed. It was the last chance for me to win, but I had to flick the last marble.

I looked back up at the window to Grandpa, and he pointed.

Jimmy saw Grandpa at the window, but before he could say anything, I took the cat's eye marble, put it against the tip of my thumb, but hesitated.

I whispered, "If I hit this marble over here, the mother of pearl, I will—"

"How do you know about the mother of pearl?" Jimmy said.

"Never mind." I said. "If I hit the mother of pearl, I win the game, right?"

"Right," Jimmy said. "But you'll never hit that marble."

I prayed, "Oh Lord, please let this cat's eye marble hit the mother of pearl so I can walk away with a banana boat smile and shut these boys up. I know I've asked for a lot of things lately, but I promise I'll keep my bedroom clean."

Leaning over, I put the cat's eye marble on my finger.

"Hurry up," one of the boys said. I jumped. "Stop trying to make me nervous."

I looked back down at the mother of pearl, focused, and flicked my marble.

Everyone held their breath. Eyes were as big as the moon. But, as the marble got closer to the mother of pearl marble, it started to roll off to the side.

"Oh, no," I said.

Just as the boys started laughing, the cat's eye hit the mother of pearl and knocked it out of the circle.

Jumping up and down I screamed, "I won. I won."

With one hand on my hip and one hand held straight out into the middle of the circle I said, "Thank you very much, but I'll take those marbles. Want to play another game?"

They didn't answer. All I heard was a lot of grumbling as they walked away, holding their heads down.

The summers weren't the same. The boys continued to play marbles, but not with me until eventually the sounds of the clacking marbles hitting and boys yelling beneath my bedroom window became silent.

The sounds that woke me up most Saturdays during the summer came to a halt.

There were many times I looked out the window but didn't see them anywhere. I missed silencing their boyish laughs.

I started spending most of my past time either playing with the girls up the road or hanging out underneath the moss-filled trees next to the railroad tracks.

I loved Mississippi and the rural colonies nestled around it. Each one had its own identity and a strong Southern comfort.

At nighttime, the trees looked like ghosts. The cascading branches formed a huge umbrella where I'd sit for hours, remembering how our family was with both Daddy and Mama.

I'd think about the smells of breakfast and dinner, of hopping onto Daddy's leg as he walked around the house, and of our private conversations. Even though Daddy wasn't here, I'd talk to him a lot wondering how and what he was doing.

The trees were also his favorite spot because they were next to the railroad tracks, where he'd catch his train going to work.

I'd stare at each train as it stopped, hoping one day Daddy would stand at the top stair with that banana boat smile so I could jump into his arms.

Summertime was about to end. In a few weeks, a desk and textbooks would replace the time I spent underneath the moss-filled trees.

####

About two months after school started, I got bored. I had friends but always felt alone. I wondered what my friends at my old colony were doing and if they were thinking about what I was doing. It wasn't the same without them. I would daydream with my arms crossed on my desk, staring out the window. That's when I came up with an idea.

At lunchtime, I'd eat underneath the moss-filled trees. The hallway was busy and I could sneak out without being seen. I'd run as fast as I could and head straight to the trees. I didn't do this every day because I didn't want the school calling my Grandma.

Sometimes I'd miss the next class and excuse myself with a note that my friends and I had written.

One day after school when I walked into the house, the telephone rang. I didn't think it was anything, so I kept walking until Grandma said, "No, Charley Louise isn't here. Is anything wrong?"

I tiptoed toward where Grandma was talking. I leaned near the wall, trying to listen to what she was saying, but couldn't hear much. I leaned in closer to the wall that separated Grandma and me. When I tiptoed across the floor, it made a cracking sound. I stood frozen, hoping Grandma hadn't heard.

There was silence until I heard Grandma telling the person on the phone that she thought I was in school. Before I took another step, I heard, "Charley Louise."

I didn't answer.

"I know you're there because I heard the door close."

Coming around the corner with my school bag hanging over my shoulder, I answered as if I had just walked into the house. "Yes, ma'am."

"How was school?"

I wasn't sure how to answer, so I said, "Good."

"Do you have any homework?"

"Not today."

"That was the principal from your school on the telephone. He said you're skipping class. As a matter of fact, you skipped class today. Now, unless the pastor summoned you to church, you'd better have a good reason for skippin' class."

We both stood there looking at each other, with me trying to think of a reason, until I finally said, "I've been underneath the trees by the railroad tracks."

With a concerned voice and softness in her eyes, she asked me why.

I told her that I was hoping Daddy would be on one of them.

She pulled me close and gestured for me to sit next to her on the sofa. She said, "I know you miss your daddy, but skippin' school isn't what your daddy or mama would want for you to do. It's near the end of the school year and starting tomorrow, I'll walk you to school."

We hugged while she told me the importance of an education, especially for colored people in the South. She told me that I wouldn't want to wash other people's clothes and clean their homes all of my life.

She cradled her hands around my face, looked into my eyes, and said, "Always set high goals for yourself."

"I'm sorry. I won't miss school again."

Silence was in the air when I got up to walk away towards my bedroom. Every step must had made a sound. Grandma's words seemed to be glued in my mind … just like the images of my family.

The next morning, Grandma called me downstairs. She was in the kitchen cooking lunch when she gave me another letter from Mama.

Dear Charley Louise,

How are you doing? I have great news. Your Aunt Louise and I have found jobs and a big house in Chicago, Illinois. We'll be coming to pick you up in three weeks. So, the week before we come, start getting your things together. The North is different from the South, but you'll enjoy it here. I miss you and love you always.
Mama

My eyes felt widened as I screamed, "Mama's coming! Mama's coming!"

"Stop jumping up and down before you put a hole in the floor. When is she coming?"

"In three weeks!" I shouted.

Those three weeks seemed like forever. I couldn't sleep, waiting to see the car pull up and Mama getting out of it.

The night before Mama and Aunt Louise were coming to get me, I kept looking at the clock next to my bed.

It seemed like the hour and minute hands weren't moving fast enough until I heard ...

Knock. Knock. Knock.

I could hear Grandma yell, "Here I come," as she stumbled down the stairs.

I jumped out of my bed, stumbled on the bottom on my pajamas, ran down the stairs, and jumped into Mama's arms.

Questions came out of my mouth so fast I had no breath. I squeezed Mama so tight. She said, "Charley Louise, you're choking me."

"Tell me all about it—the job, the house, Chicago. Are there kids my age? And—"

"Hold on. Let me get into the house and sit down. Aunt Louise and I had a long trip."

When we were all at the table eating breakfast, Mama said she found a good job working for a wealthy family, taking care of the house and kids. There are three kids, a boy and two girls. The family travels back and forth a lot to Europe. She said sometimes the kids travel with them but sometimes the wife and the kids stay at home and she takes care of them.

Mama told me that their children are about the same age as me and attend a private elementary school, but there are a lot of kids on the block where we'll live. She said that the house is big enough for all of us, including Aunt Louise and Unk.

When Mama didn't mention Daddy living with us, I asked her why.

She said, "It's for the best," She said

"Oh, I guess we're not a family," I said and looked toward the floor. I started to wonder if I'd ever see Daddy again.

"Hold your head up," Mama said. "Don't ever let me see you holding your head down. It's going to be all right. Just wait and see."

She started telling me about my bedroom and said I could decorate it however I wanted … within reason.

Mama and Aunt Louise left the room to put their luggage away in the extra bedroom.

I went to my bedroom and flopped onto the chair, gazing out the window and praying that Daddy would drive to Grandma's house before we left Mississippi. I couldn't stop thinking about what the new house would be like without him.

Every morning and throughout the day, I'd look for Daddy's car. If he didn't get here by the end of the week, I knew we would still be leaving Mississippi.

On an early morning, I lay across my bed. I heard high heels clicking on the stairs and then two knocks on my bedroom door.

I sat up when the door started to open. It was Mama. She peeked her head inside my room. "Are you ready to go?"

I smiled and said, "Yeah." But deep down inside, I didn't want to leave Mississippi because I'd be leaving Daddy all over again. I had lived with Grandma and Grandpa for about a year and had gotten attached to the colony they lived in. I'd also miss my friends.

I breathed a deep sigh, put on my traveling clothes, and went down to eat breakfast with the family.

After breakfast, Grandma carried the food that was already prepared for the trip to the car. Grandpa, Aunt Louise, and Mama carried the suitcases. When the last suitcase was shoved into the car, we hugged Grandma and Grandpa. What we couldn't get in the trunk rode with me and the food in the back seat.

Before leaving, Mama's hands were on the steering wheel with the car motionless. Aunt Louise touched Mama's hand and I touched Mama's shoulder when she started to pray. Simultaneously, we closed our eyes, bowed our heads in prayer, "Our Father, who art in heaven … and ended with a hearty Amen."

Praying isn't something our family was short of doing. This family tradition started with our church. We prayed every time we traveled, before I left for school, every time I got in trouble and talked back, and whenever the feeling hit us. It was the Holy Ghost's way. We felt that prayer would keep us safe from harm and change everything.

Aunt Louise was waving out the window to Grandma and I was waving out the back window to Grandpa. Mama looked at me in the rearview mirror and said, "We're a long ways from Chicago and will have to make the best of our time, so could you please keep the moaning and groaning to a minimum?"

As Mama drove off, she honked the horn. I told myself, *don't turn around* when my heart started pumping uncontrollably. I can't leave like this, I thought. I turned around, quickly looked out the back seat window, and then rolled down the window as fast as I could.

I looked from side to side, wondering, *Why doesn't Daddy come racing around the corner in his car, honking, telling them to stop?*

Mama said, "Charley Louise, turn around. Stop leaning out that window before you fall out of it."

I felt sadness in my soul.

The car was gradually moving when I leaned out the car window again, waving and yelling to Grandma and Grandpa, "Goodbye. Come visit us."

Suddenly I looked up and there were my friends waving from their windows and the boys, Jimmy, Don, Mike, Lewis and Joe, the ones I had played marbles with. I waved back until their faces faded away.

I looked at the suitcases next to me, leaned over to unzip one, and pulled out my journal.

Day 2, Journal Entry 2 ... Hello Daddy, it's hard to believe the time that has passed since I last heard your voice or had our private conversations. I do miss you, and one day I'll try to meet back up with you. "See you later, alligator". Love, Charley Louise

Chapter Three
Quiche, relish tray w/fruit dip,
roll or muffin, dessert ... $5.00

I wrote the last word in my journal and tied the ribbon around it. Mama and Aunt Louise talked about the trip, mostly which routes to take and which ones to stay away from. The decision was to take the same roads Mama and Aunt Louise had taken when they left Chicago to come to Mississippi.

For most coloreds traveling, this wasn't uncommon. To avoid trouble, coloreds knew certain roads not to take and could stop along the roadside to eat and use the bathroom.

And as I looked behind me, the buildings that created the rural landscape was fading away. The juke joints, kids sitting on the steps that blistered your butt, and the boys in the bypass playing marbles, making sure they woke me up every Saturday morning ... this would all be gone.

After being on the road for three hours, I couldn't hold it in any longer. The moaning and groaning was about to burst out. I said, "Can't we stop, Mama? I have to stretch my legs."

Our eyes met in the rearview mirror.

"What did you say?"

"Can we stop? I have to stretch my legs and use the bathroom."

"Let me find a good spot because we won't be at the overnight stop for a while."

She didn't yell or anything, I said to myself.

When I looked up, our eyes once again caught each other's in the rearview mirror. She must be tired too, I thought.

It was about 15 minutes before Mama pulled the car over on the road side near some tall bushes. Mama went to the bathroom first, to check out the spot. I went second and then Aunt Louise.

We poured water over our hands and ate some of the food that Grandma packed.

There was fried chicken, fresh bread, and her famous pound cake, enough to hold us over until our first rest stop.

Right after Mama drove off, she started to sing, "Go tell it on the mountain, over the hills and everywhere." She said, "Charley Louise, sing along."

Singing was another ritual our family had. Whether on a road trip or sitting around the house with nothing to do, this is what we did.

I sang quietly, "Go tell it on the mountain, over the hills and everywhere."

"Open your mouth. Sing it like you mean it."

"Go tell it on the mountain," I sang loudly. Mama looked in the rearview mirror and Aunt Louise turned around laughing. I felt a smile creep across my face until I couldn't hold it in any longer and burst out laughing. We sang so loud that the animals we passed must have heard us.

Three and a half hours later, Mama pulled up to a house on the side of the road. It was white with a picket fence. A dog chained in the front yard started barking. Then two people came out of the house, a man and a woman. Kids peeked around them and out the upstairs windows.

Mama and Aunt Louise got out of the car with big smiles on their faces, waving. Everyone hugged each other like they were kin folk.

"Charley Louise, come on," Mama said.

I walked slowly.

"Hurry up, child. This is my daughter, Charley Louise. Come

on, shake their hands."

"Hi. Nice to meet you."

That night, we ate dinner and talked. I sat on the front porch. There wasn't anything to see but the stars. I listened to the neighing sounds of their horses.

When I heard the screen door open, I turned my head. It was one of their children. She told me that sometimes the horses get a little loud, but, like the dog, they protect the property as well.

My eyebrows rose, as I was trying to understand how a horse could save anyone.

She smiled and said, "If they hear or see anything strange, they get all riled up, and it gives our family a sign that something might be wrong."

"Oh," I said.

We sat on the porch, talking about nothing much, until our families called us into the house, telling us it was time for bed.

All of us, except their kids, woke up early the next morning to get an early start.

We were sitting at the kitchen table eating breakfast when Mama told the family, "We have a long trip ahead of us. If you don't mind, we'll eat a little bit of the breakfast. We'll stop along the roadside to have lunch because there is plenty of food packed in the boxes. If I eat too much, I'll probably get too sleepy to drive."

We hugged, got into our station wagon, and drove off.

Listening to music on the radio, I began to daydream. I didn't know what to think of this trip because for once, I was going to a place I had never been to.

I stared out the window, thinking about Daddy and my friends. I visualized Grandma telling Jimmy, and his friends, the boys who played marbles, to get away from the bypass and to stop knocking those marbles against her house.

We listened to the radio, told stories, and sang hymns. At times, I'd play counting games. I'd count cows, houses, or cars we passed until my boredom was gone. It didn't help that the food we packed was right next to me on the floor.

At dusk, we weren't far from Chicago when Mama noticed car headlights behind us. She thought it was the police at first but didn't see any lights flickering.

The police knew that coloreds traveled certain roads and would bother them, making them get out of the car and lay on the ground until they searched their automobiles. They'd throw their belongings all over the ground and find nothing. Colored women and a young child in the car was worse.

Mama slowed down and sped up. With caution, she pulled to the side of the road as if to check the car tires. The car got closer and stopped behind us.

A man got out of the car. He was trying to get us to stop because one of the tail lights was out.

We all breathed a sigh of relief.

The man asked where we were headed, and Mama told him Chicago.

He said he'd follow behind us until we got to the next town so that the police wouldn't stop us. Mama tried to pay him, but he wouldn't take any money. When we got to the next town I looked out the back window. He flickered his lights and turned away from us.

Between the small town and Chicago, I fell asleep. Mama shouted, "Charley Louise, wake up! "

My body flinched. I used one arm to push myself up from the seat and the other to wipe the sleep crust from the corners of my eyes.

Looking out the car windows, it was as though we were in a race with the car next to us speeding through each street light. Cars honked and people yelled at each corner. It was a far cry from the rural lifestyle where the loudest sounds I had heard were crickets and bullfrogs serenading at night.

The car slowed as Mama and Aunt Louise looked for a parking spot. I tried to figure out which building was our new home when Mama said, "Here we are. Welcome to Chicago."

She pointed to 3200 Damon Street, a two-story, brown stone building with lots of windows. All of the houses were close together.

"The people next door will hear everything we say," I said, "And why are the kids staring at me?"

"You're new to the neighborhood. That's all. They're all nice kids, and you'll fit in just fine. Help me and Aunt Louise. Grab one of those bags out the car."

Carrying one bag in each hand, I slowly walked toward the house. The kids stared at me and I stared right back. One little girl smiled and waved. I probably would have waved back, but my hands were full.

When we got to the top stair, Mama said, "Here are the keys. You can open the door."

I opened the door and saw a big living room. Nothing like we had in Mississippi and even bigger than Grandma's home. I asked where my bedroom was.

Mama said, "Upstairs, down the hallway."

It was the longest hallway I had ever seen. There were so many doors. I yelled downstairs, asking which room was mine.

Mama yelled, "When you get to the top of the stairs, go right. The second door on the left is your bedroom."

When I opened the bedroom door, my eyes got wide. It was one of the largest bedrooms I had ever seen and had windows facing the street.

After getting all of the bags out of the car, I leaned out the window. Then I put all of my clothes in the closet and some in the dresser. I had flung my journal on the bed earlier.

After I finished unpacking, I plopped on the bed, right on top of the journal. I pulled it from underneath my body and reached to put it on the dresser. I changed my mind and wrote.

Day 3, Journal Entry 3 ... We're in Chicago, Illinois and I am in junior high school. The house is real big and I have my own room, not having to share it with company. I miss Daddy a lot and wish he was here with us. I'll miss playing in the bypass and hope that I can make friends. How many times must a person move to say, "I'm home?" Charley Louise

After spending the first night in our new home and eating a big breakfast, I went outside and sat on the stoop of our house.

The community was very different from Mississippi.

In Grandma's neighborhood, there were coloreds and a handful of whites. The community of Damon and Taylor in Chicago was predominantly white with just a few coloreds.

Many times, Mama would ask me to go play with the other kids to try and make friends. I'd say, "It's not the same. Why can't we live in an area just like down South?"

She'd always give me the same answer: "It's closer to my job."

Then she'd say, "Child, if we were able to live in the South and endure the racial climate there, we most certainly can endure it here."

In the South, the different races stayed more or less to themselves. Very seldom would I see any two races playing, eating, going to the same school, or working together. We knew our place, but I did what Mama said.

I looked across the street and noticed a girl sitting on a stoop.

That's what they called the steps. I stood just in front of the curb of the street.

We glared at each other. Finally, I yelled, "Hi, my name is Charley Louise."

She giggled and yelled back, "That's a boy's name. Who in God's sake gave you that name?"

With my hands folded across my waist, I said, "My Mama and Daddy. What's your name? Susie or Sally?" I whispered to myself, most white people I knew had such names.

"As a matter of fact, it is Susie. How did you know?"

I smiled and said, "Just a lucky guess."

We found out we were the same age. We tied the jump rope to her stoop and took turns counting and jumping.

Occasionally, her mother would look out the window, watching but never saying anything except when it was time to come in for lunch or for whatever else they had planned for the day.

Most of the summer, I'd walk across the street. She never came to my house. We'd play Hopscotch and jump rope.

One day when I knocked on her door, her mother opened it and told me Susie couldn't come out to play today, maybe tomorrow. I came the next day but was told the same thing.

"Did you two get into a fight or something?" Mama asked.

"All I know is that her Mama said that she couldn't come out to play."

While I was sitting on my top stoop, I saw Susie get into a car with some girls. She never waved my way. If she was outside, she wouldn't make eye contact and would turn away. I didn't understand. We had played together for about a month.

I was determined to find out what was going on, so I walked across the street. Susie and the girls were playing Hopscotch. When I asked if I could play, Susie said, "Not today."

The other girls glared at me. Susie told me they were her cousins and they were visiting for the rest of the summer.

I smiled and said, "Hi," but they didn't respond.

Susie said that it might be best if I went home and told me not to come over anymore.

I turned around and walked away. I sat on my stoop feeling sad and hurt.

Mama asked, "Why don't you go across the street and play with Susie and the girls?"

"Those are her cousins. Susie introduced me and told me that I couldn't play with her anymore."

Mama said, "Remember the time when we lived in Natchez and Daddy took us to town and he went to help the colored man? You know, the one the white men were hitting and shoving?"

I nodded and said, "Yeah. How could I forget it?

"The North has a racial silence to it. In the South, coloreds know where they stand. There are 'no coloreds' and 'whites only' signs in the North, but the message is silent. You have to watch the stares and reactions by the whites," Mama said.

She said that in the South, in the colonies, it represented a sense of safety and protection from Southern prejudice. People were able to laugh, enjoy each other's company, and have fellowship with one another every Sunday.

"Susie probably wants to come over and talk to you, but her parents might think different. Racism is everywhere, but is handled differently. Do you understand?" Mama said.

"I think so," I said.

It's all the years living in the South is what helped me to live and understand living in the North. It would be more challenging for you as a child, but I'm comfortable living within the mixture of the colored and white race."

"Racism is confusing," I said.

"If you don't remember anything else, please remember this, just because you see the kids hanging around and parents speaking, that doesn't mean that everyone likes you. But it also doesn't mean that everyone hates you either. I had a whole lifetime of understanding racism and will be here to help. Now let's go and set the dinner table," She said.

We got up from the stoop. Mama's hand caressed me as I turned to look over my shoulder at Susie and her cousins.

As usual, my role was to set the table and to make Kool-Aid. Since I made the drinks, I could also pick the flavor. Mama took the food out of the oven. We said grace and filled our stomachs.

For the remainder of the summer, Susie continued to ignore me and only hung around her cousins. Thank God, I met another group of girls—colored girls this time.

The summer was coming to an end. Adjusting to another school wasn't something I looked forward to. It was the first time I'd be going to a predominantly white school, and I wondered how I would be accepted.

The first day of school started just after Labor Day. It was a sunny day with few clouds in the sky. When Esther, Jill and Mona, the friends I met on Damon Street, stopped by to walk with me to school, I didn't hear, "Charley Louise, are you ready yet?" Instead, they walked up to my door and knocked. The knocking was so loud that you would have thought the police were at the front door. I jumped up from my bed, grabbed my notebook, and ran down the stairs just as Mama came out of the kitchen.

Mama opened the door, but before she had a chance to yell at them, I was at the door. I gave her a kiss and said, "See you after school."

When I looked around, she was still standing in the doorway pointing her finger, but with a smile.

The school was larger than the one in Mississippi. The constant stares from the white students was uncomfortable. My friends and I were walking down the hallway. I turned and stared back at the white students.

"Come on, Charley Louise. You'll get used to it."

"Why? How did you guys get used to it—the stares and the giggling?"

"Our families helped us, and we'll help you."

We checked to see what classes each of us had. At times, we saw that we were in the same classroom. The first hour was not one of those times.

I walked into the classroom shyly and stopped. The teacher asked me my name. "Charley Louise," I said.

"Welcome, Charley Louise. Your desk is right over there."

It wasn't quite in the back of the room, but close enough. It seemed like every step that I took, they were all staring, except the colored kids. I wanted to shout, "What the hell are you looking at?" but stayed silent, remembering some of the things Mama and my friends had told me.

After the school bell rang for class to start, the teacher took roll call. She asked all of the new kids to stand up and say their names. I was the last one. Slowly, I stood up and cleared my throat.

Laughter started to fill the room.

"My name is Charley Louise."

The laughter grew louder.

"Stop laughing," the teacher said. "What is your last name?"

"Charley Louise Dorsey. I'm from Natchez, Mississippi."

I knew it was coming, so I prepared myself. Someone asked, "Isn't that a boy's name?" Sweat started to roll down my forehead. "No," I said. "I was named after a great man."

The teacher told the class to settle down. I sat down in my seat.

I guess that's another first, I thought. *Another one of those firsts Mama told me I will get past.*

For me, the best sound of the day was the last bell ringing.

By the time I got to my locker, my friends were already there, waiting to walk me home. I had never been so happy.

While walking home, talking about the day and how I had survived it, we heard giggling.

When we turned around, the giggling stopped, so we continued walking.

"Look at those niggers," a voice said.

We turned around. There were a group of kids around us, so we weren't sure who said it. They all stared.

"N-I-G-G-E-R," someone shouted, spelling it out.

When I turned around, they were closer to us and Susie was with them.

We all glared at each other. I said, "Hello, Susie. Did one of you call us out of our names?"

One of the girls said, "Someone from across the street must have said it."

"Susie, how about we walk with you guys? We live close to each other."

In unison, the girls said, "We all have to be somewhere else."

I looked into Susie's eyes. "You too?"

"I'll talk to you later. Right now we have to go," she said.

"She's a coward." Esther, one of my friends tugged at me.

"Let's just go," I said.

Normally, I would have stood my ground, but this was a new experience. I had never felt a sense of hatred toward me.

My feet didn't want to move. I looked at Esther. "Is this how it's always going to be?"

"Not always, but a lot of the time. You'll get used to it and, at the same time, learn how to handle each instance. Let's go home."

After everyone turned down the street where they lived, I ran home as fast as I could. I reached for the doorknob, but it didn't want to turn. My hands were wet and sweaty from all of the excitement.

Mama was opening the door at the same time. I fell into her arms.

"What's wrong?" She asked.

"My friends and I just had the worst experience. I want to move back home. Why can't we go back to Natchez?"

Mama rubbed the sweat from my forehead. We sat and talked. She told me everything would be all right and I'd have to give it a chance.

The more she said that it would be all right, the more I said it wouldn't and that I wanted to move back home.

"Wait after school," she said, "I'll walk you and your friends home to see that you all get there safely. I'll talk with their parents as well."

I went upstairs and laid across my bed, thinking about what had happened. I remembered that day when I went to town with Daddy and Mama in Mississippi and saw a man attacked by some white men.

This time, my friends and Mama were around and it was happening to me. I asked myself how to handle the same adversity when no one is around. Should I back down or fight for what I believed in?

At the dinner table, it was quiet. I thought about the day and about Daddy. I wondered what he was doing and how he was doing.

"Charley Louise, you have to eat something," Mama said. "We didn't move from down South because of the racism."

"But why? And why did we leave Daddy?"

Her forehead wrinkled. Aunt Louise dropped her spoon in her soup bowl when Mama said, "Don't question me, child. This will be a better life than we had down South."

A better life for who? I thought. *So far, this doesn't seem better for me except that now Mama and I live in a big house together.*

I didn't eat much dinner and Mama noticed. Later on, she came up to my room and sat on my bed.

"Charley Louise, look at me. This will not be the last time you experience racism and trying to find ways to defend yourself. I'll be right here by your side to help. You won't be alone. I promise."

"I know you will, Mama," I said, caressing her.

It seemed as though she didn't know a lot of my thoughts weren't about racism but about Daddy, and I didn't see any need to tell her.

Mama left my room. I pulled out my diary and wrote as if Daddy were here, telling him everything that happened to me that week.

Day 4, Journal Entry 4 ... Dear Daddy, this week I started school. For the most part, it was not that bad, but on the way home some white girls were behind me and called me a nigger. I remembered that day when I went into town with you and Mama and watched that colored man get pushed around. I tried to be strong, but there were five white girls and three of us—myself and my friends. Although I'm too big to ride your feet, many days I sit up in my bedroom wondering if I fit in this big city life, missing our private conversations. I pray for the day that we can see each other again. Love, Charley Louise—A name I'll always be proud of, even if it is a boy's name.

Chapter Four

Chop suey, rice, salad
w/condiment, dessert ... $4.50

Uncle John, Mama's brother, stood 5'9", heavyset, with a round face and a fat nose that seemed to spread across his face. I called him Unk.

Even though I found myself staring at his nose most of the time when we talked, I loved the different hats he wore. All the men wore hats. When I rubbed the hats on the rim between my thumb and pointer finger, they felt like silk.

There were bright colored hats and dark colored ones, but Unk always wore the brown-tone ones, snuggly fitting around the top of his head and tilted to the side.

He was a very stern and determined man who always walked with confidence. When Unk spoke, you didn't talk back but stood still and listened.

Our family strongly believed in getting an education, so when Christmas came, Darlene and Rose, my cousins, and I never wondered what our gifts would be from Unk. All the kids got the same thing... books.

We didn't just get books. We had to do book reports and read them to him within a certain time that Unk gave all of us.

Mama had one sister, Aunt Louise, who stood 5'2", not too heavyset, but plump. She was the youngest and very observant.

They were inseparable and shared the same family disciplinarian belief that a child never talked back. When it was time to discipline, the whole family disciplined you—Unk, Aunt Louise, and Mama.

That didn't seem fair to me, but I wasn't about to share those thoughts.

When I heard a high-pitched voice and my full name called, most times that meant I was in trouble. Unk was the only one who didn't call me by my full name, but that didn't mean the punishment wasn't just as bad or worse. I'd prepare myself to read, read, and read. Sometimes I'd use the excuse of "I have homework to do" to get out of the punishment.

Just when I thought that worked, Unk would say, "Remember that time when you did so and so? Or do you have any homework ... school projects?" He'd wink because school was out. "Here is a nice book for you to read, and I expect a book report."

"For God's sake, Unk, it's summertime."

A bulldog frown came on his face. He'd say, "Are you talking back? Would you like to add another book to your list?"

"No, sir." I walked up the stairs to my room muttering, "Boy, I wish Daddy was here."

It was a hot Friday night, so I slept with my window open, hearing all the sounds from the street. Early the next morning, a rhythmic car horn that sounded like it was right under my bedroom window awakened me.

At first I didn't pay attention. I curled up with my pillow, trying to fall back asleep.

The honking continued. I leapt out of the bed, hurried to the window, and saw a big, black, shiny car full of people. I didn't recognize the car or the people at first. Then a man wearing a familiar dress hat got out from the driver's side. I leaned out of the window and yelled, "Unk! Unk!" As grumpy as he was, I had missed that man, and Darlene and Rose, who was named after Mama.

He looked up toward the window and hollered, "Hey, Charley Louise."

I grabbed my house coat, slid into my slippers, and ran down the hall to Mama's room, knocking on her door. "Mama, Mama, Unk's here."

"Calm down."

"Unk, Aunt Pearl, Unk's wife and Darlene and Rose are ..."

"Okay. Okay. Go open the door and I'll be right there."

I ran down the stairs, opened the door, and jumped onto Unk's big body, hugging him until I could hardly breathe. After that, there was a hugging fest. Unk asked how I was doing and if I had conquered the world or if the world was conquering me.

Before I answered, I looked up at Mama, who was standing next to me. She's a private person and didn't like all of the family business getting out unless she told it. She looked down at me with hesitation but said, "Go ahead."

I put my hands on my hip and blurted, "Racism, Unk."

Mama pinched me and frowned. "Charley Louise," She said with her arms crossed.

"Unk asked what happened."

I looked back up toward him and before Mama could say anything else, I said, "These girls were—"

Mama said, "Sit down, John, while I go into the kitchen to fix us all some breakfast." She turned around, looked at me, and said, "Charley Louise, you come with me and help in the kitchen."

"What did I do? Why did you stop me from telling the story? You told me to tell them." She told me it wasn't telling the story, but how I told the story. She said that I sounded so mean and hateful.

I asked Mama how she wanted me to talk about racism, that it's hard not to be mad or upset.

As usual, when guests or relatives were at our home, she said that we'd talk about it later.

"You got something smellin' good in that kitchen," Unk said. "What's that awesome smell?"

Mama yelled from the kitchen, "Homemade waffles, fresh eggs, bacon from the market, and grits with a little cheese mixed with them."

About an hour later, everyone was sitting at the kitchen table. Unk sat where Daddy should be sitting, at the head of the table, and said grace over the food.

I bowed my head, pretending that it was Daddy saying grace.

After grace, I decided to give Mama the letters I had written for Daddy so that she could mail them. I had written one almost every week while living in Chicago, telling Daddy everything that had happened since we were separated and how I missed him. I didn't know how to get them to him without Mama knowing, but decided not to hide it anymore.

I noticed Unk and Mama whispering, talking about things they didn't want me, Darlene or Rose to hear. We never asked what they were talking about. We knew better.

Then I heard Unk and Mama talking about another house and since Grandpa and Grandma passed, his family was the only ones left down South. That's why Unk had decided to move to Chicago.

I wondered why there were no suitcases in their car or with them at the door.

I smiled and asked, "Where will you live … with us?"

Mama said, "No. Unk has found a house in a different part of Chicago, not far from where we live now."

I looked around the breakfast table. Unk and Mama glanced at each other with a "I know something you don't and how do we tell you?" look on their faces.

As usual, my curiosity got the best of me and I had to ask "What's wrong?"

"Nothing," Mama said.

I looked around the table. "Then why is everyone looking at me like they know something I don't?"

It looked like Mama was going to begin with a long, "Well." That always meant something was up.

"Well, Unk, his family, Aunt Louise, you, and me will all be living together, in the same house, but not this house. We'll still live in Chicago."

"We're movin' again? We've only lived here almost two years. I'm sick and tired of moving. I'll have to make new friends all over again. Can't we just get one place and stay there?"

I was told that Unk was having a hard time finding a house in this area and that the family had always lived close to each other. With the house he found, the whole family could stay together and help each other.

I put my fork down on my plate of food, pushed my chair hard from underneath the table, stood, and threw my napkin down. "It seems like we're always moving further away from Daddy and my friends. Can't we just stay in one place long enough for me to adjust and make friends since I can't see Daddy?"

Again, I was told, "This is good for the family … the whole family."

"How is this good for the whole family when I was taken from Daddy?" I muttered.

"Charley Louise," Mama said. "Watch your mouth, young lady. It's getting the best of you, and believe you me, I will win that battle. The decision is made. We're moving."

I told myself, *Somehow I've got to get Daddy these letters.*

The bright sun usually woke me up and on Sunday morning, as usual, we got ready for church. The family now, which included Aunt Louise, Unk, Aunt Pearl and my cousins, had our usual large Southern breakfast. Afterwards, we all cleaned the kitchen.

The plan today was to go to church and drive over to see the house Unk had found. It wasn't too far. Although you could drive six blocks in another direction and it seemed like you were in a different city.

We drove in two cars because there wasn't enough room for all of us in Mama's station wagon. The cars began to slow down. *"Oh God, where are we? I must have died and gone to hell."*

The neighborhood didn't look like Damon Street. They houses were close together, and the houses weren't as nice looking. Trash was scattered across the streets. But, hallelujah, colored people were everywhere.

Doesn't anyone know how to pick up their trash? I thought to myself. I'd rather get in trouble and read ten books than move here.

As we got out of the cars, Unk said, "The house is three stories high."

When you first walked into the house, there was a large foyer. All of these homes had one. Next, Unk took the family through the living room and the dining room. Both rooms had large fireplaces and plenty of room for all of the furniture.

We went into the kitchen—Mama's favorite place in the house. It was big and had plenty of room for the whole family to eat. There was a big metal stove with plenty of oven space for Mama to bake. Cupboards went all around the kitchen, and there was plenty of counter space. Our kitchen table would definitely fit. Mama had the biggest smile, almost like Daddy's banana boat smile. I was happy for her, but sad for Daddy.

We walked up the winding stairway when Unk said, "Aunt Pearl, Darlene, Rose and myself will live on the third floor. Aunt Louise will have a room on the second floor with you and Charley Louise. The remaining rooms would be for possible renters."

Chapter Five

Casseroles
Choice of chicken noodle, beef noodle,
vegetable rice & chicken served
w/tossed salad & dessert ... $5.00

When we returned to our home on Damon Street about a week later everyone helped pack our belongings for the move to 1509 West 14th Street.

I packed all day. The mood around the house, the quietness, felt different. For me, there was a sense of uncertainty for the future because in a short time, I have moved and left my Daddy and friends.

While getting ready for bed, I start thinking of those friends I'd leave behind. Already, I missed our silly conversations and the many times they helped me understand racism. One of the good things, if this is a good thing, is I'd be able to say good-bye.

Each picture I took off the wall held a memory I wouldn't forget. Especially pictures of us looking goofy and playing dress up. I had one frame with a picture of Daddy. That was the only picture I had of him, and it traveled with me every time we moved.

I picked up Daddy's picture from the small table next to my bed and while looking at it remembering all the times I grabbed the bottom of his jacket, hopped on his foot, and wrapped my arms around his leg while he walked me around the living room before he left for work.

I told myself one day we'd see each other again, but I just didn't know when.

Our family always took pictures. There were pictures each time I went to another grade, Sunday pictures, and family gathering pictures.

Although if someone else told me to pose for another picture, I'd gag, But I understood why picture taking is a good thing. It helps you remember people and events in your life. This time, I was happy there were so many pictures I could take with me.

I used to be left out of conversations involving family matters. I was happy that, at the breakfast table, they decided to include me to hear my opinion about the move.

####

While I was packing upstairs in my bedroom, Mama called me to come downstairs. I galloped down the stairs, and when I got near the bottom, I saw Unk sitting next to Mama on the sofa. Boxes were everywhere—some packed and some empty. Our house sounded hollow every time someone walked on the hardwood floors—a clunk, clunk sound.

Mama yelled, "Charley Louise, how many times have I told you not to gallop down those stairs like a horse?"

"Sorry," I said.

She asked me how far I had gotten with packing my room because the last time she saw it, there was still a lot of packing to be done.

"Almost done," I said. I looked at Unk and asked, "How are you doin'?"

Unk's eyes wandered up and looked behind me.

I twisted the upper part of my body. Mama stood with her arms and hands in a crossed position over her chest, glaring at me. How her arms were able to cross is a mystery to me since the Dorsey family was known for having huge breasts. The wrinkles in her forehead were deeper than ever.

"Don't give me that look," she said. "You're supposed to help me pack the kitchen."

Besides the living room, the kitchen is the room I hated to pack, putting pans, dishes, silverware, and hundreds of knickknacks in boxes.

Mama asked me to go on the back porch to get some more boxes and to ask Unk to help me.

Unk was sitting in Aunt Louise's favorite chair. It was right in front of the large picture window, in view of everything.

I told him what Mama needed. Then "book" came out of his mouth.

He asked me if I thought he'd forgotten.

I stopped surprised and asked, "Forgot about what?"

"The reading!"

I knew exactly what he was talking about, but if he thought I was going to remember, he was wrong. I said, "The reading?" I looked down at the ground and he stopped walking.

"I'll start reading after we move," I said.

He told me that since I had to help Mama pack, he'd let it go for a while, but not much longer after the move. I breathed a sigh of relief, trying to hold a smile inside.

We were coming back into the house from the porch and heard, "Oh my God."

I turned around and ran back into the kitchen, "What's wrong?"

"Everything's fine," Mama said. "It looks like a tornado has gone through this kitchen and we'll never get everything packed in time."

"Mama, it'll be all right." But looking around the kitchen, I thought, *If another knickknack makes it into this house, I'll scream.*

Some of our cupboards had doors, and some were covered with curtains for doors. I pulled back the curtains, praying that the pans behind them had been packed. Sure enough, they weren't. I opened one of the cupboard doors. Thank God, they were empty.

"And don't forget to pack your book."

Every time I walked through the house, Unk had to remind me of the reading punishment. He yelled into the kitchen, "I don't want you to miss out on the pleasures of reading and helping your mind to grow."

What is it with him and all of the book reading? Grandma must have punished him, and he is taking it out on all of us.

Mama and I had finished packing the kitchen. I went back upstairs to pack more of my room. I bent over to pick up something near the window and saw Susie. She was sitting on her stoop, talking with some of her friends from school.

I'll never forget the day when Susie was walking with her friends and I was walking with mine and they called us niggers. How could she act like a friend to me one day and then turn her back against me the next?

I don't know if I'll ever forgive her or understand another race thinking that they're so superior or how parts of the country can be so different when it comes to the coloreds and whites. I just know that this race thing is confusing, and it's hard not to have hatred.

"Charley Louise," Mama hollered. "Your friends from up the street are here."

I asked Mama if I could go outside with them for a while to say good-bye. She told me to follow her up to my room first and the girls could sit on the couch.

When Mama opened the door to my room, she said, "Charley Louise, you've done better than I thought. You can hang out with your friends, but don't stay out long. We have to be up early in the morning."

Mama was leaving my room and just about to close the door when I grabbed my sweater and sneaked the lipstick into my pocket. When she turned around and asked what I was putting in my pocket, I jumped.

I had to think quickly. "Oh, just some gum that was sitting on my dresser." I pulled the gum from my pants pocket and showed her.

"Now remember, don't stay out too long."

Earlier that summer, the group of friends I had hung out with had created a self-proclaimed hairstyle that we all wore from time to time.

I'd roll my hair up into a bun, tighten it with bobby pins, and brush my bangs to the front of my forehead.

If Mama knew I wore lipstick, she would have a church fit. Girls who went to church didn't wear lipstick. It was a church sin. The church felt that girls who wore lipstick were worldly girls—the ones who stayed out late at night on the corners taking money from men, or those who didn't go to any form of a church. Good girls didn't do such things.

I ran down the stairs and yelled, "Mama, I'm going next door, okay?" When we say 'next door,' sometimes it's literally next door, but sometimes it's three or four houses up or down the street. In this case, it was three houses up the street.

Me and Esther picked up our other friend at her house and saw her sitting on the stoop. I said, "Stop a minute." I walked ahead of them, one hand on my hip, and the other hand slightly bent at the elbow. My hips were swaying from side to side. When I approached stoop I said, "Hey girls."

We all sat down and turned around to make sure our friend's Mama wasn't looking out the window. I took my spot on the stoop and we helped each other put on lipstick. We all chose a red color because, according to the fashion magazine, it was the most popular color of the summer.

We talked about boys, people, and sung our favorite songs as we swayed from left to right, laughing in between. Then I heard Mama calling me. We stopped singing and looked at each other.

Mama yelled, "Charley Louise, don't make me come down there and get you."

I yelled back, "I'm coming." We hugged and cried, saying how much we'd miss the Four Stylists. We called our group that because we always tried to dress alike and look good. We wiped the lipstick from our face. Before I walked away, I gave each of them my new address.

"Don't forget me," I said, wiping tears from my face.

"We won't," they all responded.

I turned around and walked away, but this time I didn't have the same sadness like when we moved from Natchez, Mississippi. I had actually been able to say good-bye.

####

I was sleeping when I felt someone pushing me. "Charley Louise, wake up. Your uncle will be here soon." I tossed and turned and opened my eyes to look out my bedroom window.

"But Mama, it looks dark outside. What time is it?" I asked.

"Just wake up. When I come back to your room, you had better be up, you hear me?"

A few hours later, I heard a knock at the door. Mama must not have heard it because whoever it was knocked again. I ran down the stairs and peeked out the living room window. It was Unk, Aunt Pearl, Darlene and Rose.

As soon as I opened the door, they came in, all excited and happy. I couldn't understand why. Mama and I were going to leave my friends and move.

"Why the sad face, Charley Louise?" Darlene asked.

Unk asked if we were all packed and ready to move. I smirked when he said we could start with the upstairs first. He told me, Darlene and Rose to start in my room and to be careful not to break anything. He and Mama started in her room.

I couldn't count how many boxes and bags we carried. As soon as I put the last box in the car and closed the car door, I saw my friends from next door. We waved at each other. Then I looked out the back window of our station wagon and saw Susie. We kept staring at each other. All of a sudden, she ran into the middle of the street and waved. I leaned back from the window with surprise.

I went to put my hand up and quickly put it back down before she saw it. I never waved back. Maybe I should've, but I hadn't forgotten her group of friends calling us niggers on my first day of school. That memory will probably stay with me forever.

Our car turned the corner. I turned around too, my last vision being of Susie. Someday I might be able to forgive her, but not now.

Thirty minutes later, we pulled up to 1509 West 14th Street. I didn't know which was worse, living on Damon Street in a predominantly white neighborhood where at times the stares went right through my body and the houses were well-kept, or the stares from the coloreds on moving day where the houses weren't well-kept and garbage was scattered.

I liked to put on make-up and listen to music, usually singing to the radio. Other than that, I sat on the top stoop of the stairs with one French braid across the front of my head and a braided ponytail pulled to the back, popping bubble gum and dressed in my ironed summer shirt and pants.

When kids walked by, I'd say, "Hi." They either turned their heads and kept walking or giggled as they walked by. I wondered what was wrong with me. I looked like them, talked like them, and had the same kind of hair.

The only difference I noticed was that on Damon Street, all of the kids seemed to take pride in how they looked. Their Afros weren't as big and out of control. We always had pressed clothes.

On West 14th Street, there were uneven Afros like the wind

had blown through them, and a lot of the kids didn't have pressed clothes.

That was something Mama didn't tolerate. She always told me, "No matter what, carry yourself with dignity and pride."

One day, I asked Mama if I could go outside without ironing my everyday clothes.

She was cooking and looked at me. With a firm but gentle voice, she said, "No."

I said, "The other kids on the block don't iron their everyday clothes, so why do I?"

I will probably never forget the reaction on her face. She said, "As long as you're living under our roof, you will follow our rules." I turned around and went outside. I never asked that question again.

I was sitting on the top stair of our stoop in a crouched position. My arms were on my knees and my head was propped up by my hands when two girls came down the street and said, "Hello."

One of my legs slipped off the stair and my hands no longer held my head. The girls giggled as I tried to act like it was an accident.

I said, "Hello, my name is Charley Louise. What are your names?"

They told me their names were Laura and Dorothy. That was the beginning of a new friendship, and a different type of summer growing up.

There were different groups of people that lived in the West 14th Street area, women of the night standing on corners where nightclubs blasted music, street hustlers and gamblers, men with processed hair and finger waves, driving pink Cadillacs, and drug dealers.

The other groups were the everyday people trying to earn an honest living and the church goers trying to convince the hustlers, gamblers, pimps and women of the night to change their ways, telling them that God is the only way and to repent.

It didn't matter to me how a person looked, talked, or dressed. That's not how our family was raised. So, throughout the summer, my two friends and I occasionally spoke to the worldly women and asked them why they do what they do.

Most times, we were told to mind our own business as they walked away, swaying their hips and puffing on cigarettes. We'd run across the street, laughing, before Mama caught me acting out. We sat back on the top stoop. It was always the top stoop because you could see more of what was happening up and down the street.

We also talked about the boys on the street and who liked who or who was going out with who. On a few occasions, we saw children and grown-ups running from what we thought were gangs.

When Mama was at work, we danced to the neighbors' music playing on the Victrola, acting like we were at the Apollo in New York.

That summer, I learned how to laugh again, but I never forgot my friends on Damon Street. Sometimes, on her way to work, Mama would drop me off at my old friends' houses on Damon Street. Other times, we would write to each other, giving our letters to Mama for hand delivery.

I was too old to hop onto Daddy's leg and have him whisk me around the house, but I missed our private conversations. If we would stop moving so much, I probably would have written him more letters, I lifted my mattress, where I hid my diary.

Chapter Six

Sweet & sour chicken, rice, salad,
rolls w/butter, dessert ... $5.00

Day 5, Journal Entry 5 ... Well, Daddy, we've moved again for the second time, getting further and further away from you. I have made some new friends along the way, but life and racism is hard to understand. I keep thinking about the day we went to town ... you remember, in Natchez, and you tried to help that man. I was a little girl then, but how do you live with racism and still smile and turn the other way. Mama and my friends are helping me along the way, but it seems like each place we move, it's handled in different ways. I do miss you and I know that we will see each other soon ... I just don't know when. Love, Charley Louise

I laid half-asleep and heard footstep in the hallway. My bedroom door creaked. I lifted my head a little, opening my eyes. "Charley Louise, wake up. It's time to get ready for school."

I moaned.

"Wake up and get ready for school."

"Yes, ma'am." I rubbed sleep crumbs from the corners of my eyes.

Already, I could smell biscuits, eggs, and bacon, our usual breakfast on weekdays. Sometimes Mama added hot or cold cereal.

Usually, I'd hurry to get dressed and out the door. This time I wasn't in such a hurry. I didn't know if I wanted to attend a school other than the one on Damon Street.

There was a knock at the door. When I opened it there was Laura and Dorothy sitting on the bottom step. I felt a banana boat smile spread over my face.

Mama couldn't go with me because she had to work, and so did the rest of the household. My cousins weren't in the same school. They were younger than me and still attended elementary school.

My friends and I were giggling and laughing when all of a sudden I looked up and saw a big, tall, dirty building with cracked steps. I stopped.

"Is that our school?"

"Yes. What's wrong?"

"I guess nothing," I said.

"What did you expect?"

"I don't know. Just …"

"Just what?"

The hallways seemed dark, like someone hadn't paid the electric bill. On Damon Street, there were so many kids that you were pushed and shoved as you walked through the hallways.

The majority of the kids were colored. When the teacher called roll, I wasn't out of place, although I still saw stares when my name was called.

There were a lot of empty desks and kids who walked into the classroom late. The teacher would call roll and say, "Johnny?"

There'd be no answer or the student would run into the classroom and yell, "Here." It seemed like for every two or three names, there was either a "here" or no answer. I wondered how so many kids could be sick.

When the bell rang for lunch, kids leapt from their desks, hustled to put their books away in their lockers, and practically ran to the school cafeteria

We could sit anywhere as long as we sat by our classmates. There wasn't a section for coloreds or whites.

Lunch was the perfect time to ask where all of the kids were and so I did.

I was told, "Most of them hang out late in the streets and don't get up for school. Or their mamas ain't home yet from hanging out in the streets."

They said that the truancy officers would go to their houses and either pick them up to take them to school or let their parents know that the school is looking for their child.

My friends told me to not hold my breath because they won't get to their houses right away. The truancy officers were always looking for someone.

I knew they'd never come to the Dorsey house because if I skipped school, Mama would whip my butt. She'd then say, "It's a sin not to get all of the education you can. The world isn't going to hand you nothin' free."

Walking home was much different than when I walked home with my friends on Damon Street. Kids were running around, some who should have been in school. Women leaned out of windows, yelling, "Tony, get up here and help me do somethin'" or "Child, if you don't get out of those streets, I'll bring my belt down there and whip you in front of everybody."

There wasn't the insulting name-calling with the continued giggling afterwards.

When I came home, I opened the door and smelled food cooking. Mama was in the kitchen, as usual, making supper. Our house always smelled good because either Mama or Aunt Louise was cooking.

"Charley Louise, how did your first day go at your new school?"

"It was different."

"How so?"

"A lot of kids didn't come to class. I don't know. It was just different."

"After you make a few more friends, you'll like it. Give it time. The neighbors next door seem like good people, and they have a girl about your age. Have you met her yet?"

"I have. She isn't in the same grade as me, but I'll get to know her better."

When I was coming home from school, I saw her sitting on the top stair of her stoop. I said, "Hi," and she waved. She never got up and I kept walking.

After Darlene, Rose and I came home from school, it was a rule in our household to change from school clothes into everyday clothes. They were the clothes that had been torn and fixed by Mama or Aunt Louise.

I did my homework and went outside to sit on the first stair at the top of our stoop. I leaned over to see if the girl next door was outside. I said, "My name is Charley Louise. What's yours?" She looked at me and turned her head.

"You don't have to be so mean. I'm just being friendly." I leaned back and sat down.

"My name is Wanda. Wanda Smith."

I walked to the bottom of the stairs, peeked around the corner, and smiled. "Nice to meet you … Wanda Smith."

We sat on the top stoop saying nothing, so I was surprised when she said, "Look at those fools across the street. That man is always trying to hustle someone."

Staring at the people across the street, I asked, "Have you lived around here for a long time?"

"Nah, I grew up a little further over, but I know this neighborhood."

"My family is from Natchez."

She frowned and tilted her head at me. "Natchez? Where the hell is Natchez?"

"Your Mama lets you cuss?" I said, startled.

She smiled. "No, but I do it anyway."

Answer the question, "Where the hell is Natchez?"

"Mississippi ... down South."

She looked confused. "I was told that the South is all rural. Countrified people live there with no street lights, just roads"

She was right, but I didn't let her know. I said, "My mama and my family moved to Chicago on Damon Street, and now here on West 14th Street. We've moved too many times to make friends, but I hope this will be the last."

Looking at me with a soft expression, she said, "My family moves a lot too, but I don't have any problems making friends."

When I asked her why they moved so much, she changed the subject and started talking about a pimp across the street. I figured that somewhere inside her, there was a secret, and she wasn't about to tell me.

When I heard her loud-pitched voice from inside of the house calling me, I stood up. Halfway down the stairs, I turned around and said, "See you later, alligator." She was already walking away, but turned around with the strangest look on her face. "What?"

"See you later, alligator."

Wrinkles formed at the top of her forehead. I shrugged and said, "When I say, *see you later alligator, you say, after while crocodile.*"

"That's stupid."

"Just say it. It will be our secret saying."

She smiled and said, "After while crocodile."

We both smiled. She went into her house and I went into mine, running up the stairs. Every night, that's how we ended the day. It brought back memories with Daddy.

Soon, we became closer friends than the Laura and Dorothy, the girls up the street. She started walking to school with us. The only time we didn't hang out together was when she'd go away for the weekend to spend time with her daddy. He didn't live with her family either. I think that was another bond that kept our friendship. Laura's and Dorothy's fathers were living with them, but sometimes they wouldn't come home.

One day, a silence brought our laughter to an abrupt stop. Wanda looked down at the stairs beneath us and then back at me. "Can I ask you a question?"

"Sure," I said. "Why do you have that funny look on your face?"

"Why do you talk funny?"

I wrinkled my nose. "What do you mean?"

"You know ... like a white girl. Aren't you from the south?"

I stood up and stomped my foot. "No I don't. Take that back right now."

She stood up, leaning into my face. "Well, why do you dress and sound that way?"

I looked at my clothes and shoes and then at hers. "This is how my mama and our family talk and dress. On Damon Street, I didn't have any problems with the way I talk."

She said with a laugh in her voice, "Oh, where everything is pretty and clean. Kids have a mama and daddy that live in the same house and sound like you. Look around. What do you see? Maybe I missed something."

As I looked around the block, I saw kids playing, fighting, and men with pink Cadillacs and more than one woman in the car. She was right. Why is it that the colored families seemed to have a hard time staying together?

"Now describe Damon Street."

I stood there staring, thinking, *Damon Street had nice homes, families that were together. Fathers went to work, most mothers stayed home, and kids went to school - A predominantly white community.*

She was right, but I kept my thoughts to myself. I said, "Damon

Street has problems … racial problems. There are racial problems everywhere. Would you rather live with racial problems or live in an area where people see no hope?"

In the midst of silence, Mama yelled, "Charley Louise? It's time to come in. You have school tomorrow."

I got up from the stoop, wondering if I still had a friend. I held my head down walking down the stairs. Near the bottom of the stairs, I heard, "See you later, alligator."

Smiling, I turned around, "After while crocodile."

If that argument didn't take away our friendship, nothing could. I hurried down the rest of the stairs.

####

On the way to school the next morning, I knocked on Wanda's door, but there was no answer. I knocked several times and looked at the windows to see if the curtains would move, but nothing happened.

For a week, I knocked on the door. While walking away, someone yelled out of a window, "They moved."

I looked up and asked, "When?"

"A couple of days ago."

How could they have moved so quickly? I thought. How did I not see them moving?

After school let out, I hurried home and ran through the house looking for Mama until I found her in one of the bedrooms. I asked, "What happened to the neighbors?"

She said, "Slow down and sit down on the bed. I don't know everything, but the family has moved. I don't know the day or time. People in the neighborhood said, they moved in the middle of the night."

Since I never went into her house, I couldn't see if they were packing boxes.

"How do people all of a sudden move, let alone in the middle of the night?" I asked.

Mama chuckled. "It's not uncommon. People do this all the time. They are here one day and gone the next. Now go and get everyone. Supper is ready."

At the dinner table, I picked at my food.

Mama said, "Eat everything on your plate. We can't afford to waste any food. I know Wanda became a good friend of yours and you'll miss her, but it'll be all right. You have your other friends up the street around the corner. Eat your supper."

Why do grown-ups always say it'll be all right when maybe sometimes it won't be all right? I ate the peas and chicken left on my plate and went upstairs to do my homework.

I went to sleep sad that night, wondering how Wanda was doing and where she was at. Before I closed my eyes, I said, "See you later, alligator ... After while, crocodile." I turned over and went to sleep.

####

Pop. Pop. Pop.

I leapt out of bed, yelling as I ran down the hallway toward Mama's room, "What is that noise?"

Unk ran into the room. "Is everyone all right?"

"Yes," Mama said.

Unk headed downstairs to peek out the window and told us to stay upstairs. I started to walk behind him, but Mama pulled me back and told me to let Unk see what's going on. He didn't need my help.

When he came back to my room, he said it was just some commotion going on down the street. He didn't see any guns, but he saw a gang of boys fighting. We immediately made sure that all of the windows were closed and the doors were locked.

"Are we going to be safe?" I asked.

"We'll be fine, but everyone should sleep on one floor for the rest of the night," Unk said.

I was never so scared in my life. Between the gun shots, kids wanting my school money, and my friend moving in the middle of the night, I was ready to move back to Damon Street.

The weekends seemed to be when most of the problems happened. After that incident, sometimes on the weekends I'd wake up in the middle of the night, not able to sleep, I'd peak out the window.

The street hustlers were on the corners, and the ladies of the night stopped anyone who passed by, trying to meet the weekend quota for their pimps. Some kids were sitting on their stoops way past their bedtime, and Fred the drunk was walking with a limp, dragging his left leg, doing his usual job of asking people for money.

Every weekend, Mama gave me my allowance, and every weekend, if Fred saw me sitting on the stoop, he'd come across the street wearing the same dirty, smelly, oversized trench coat. His face was withdrawn and sagging with wrinkles. He'd look up and say, "You got any spare change? I need to buy some food."

Although I felt sorry for him, I always said, "No." I knew he wasn't going to buy any food for himself. He'd head straight to the liquor store.

"I don't have any money, Fred. Go and bother someone else."

"Yes you do, Charley Louise. You just got your allowance."

"How do you know?"

"Fred knows everything," he said.

"My money is for me."

"Come on, Charley Louise. I just want to shoot some pool."

"I thought you wanted the money to buy some food. Now you

tell me you want the money to shoot pool." I looked at him and told myself that although he was the best pool player in the area and that probably was his life, if I gave him any money, he was going to go straight to the liquor store. I said, "Go about your way."

He walked away, hunched over. I felt bad for him, but I knew he'd find someone else.

Even though girls came from up the street and around the corner to talk, I continued to sit on my stoop, peeking over the concrete divider, wondering how the girl who lived next door was doing. I missed my friend. Without her, I found it hard to want to fit in and began to miss the Damon Street community.

The school year was long, and I didn't care for the community or the school. I was tired of the gangs, pimps, and even old Jimmy. Monday morning would arrive too soon and I'd have to get up and walk to school.

During the school year, I stayed in touch with my friends from Damon Street. Their letters were substitute for friends I could not talk to in person. We talked about the same things, boys, what was happening in their community, and what was happening in mine.

On Sunday evening, I had just written a letter to my friends on Damon Street. Mama called to let me know that dinner was ready and the family was waiting for me.

I moped and plopped down in my chair at the dinner table.

Mama asked, "What's wrong?"

"Why can't I go back to the school on Damon Street?"

"Your Uncle John found this beautiful house for the family where we could all live together. Don't you like it here?"

"It was better on Damon Street. The school was better and I was starting to feel comfortable."

"You'll be all right. Now eat your dinner."

####

Our family was at the dinner table talking and laughing when we heard three knocks at the door.

Mama walked toward the front door, yelling, "Coming." The person knocked three times again. "Here I come. Just a minute," Mama said.

The rest of us leaned backward in our chairs, trying to see who would come through the door.

"Hello, Madam. My name is Mr. Yakes, the truant officer from the West 14th Street school. Is Charley Louise Dorsey your daughter?"

"Yes," Mama said. "Please come in. Is there a problem?"

The man said that he was here to let Mama know that I had been skipping school and didn't attend class today. I gulped my Kool-Aid.

Mama asked, "Are you sure? She wouldn't do anything like that."

"It's true. I have the teacher's attendance report. If you have any questions, contact the school office." Then he left.

Mama closed the door and yelled my name so loudly that God probably even heard.

I jumped in my seat while Darlene and Rose giggled and said, "Ooh. You're in trouble."

Mama stomped into the kitchen. In a stern voice, she said, "You're my daughter who I raised not to lie and to get a good education. Follow me into the living room."

I walked slowly behind her, not trying to figure out what she was going to say but how she was going to say it.

Mama stopped and said, "Have a seat on the couch."

I sat on the couch, nervous, and she sat in the chair facing me. For a second, she just looked at me. I started to sweat.

"How was school today?"

"Why?" I said slowly. "Did someone get hurt?"

"Today I had a visitor."

"Yes, we saw him. Who was that?"

"Do you know a Mr. Yakes?"

"No, ma'am."

"Mr. Yakes is your school's truant officer. Do you know why he would visit our home?"

I hesitated to make sure I said the right thing and answered, "No ma'am."

Mama glared at me. "Are you sure? Don't lie."

I blurted, "Mama, I don't like going to that school. These kids don't go to school anyway. Can I please go back to the Damon Street School?"

Mama said, "We had the same situation when you stayed with Grandma Emma."

I whimpered. "I was taken away from Daddy and moved to two communities in three years. How fast am I supposed to change?"

Mama sat up straight, and I got scared. I had never talked back to her like that and wasn't sure what she was going to do. Usually she'd say, "Get me the belt" or "Go to your room."

I moved to the back seams of the couch, tucked into the cushions.

Darlene, Rose and the rest of the family peeked out of the kitchen, listening to every word.

I decided that the West 14th Street community wasn't the problem. It was me. But I still wanted to go back to Damon Street and was determined to figure out how to accomplish that. I was tired of going to school with undisciplined kids who didn't want to learn anything.

The Damon Street kids weren't perfect either, but at least I didn't have to worry about gun shots in the middle of the night. And, for the most part, the whites and coloreds seemed to get along. We left them alone and they left us alone.

####

I walked home from school with my friends. Mama met me at the door with a smile on her face.

"Why are you smiling?" I asked.

"Come in and have a seat. I have something to talk to you about," She said.

"Is Daddy coming?" I asked.

"No." She paused a moment. "Are you sure you want to go back to the Damon Street school?"

I jumped up from the sofa and shouted, "Yes! Can I go? When do I start?"

"Calm down and stop bouncing up and down on my sofa. I worked hard to get that sofa."

Then she looked at me and said, "I made an appointment to meet with the school boards, Damon Street and West 14th Street, to discuss if you can transfer. I want to make sure this is what you wanted. If it's approved, don't even think about transferring back to the West 14th Street school district."

I was sitting in the living room when letters fell through the mail slot onto our floor. I yelled, "Mama, the mail is here."

"Well, pick it up off the floor and bring it into the kitchen."

I walked to the kitchen with excitement, looking through the mail. I gave Mama the one that was addressed from the West 14th Street school district.

"Hurry, hurry," I told her as she opened the envelope. She read it silently with her eyes going from one line to another.

Her voice was getting louder and louder: "Charley Louise Dorsey, a student at the West 14th Street School System, has been granted permission to attend the Damon Street School System beginning the next semester in the fall year. Please contact that school system for further instructions. They will help with the transfer process."

Mama reminded me that this decision was non-negotiable. I asked her what that meant and she told me that I wouldn't be able to transfer back if I decided I didn't like the Damon Street School.

Although I lived 30 minutes away by car, the bus ride would take longer because I'd have to transfer before reaching the Damon Street School.

After the decision was made that I could go back to the Damon Street School, the family had a group meeting and decided Mama would take me to school on her way to work and Unk would pick me up when he got off work.

That summer, I spent time with my friends across the way on Damon Street. That's what my friends and I called it—across the way. One day, after we sang songs by our favorite singers, I blurted, "This fall I'm coming back to Damon Street School."

Everyone stared at me with their mouths open wide.

They told me to repeat what I just said, and I did. We all screamed until one of their mothers asked if we were all right.

"Yes," we said in unison.

During that summer, we laughed, played music, and acted like we were at the Apollo in New York City.

####

On September 1, I woke up extra early. Mama didn't have to knock on the door, come in my room, and tug me to get up for the first day of school.

I must have had a glow because at the breakfast table.

Darlene looked at me and said, "She's happy because she's going to Damon Street School with the rest of the Bouswai coloreds … the ones who think they're better than all of us. We don't know why she wants to go to that white school and not stay with her own kind."

"Stop arguing. It sounds so ugly," Mama said. "Let's go, Charley Louise, before you're late."

When the car pulled up to the Damon Street School, I was a little nervous. I hadn't been to this school in a few years. The kids looked bigger. Some I didn't recognize.

I saw my friends, Esther, Jill and Mona as they passed our car, not noticing until I got out and put my hands on my hip with my pinky extended. "Hey girls."

"Charley Louise!" They screamed. "You're here. You're actually here."

"Yes, girls, I am."

After school, I was sitting on the top stairs, waiting for Unk to pick me up, when someone tapped my shoulder. It was Susie. I quickly stood up. Before I could get the right words out, Susie said to let her talk first. I didn't let her. I said, "I'm not that same little girl where you can call me names. I'm—"

"I don't hang around with the same girls."

"Why not?"

"I feel bad about that day and have thought about it ever since."

I felt my mouth drop open.

"You want me to believe that you've changed that quickly over a few years?"

"Yes," she said.

She told me she was older and, through her family's travels, had seen a lot of the world.

"I'm truly sorry for what happened," she said. "It wasn't the right thing to do. Will you accept my apology?"

"Let me think about it and get back to you," I said.

Her ride came and she left. At that moment, my friends came up from behind me and told me that they heard everything.

"Are you really going to forgive her?"

"I'm not sure."

A car pulled up and honked. It was Unk. I asked him, "Could you give my friends a ride home? It's on the way."

"Sure," he said. "Get in the car."

While we were in the car, I asked Unk, "Do you remember the story of the white girls from this school who called me out of my name a few years ago?"

"I remember. Are they bothering you again?"

"No. One of the girls asked for my forgiveness."

"What did you think about that?"

I looked over at him. "I don't know. One part of me wants to forgive her, but the other part of me doesn't."

He said, "Forgiveness is a hard thing to do. Dig deep inside of your soul and you'll do the right thing."

"How will I know what the right thing is?"

"When the right time comes, you'll know." He grinned.

####

The day had started out warm and gotten cool after school. My friends and I were waiting for Unk to pick us up when I saw Susie waiting for her ride, too. Some kids were teasing her.

"Susie has changed," I said. "I don't know how, but she has changed. Let's help her."

"Why?" My friends had their arms crossed. "Have you forgotten a few years ago? Did she help you?"

"No, but two wrongs don't make a right." I walked over to Susie. "Are you all right?"

"Go away," she said. "I'll be fine."

There was a pause for a moment when our eyes met. "I forgive you," I said.

She looked at me in disbelief. Then a banana boat smile appeared on her face.

From that point on, Susie and I were friends again, but at a distance. We'd smile at each other and say, "Hi." Sometimes she'd eat lunch with us.

"We'll probably never understand you, Charley Louise," Esther said.

Day 6, Journal 6 ... Daddy, I was finally able to transfer from the West 14th Street School to Damon Street School. Mama met with both school boards and everything worked out. The white girl who called me outside of my name has changed a lot. She said that her family traveled around the world and she now sees people in a different way. We don't see each other all the time ... just a "hi" here and there. I miss you a lot and hope one day we'll see each other again. Love, Charley Louise

Chapter Seven

Bar-b-q chicken, potato salad,
jell-o, cookies, rolls w/butter ... $5.00

Every Sunday night, there was one ritual. Mama, Aunt Louise and Aunt Pearl would get together and plan a menu for the week. Once the menu was made it was then placed on the front door of the refrigerator. The menu changed only for holidays or for special guests.

####

The aroma of baked yams, collard greens, and fried chicken flowed through the Dorsey house. Mama, Aunt Louise and Aunt Pearl were in the kitchen cooking and singing to gospel music ... mostly Mahalia Jackson, "Go tell it on the mountain, over the hills and everywhere. Oh, go tell it on the mountain that Jesus Christ is born," tapping their toes and saying, "Hallelujah" with each pause in the music.

From upstairs, I heard the tapping of spoons against pots and pans and the clanking of silverware. The scent of food cooking wandered underneath the doors and around the curtains. The smell went through the open windows in the summer and when the front door was opened in the winter.

But, on this particular morning, they opened the kitchen drawer where the aprons were kept, and picked one out for a special meal they were going to cook—the Thanksgiving meal. It didn't matter which apron. Mama had no favorites. She said, "Anyone would do."

She unfolded an apron, wrapped her hands around the top, flung it up in the air, and yanked it up and down until she heard a loud "pop."

When I was a little girl, I'd copy Mama's every move in the kitchen. Now that I was a teenager, I'd rather do any other chore than help the kitchen. But no matter where I was, I'd hear, "Charley Louise, come help me in the kitchen. And bring Darlene and Rose with you."

We moaned and groaned, but if we didn't walk in kitchen fast enough, Mama would say, "Don't let me call you again. The next time I'll bring the belt with me." No one was too old to have the belt, so no matter where we were, we ran into the kitchen ... sometimes out of breath.

We'd come downstairs, dragging our feet and hanging onto the stair's rails, or from outside with friends and into the kitchen. All of us had long faces except for one cousin, Rose. She was always happy about cooking and working in the kitchen.

She pushed us aside, knocking me against the doorway, saying, "Good morning, Aunt Rose, Aunt Louise and Mama. How are you doing?" Then she scurried to the apron drawer like candy was inside it.

Darlene and I walked slowly to the drawer and fought over who got which apron and what color. "Just pick out an apron and stop fighting," Mama would say. "You don't have to look through them. They'll all serve the same purpose."

After Mama gave us our cooking assignments for the morning, Darlene and I would say to each other, "We knew little Ms. Homemaker would jump ahead of everyone. It's just aprons."

Rose frowned at us. Then she looked up at Mama smiling. "What's on the menu today?"

Mama said, "You mean 'What is on the menu today.'" She constantly corrected us and told us the proper way to speak. While the rest of us prayed that our names were next to the easiest thing on the menu to make, Rose looked forward to helping make the most difficult thing.

Since there were guests in the house renting rooms and a long way from their own families, we invited them to share our Thanksgiving dinner.

The menu included: Two large turkeys, one large pan of homemade dressing, one large pan of potato salad, two pans of fried chicken, one large ham glazed with brown sugar, one large pan of fresh string beans, one large pan of macaroni and cheese, one large pan of fresh yams, one large pan of fresh collard greens, two large pitchers of grape and strawberry Kool-Aid, two freshly baked cakes, two large freshly baked apple pies, and two large sweet potato pies.

We usually peeled potatoes, plucked little thin hairs from the chicken, snapped off the string bean tips and cleaned the collard greens.

Mama said, "Isn't this the start of a blessed day that the Lord has allowed us to wake up?"

The record started skipping. Mama left to fix it and came back into the kitchen singing and clapping her hands, swaying back and forth. "Hallelujah, hallelujah. Sing that song, Mahalia."

She walked next to Aunt Louise, and she started swaying and singing, mixing up the corn bread stuffing. Then Rose started singing and bumped Darlene and she bumped me. Soon we were all singing and laughing.

I looked around at everyone and began to think about Daddy, wondering what he was doing and if he was spending Thanksgiving by himself.

Darlene looked at me and said, "Charley Louise, I know what you're thinking about. Your Daddy is okay. He's probably visiting his family and thinkin' about you, too. He's fine."

I looked at her and said, "You're probably right. But that doesn't stop me from thinkin' about him." I turned around and kept plucking and cleaning. With a low voice, I started singing to a Mahalia Jackson song. I don't remember which song it was.

We ate until our bellies couldn't hold anything more. We left some of the food out in case we wanted to come back for seconds and thirds. Unk watched television. Darlene, Rose and me went upstairs to nap.

"Clean up time. Clean up time."

I turned over in my bed, looked up, and saw Mama. "Go wake up Darlene and Rose. It's time to clean the kitchen."

The worst time to clean up a meal is Thanksgiving, Christmas, and Easter. We walked into the kitchen and stopped at the door. It seemed like there were more pots, pans, and dishes than we started with. We looked at each other and said, "We might as well get started."

After a while, to make it fun, we started joking and laughing with each other, making a game out of it, when I heard a loud snore.

Rose peeked around the corner and said, "Daddy's snoring." She tiptoed into the living room and placed her two fingers across his nose. The loudest snore came out. She ran back into the kitchen as fast as she could. He tossed in his chair and cocked his head the other way.

"That was close," I said.

Unk's snoring was louder than the TV show he had been watching and didn't have any rhythm.

"That was funny," Rose said.

"Yeah, but not as funny if we don't get these dishes done soon before Mama walks down those stairs."

Day 7, Journal Entry 7 ... Hello Daddy, the family spent another Thanksgiving without you. The house was full of prayer and the aroma of food. Of course, Mama, Aunt Louise and Aunt Pearl had to invite Mahalia Jackson, the greatest gospel singer in the world, to our home. You know what I mean. The Victrola was loud as could be. I pray for the day we can reunite again. I hope that you're not alone and your health is good. Love, Charley Louise

####

On a hot Saturday evening, I woke up thirsty and went downstairs to the kitchen to get a glass of water. I closed the refrigerator door and choked on the water when I saw the weekly list of chores that Mama had hung for everyone to see on a big sheet of white paper and written in black ink so Darlene, Rose or myself couldn't change it.

I wouldn't have paid it much attention but noticed an added job was put underneath my name. I was supposed to clean the living room and help clean the smaller guest room.

Normally, the guest rooms were off limits. Aunt Louise was the only person who cleaned those rooms. The rooms were rented to grown-ups, and the family didn't want us to find anything that didn't need to be found.

The list of chores changed every week. The only thing that didn't change was cleaning our own bedrooms every weekend. Every morning we also had to make our beds before going to school. My family was disciplined, and there was no room for negotiations.

It seemed like there was a rule for everything. The dishes had to be washed by a certain time in the evening. We couldn't watch television on Sundays because it was God's day. We couldn't have our friends in the house if a grown-up wasn't there. We had to study at a certain time after school.

Sometimes when I was sitting outside on the top stoop with a friend, I'd hear, "Charley Louise has to come in the house now and you'll have to go home." How embarrassing.

My friends and I came up with a plan. I'd go into the house and up to my bedroom. They'd walk until they got to the corner of the building and would peek around the corner. When they saw me open my bedroom window and poke my head out, they'd return and we'd whisper to each other.

This lasted for a little while until Mama walked into my room one night and caught me leaning out of the window. She yelled, "Charley Louise, what are you doing?"

Startled, I bumped my head against the window. Mama leaned out of the window to see who I was talking to, but my friends ran around the corner, out of sight. Mama shut the window hard. She turned around and pointed her finger at me as she continued yelling. It was so loud that everyone down the hallway could hear it.

Darlene and Rose peeked into my bedroom door and quickly moved out of Mama's way or they would have gotten walked over.

"See, that's what you get for trying to act all grown up," Rose said.

I rubbed the back of my head, laid on my bed, and thought about what my punishment would be.

Two days had passed. Then I heard, "Charley Louise, come down here."

Not only was I supposed to do my list of chores, but I also had to wash dishes for Rose and Darlene the remainder of the week. I don't believe there was any stricter house than ours. We had bed curfews for the school nights and weekends. And we couldn't curse or say phrases like "I can't do this" and "I ain't gonna."

In our neighborhood, most of the kids cursed, even at school. But on Damon Street school there wasn't much cursing. A lot of the people talked properly. When I came home, I found myself changing the way I spoke and acted. The cousins didn't have a hard time because they went to school in the same neighborhood.

Around our friends and away from Mama, we decided to talk just like everyone else. We had to fit in or we'd be laughed at and teased.

Other big rules in our house were that we could not wear make-up, wear our dresses above our knees, no drinking, playing cards, or playing what was called "worldly music" … street music.

The only time I'd listen to street music was when I visited my friends on Damon Street over the summer weekend or when I heard it blasting from the closest bar or in the neighborhood. I had a churchgoing, God-fearing family, and that just wasn't tolerated.

We didn't have many family vacations because Mama worked all the time. Our family vacations consisted of driving around the Chicago areas that we hadn't seen before or going to the park for a picnic. There were times that Mama traveled, but it wasn't for vacation. She traveled with her employer, the Rosenbergs.

####

The Rosenbergs' were a very wealthy Jewish family who lived in a gated community that had some of Chicago's biggest and most beautiful homes.

One day Mama took me to work with her. There was a man who guarded the community. No one was allowed inside unless invited. Mama walked up to the gate and told the guard, "Call the Rosenberg home and tell them Mrs. Dorsey and her daughter are here."

The guard went inside of a small building the size of an outhouse, but with glass, and picked up the telephone. I walked closer to the gate, wrapping my hands around the bars, my face almost touching them, to get a closer look at all of the homes. The guard leaned outside of the little house with a mean look on his face and pointed his finger at me. Mama yanked my arm and pulled me closer to her. The gate opened in slow motion.

There were black limousines with chauffeurs everywhere opening the car doors for people or sitting in them as though they were waiting. Lawns were being mowed and hedges cut.

I didn't see stray cats or dogs, kids in the streets, corner girls, or bars anywhere.

We walked up to the house where Mama worked and rang the bell. A tall, colored man wearing a tuxedo and gloves opened the door. Mama told me his name is Mr. Johnny.

"Good morning, Mrs. Dorsey. How are you doing?" Then he looked toward me. "Charley Louise, I swear you are growing taller than in your pictures."

I returned the smile and said, "Thank you, Mr. Johnny."

The Rosenberg family consisted of his wife, three kids, one dog and Mr. Johnny, the butler. Although Mr. Johnny was a well-dressed man, my eyes always went to his potbelly stomach that hung over his belt.

He wore black suits and matching vests. Inside his vest pocket, he had a gold watch that was attached to a long chain. When Mr. Rosenberg didn't ask Mama for the time, he'd raise his right eyebrow and prop a round piece of glass up against his right eye, pull out his clock from his pocket, place his thumb against the cover, and flip it open. Every time I saw him open it, I'd think, *if Daddy was here, I'd buy him one of those clocks.*

When I first walked into the Rosenbergs' home, I entered a big room called a foyer, then the living room, and then the formal dining room. Our whole house could fit inside.

When I walked into the living room, I saw the largest fireplace I'd ever seen. I believe five people or more could stand inside without bending a knee.

Their family traveled three times a year in summer, spring, and early winter to Europe, what they called "homeland," for a month. A lot of the time the whole family traveled, but sometimes Mr. Rosenberg traveled alone. There were times Mama traveled with them, taking care of the kids. The only time Mama didn't travel is when the rest of the family stayed home.

There were many times I felt jealous, like they were taking her away from me. I always thought Mrs. Rosenberg must have felt the same thing and would invite me over to visit with the children. Two of them were just about my age. We didn't have everything in common, but we had enough.

Mama raised me to socialize with any group of people, black or white, rich or poor, so the transition wasn't hard. Only the oldest Rosenberg child didn't care for me. She'd tell her sister and brother, "Don't play with her. Don't play with the hired help ... a colored girl."

Chapter Eight

Dessert selections
Cakes: carrot, cherry, cherry chip, lemon, chocolate,
cheese cake, tart cake w/strawberry or cherry pie filling

Ca-thump.

"What's that?" I heard someone say.

"Sounds like it came from the other room," the butler said.

The Rosenbergs had hardwood floors in their home and this sound was so loud that it seemed as if it was right next to me on the first floor of the house. The kids and I were sitting in the foyer, talking and giggling when we all jumped.

The butler ran into the dining room yelling, "Somebody come help. Mrs. Dorsey is lying on the floor."

We ran into the dining room. "Someone help Mama," I screamed. "She's not moving."

The Rosenbergs ran into the room, asking what happened. Mr. Johnny said, "All we know is that we heard a loud thump and then Mrs. Dorsey was found lying on the floor with her eyes closed."

I started to cry and asked, "Is my mama going to die?"

"She isn't going to die. Let's wait for the doctor to arrive," Mr. Rosenberg told me.

The Rosenbergs had a grandfather clock in the same room, and I couldn't keep my eyes off it. It seemed like every minute I'd ask the same question, "When is the doctor going to get here?"

I'd get the same answer, "He'll be here soon. Be patient," Mr. Johnny said softly.

Mrs. Rosenberg and I hugged when we heard the doorbell.

Everyone jumped. Mr. Rosenberg told the butler, "Hurry, go and answer the door. If it's the doctor, bring him in the dining room."

The doctor came in, leaned down, put his stethoscope on Mama's chest, and listened for her to breathe. He whispered something to Mr. Rosenberg, at times looking toward me.

"What's wrong?" I asked with tears coming down my face. "Is my mama going to die?"

"No," the doctor said. "But your mother's health isn't the same."

"What do you mean?"

"She needs to rest for a while," the doctor said. "Her body is tired."

Mama had worked for the Rosenbergs ever since we moved to Chicago. They had treated our family very well and on many occasions told us that we were part of the family.

When the doctor said that Mama needed some rest, the Rosenbergs told her to take all the time she needed. Mama, being stubborn, didn't want to let their family down and tried to come back to work sooner than the doctor said.

One day Mama when was cleaning their dinner table, Mrs. Rosenberg passed by and saw her sitting in a chair, leaning over the table and holding her head.

Mrs. Rosenberg touched Mama's shoulder and said, "Go home and rest. Don't worry about the rest of the night."

The next day Mama met with the Rosenbergs. She told them that her sister, Louise could help until she is gets better and to please let her know their answer. A few days later the telephone rang. It was Mrs. Rosenberg. She said the family had made a decision. There was a slight pause on the telephone. She told Mama that would be a good idea because the family and the kids knew Aunt Louise.

Every day Aunt Louise woke up before daylight, went down to the kitchen, and made morning coffee and breakfast for Unk before he left for work.

I didn't have to wake up as early, but with the aroma of the coffee and breakfast cooking, who wouldn't?

At first I thought everything would change. Aunt Louise was the one who woke the cousins and me up for school, prepared our breakfast, and made sure we got out the house on time to catch the city bus for school.

With Mama being sick, I wasn't sure what would happen, but at the family meeting a few days ago, we were told that the kids would have to take on more responsibility.

The family had bought us clocks, and one responsibility was that we had to set our own alarm clocks to get up for school and lay our clothes out. Lastly, most mornings Aunt Louise would still make our breakfast and keep it warm in the oven, but other days we would eat cold cereal.

This is where the chores, breakfast, lunch, and dinner lists that adorned the refrigerator door came in handy.

For about two months, Aunt Louise took on the role of Mama. The coffee was made, and out the door she went to catch the two buses it took to get across town to the exclusive gated community where the Rosenbergs lived. She left the car home for Mama just in case there were any emergencies.

Before going out the door to school, I'd peek into Mama's bedroom to see how she was doing. Many times she'd be asleep. I kissed her forehead and say, "I love you, Mama."

About one month later, Mama would up get from time to time, roaming the hallways.

There were times that I peeked into her bedroom, rubbed her forehead, and worked up enough courage to tell her, "I was scared … scared you were going to die and I'd be left alone."

In our family, we didn't like to hear negative words. It was against our family values. We were raised to think positively and that

God would fix everything.

"Mama, have you tried to write Daddy ... you know, about your health and everything?"

She looked at me with a blank stare, closed her eyes, and didn't answer. I kissed her on the cheek and said, "I'll check on you later. You get some rest."

Mama's health was constantly on my mind. Over the past year, I had gone from writing Daddy notes in my diary to writing him letters at the last known address.

The person I trusted to mail the letters without Mama knowing was Unk. I wondered if the letters had been mailed. The only way to know was to ask Unk.

I had to find that courage because I thought that Daddy needed to know about Mama.

I started walking downstairs and stopped. The living room had what we called a picture window and offered a perfect view of the street.

Unk was in the raggedy chair where he sat every day, either sleeping or reading the newspaper. Today he was reading the newspaper, and when he did that, he didn't like to be disturbed.

My hands were sweating, and with each step, my heart beat faster and faster. *You can do this,* I kept telling myself. *Just ask him.* Here I go. "Unk?" I said quietly.

He must not have heard me.

"Unk?"

"Speak up, Charley Louise. What do you want?"

"That's all right." I started walking away and heard the newspaper wrinkle.

"What do you want, Charley Louise? Don't you see I'm reading the paper?"

I turned around and the newspaper was on his lap. "I was

wondering ..." I paused. His face had the stern look of a bull dog.

"Did you have a chance to mail my letters to Daddy?"

"I gave them to Aunt Louise to mail. She passes the mailbox on her way to work every day."

Not Aunt Louise, I thought. I knew she'd go straight to Mama. Daddy probably never got the letters. But the only way to find out was to ask.

I could smell food coming from the kitchen. Since Mama was upstairs, sick, it could only be Aunt Louise.

"Hello, Aunt Louise," I said as I walked into the kitchen. "Can I help you with anything?"

She dropped the spoon she had in her hand and looked at me, surprised.

Everyone in the house knew that cooking wasn't my favorite thing to do unless I was eating. But I stood next to the stove with a big banana boat smile.

"Not at the moment, Charley Louise, but I do enjoy your enthusiasm for cooking."

"Aunt Louise, did Unk give you anything to mail for me?"

She turned her head toward me. "Like what?"

I could see she knew exactly what I was talking about. "Letters written to Daddy," I said.

"No. I gave them to your mama," She said.

I prayed to God to please come down and save me right then because I knew I was going to get in trouble and be punished for the rest of my life. I probably wouldn't see the outside of the house again.

Voices came from the living room. I knew we didn't have any guests. I peeked around the corner and saw Mama talking to Unk, but I couldn't hear them. When I walked closer, they stopped talking.

Mama and Unk turned around and asked, "How are you doing?"

I smiled. "I'm doing just fine. Mama, the doctor said to stay in bed. What are you doing down here?"

"I'm feeling better and tired of lying on that old lumpy mattress."

I felt that if there was any time to ask Mama about the letters to Daddy, it was now. I walked up to her, gave her a big hug, and said, "Mama, do you think Daddy is doing okay down South? With you being sick, maybe he could help."

She pulled away from me and put her hand underneath my chin, turning my face up toward hers, and said, "I'll be fine. Your uncle and aunt are here and the Lord will take care of me. Then she said, "I know about the letters you wrote to Daddy. Aunt Louise gave them to me because the family felt that I should know."

"Mama, did you have a chance ..."

She turned away from me and started talking to Unk.

"I know you told me not to write him about what was going on in the house, let alone that you were sick. Mama, do you remember mailing the letters to Daddy?"

"Child, don't interrupt. Can't you see I'm talking to your uncle?"

"But Mama ..."

She pointed a finger at me. "Charley Louise, didn't I tell you not to interrupt grown-ups? I'll talk to you later."

I walked upstairs to my bedroom feeling helpless, stomping up each stair.

"Charley Louise," Mama yelled. "How many times have I told you not to stomp on the stairs? They haven't done anything to you."

I jumped on my bed with my arms crossed behind my head. Then I came up with the idea to search the house for the letters. They had to be somewhere.

While everyone was downstairs, I decided to search upstairs in Mama's room, Aunt Louise and Unk's room and in the two vacant rooms. No one but the grown-ups were allowed into the vacant rooms.

"Where would the most likely place be to hide the letters?"

Walking past the vacant rooms, I couldn't help but glance at them.

Don't you dare go into those rooms, I told myself. Keep walking.

But I couldn't help it. It was the most likely place. I turned around and put my hands on the doorknob, looking back and forth to make sure no one saw me, especially loud Rose.

I opened the door slowly, trying to make sure it didn't squeak. Mama didn't oil the hinges on purpose. This way the family would know if someone was coming in or out of the rooms.

Once it was open, I tiptoed into the room, carefully closing it behind me. Thank God there was daylight and I didn't have to turn on any lights.

There was a dresser in the room that had three drawers. Mama made sure that there was night clothing for all guests. That's what was in the first drawer. The second and third drawers were empty, and I looked in all of the cubbyholes.

Darn it. No letters.

I leaned my ear against the door to hear if anyone was coming. Then I opened it just a little, peeking into the hallway, and left the first vacant room.

I walked down the hall to the second vacant room—my favorite. Sunshine from the windows cascaded throughout the room. I called it the banana boat room. No one knew, but when the room was empty with no guests, I wrote most of my letters to Daddy here.

It had the most pleasant feeling and smelled of Mama's perfumes. Most female guests stayed here. It was also the room where Mama kept one of her favorite pieces of furniture—a dresser with three mirrors. Mama had another one just like it in her bedroom, but I couldn't touch anything on it.

The mirrors would unfold from one to three. There was one mirror in the middle and one on each side that folded backward or forward. The countertops were adorned with perfumes, and inside one of the drawers were dusting powders.

I got distracted and began to play with things on top of the dresser, pretending I was a famous singer.

The brush served as the microphone. I picked up the pearls that were hanging on the dresser corner and put them around my neck. I started to reach for the perfume and dusting powder, but stopped. If I put on the perfume or powder, the smell would spread throughout the house.

I heard a creak, jumped, and bumped the dresser. One of the perfume bottles started to twirl, and I held my breath. "Please, please," I whispered. "Don't fall." But it kept twirling and twirling. And, if I moved to catch it, the bedroom floor would creak.

I had no choice. There was a bed right next to the dresser. I dropped the brush on the bed and put both of my hands around the bottle just as it started tipping toward the floor.

The doorknob started to turn, and the door opened. I thought for sure it would be Mama, but it was Darlene.

She put her hands to her mouth and said, "Ooh. I'm telling."

"Wait. Close the door. Don't tell."

"What are you doing in this room? You know we're not supposed to be in here."

"I'm looking for my letters to Daddy. Mama didn't mail them. Please don't tell." Thank God it was Darlene, the better of the cousins and the one I was closest to.

"I promise not to tell," she said. "I'll help you."

"I don't need anyone else getting in trouble."

After she left, I didn't want to look too much longer in the room. The only other place I could think of to look was in the closet.

On the floor of the closet were shoe boxes, but no letters. There were hat boxes on the top shelf, but they were too high for me to reach.

I turned around and saw a chair in the corner of the room. I picked up the chair and set it close to the clothing in the closet and then stood on my toes and reached for one of the boxes. It slipped out of my hands and fell to the floor.

Darlene stood watching saying, "Charley Louise be careful."

Again, I prayed that no one had heard the noise. I waited a minute to make sure, and when no one came to the room, I said, "Hallelujah."

Letters were scattered all over the closet floor. I gasped. Daddy hadn't received my letters. They were all marked "Return to Sender," but I didn't know what that meant.

After tucking one of the letters inside my pocket, I put the box back on the shelf and the chair in the corner.

While walking back to my bedroom, I heard Mama's voice from downstairs. I paused, trying to decide if I should tell her that I'd found the letters, but that would take more courage—courage I wasn't sure I had.

It was a cool night. I stood looking out my bedroom window and put my hand in my pocket, feeling the letter.

Daddy needs to know what's going on up here in Chicago. I decided to go downstairs and talk to Mama. I wasn't sure what I was going to say.

By now, Aunt Louise, Rose and Darlene were upstairs in their rooms. I walked downstairs, hesitating. Unk sat in his favorite chair, snoring.

Although the doctor told Mama to rest, she couldn't help but be in the kitchen, washing the dishes or cooking something.

I walked into the kitchen.

"Hello, Charley Louise, do you want something to eat?"

"No, but I'd like to talk to you about something."

"What is it?"

She watched me as I started to pull the letter from my pocket.

"Are you sure Daddy's letters were mailed?"

"Yes. Why?"

I saw her eyes following my hands. I pulled the letter out and asked, "Why does this letter have 'Return to Sender' stamped on it?"

Mama said, "Let me explain." I couldn't understand why she wouldn't tell me, why she'd hide the letters. She just said, "I thought it was for the best. You haven't seen your Daddy in years, so why now?"

I ran out of the kitchen with Mama calling after me, "Charley Louise." But I kept running up the stairs to my bedroom, crying and vowing to see Daddy again. I decided to write Daddy again. This time I'd mail the letters.

Every day I looked out of my bedroom window, waiting for the postman, running down the stairs each time to catch him.

There was still no reply.

I'd ask everyone in the house if I had received any mail, and they said no. By this time, the whole family would wait to see if Daddy wrote me back. No such luck.

Finally, one day Unk said that he'd take some time off from work and go to Natchez to see what was going on and that he wouldn't return back home until he had an answer for me.

####

Ring. Ring. Ring.

I stopped coming downstairs when Mama yelled, "I'll get it."

"Okay. Okay. We'll see you when you get back home." Then she went into the kitchen with Aunt Louise and started talking.

I leaned near the kitchen doorway and heard them say that Unk had located Daddy. When he had knocked on Daddy's door, he saw a woman in the doorway. She had asked Unk to have a seat, offered him coffee, and went to get my daddy.

When Daddy entered the living room, he was shocked to see Unk and asked what he was doing in Natchez?

Mama said John told him it was because of Charley Louise. He asked Daddy if he didn't want to know how I was doing.

Mama told Aunt Louise that Daddy had a sullen look on his face, hung his head, and said, "It has been a long time since I've seen my child. They left without me knowing and took her away. Of course I'd like to know how she's doing."

They said Unk had pulled his wallet from his back pocket and had showed Daddy pictures of me. Unk said tears fell from Daddy's eyes when he saw I had grown into a beautiful young lady.

Aunt Louise asked, "What did he say about the letters that Charley Louise wrote him? Why didn't he write back?"

Mama said Daddy didn't know that I was writing and had asked when the letters were mailed. Unk told him he didn't know exactly, but the family was aware of me trying to locate him.

Mama said that when Daddy had called this woman friend into the room and asked her about the letters, she admitted that she was the one stopping the letters from reaching him and had written *"return to sender."*

They said that Daddy was furious with her and told Unk that he'd get in contact with me. He sent a message to Unk to tell me that he loves me and misses me.

It was at that moment that I walked into the kitchen and acted like I didn't hear anything. I asked, "Did Unk find Daddy?"

Mama said, "Yes, he did. He wants to reunite and keep in touch with you, but now it will be up to him."

Chapter Nine

Pepper steak, noodles or rice,
salad w/condiment, dessert ... $4.25

It was fall, and the streets weren't as busy. Pimps and prostitutes were still on the corners, but the kids weren't cluttering the streets and chasing each other.

Although Mama's health still wasn't the best, she was back to work taking care of the Rosenberg family and still no letters from Daddy. But I was an official teenager, entering ninth grade. By now, our family had lived in Chicago for four years.

The family was having dinner when Mama all of a sudden said, "I'm growing tired of city life. My health hasn't been good and I'm looking to relax in a rural location but don't want to move back home to Natchez, Mississippi." Mama turned and looked at me. "What do you think about the family moving out of the city?"

I dropped my spoon and all the food it was holding. "You're asking for my opinion?"

She smiled and nodded her head.

I said, "I don't know." Then I paused to think. "If this is good for your health, I'm okay with it. I'm older now and moving further from Daddy ... we haven't spoken or seen one another in some time now. So, if it's for the best, I say okay. Where and when are we moving?"

####

It was just about two weeks later when a lot of cooking was going on in the kitchen. A few hours later, Mama and Aunt Louise set the table with what should be a holiday dinner, except it wasn't a holiday. We had turkey, dressing, Aunt Louise's fresh greens, fried corn from the cob, Mama's famous sweet potato pie, and Kool-Aid.

Mama asked, "How is everyone enjoying dinner? Does everything taste all right?"

I looked around the dinner table at everyone, asking myself, *"Doesn't anybody else notice something different? This kind of meal is usually cooked on holidays or special occasions."*

When I started to ask what was wrong, Aunt Louise pinched my thigh. I looked across the table. Darlene and Rose were snickering.

I asked, "What is—"

"Be quiet," Aunt Louise said.

Just about the same time, Mama asked me, "What's going on? What's so important that you have to yell?"

"This might not seem strange to anybody else, but why are we eating turkey in the middle of the week? It's not Thanksgiving or Christmas. Why today?"

Everyone's eyes turned toward the end of the table at Mama. She started stuttering and acting funny. She paused as though she was thinking of a perfect answer and told the family, "I met a young man who sells things."

"What kind of things?" I asked.

"Property," she said, "Land. His name is Mr. Little and I asked him to locate a plat of land for me to buy."

Unk slammed his spoon down so hard everyone jumped. He asked Mama in a stern voice, "Where is this land?" I had never heard him talk to Mama that way.

Mama said, "Everyone, calm down and think about all of the open space, fresh air, peace, and quiet, and no noisy neighbors blasting their music all night long. Mr. Little is a nice man and has found families land in Michigan before."

"Michigan?" Everyone shouted in unison.

"Where the hell is Michigan?" Unk asked.

I don't think anyone was prepared when I repeated, "Where the hell is *Michigan?*" I immediately gasped for air and covered my mouth. I just knew that was going to be my last breath on earth.

Mama slammed her napkin to the table and said, "Charley Louise Dorsey, this is the house of the Lord. Where did you hear such cuss words? Do you want me to get the soap?"

"No, Ma'am. I'm sorry."

"Since you seem so well educated and have such a fluid vocabulary, go and get the U.S. map from the dresser in the living room."

I jumped up from my seat before she changed her mind. Getting the map was a much better punishment than helping to cook or doing one of Darlene or Roses chores.

"Have you found that map yet?" She yelled.

"Yes, Ma'am. Here I come."

"Could you please find the state of Illinois for us, genius?"

I circled my fingers up and down looking for Illinois. With a banana boat smile, I said, "I found it."

She then told me to find Chicago.

Again, I moved my fingers along the map. "Here it is."

I looked up and saw Unk glaring at me. I immediately thought, *Oh, no.*

"Now, let's continue your education," he said.

I looked across the table at Darlene and Rose giggling. Unk looked toward them and said, "If you continue to giggle, you'll have to show how educated you are."

"Look on the map for Michigan," Unk told me.

Just afterward I heard Darlene and Rose whisper, "I bet you she can't find it," I looked up at both of them with a big grin.

"Here it is."

Mama told Darlene and Rose, "Why don't you help her find the town of Baldwin, Michigan?"

I looked up from the map and said, "There is no such place called Baldwin, Michigan. We couldn't find that place and probably nobody else could either."

"Young lady," Mama said with a stare, "You're working my last nerve today. Hand me the map."

"Hush up. I think there was a knock at the door," Mama said.

Everyone was quiet. Sure enough we heard ... Knock. Knock.

Unk jumped up from the dinner table and hollered, "Just a minute. Here I come."

We turned around. At first we couldn't see him because Unk only cracked the door.

Unk yelled to Mama, "Did you invite a Mr. Little to dinner?"

She leapt up from the dinner table. "Yes. Let him in." A tall, thin, well-dressed colored man stood at the door, waiting for Mama to greet him.

Mama said, "Come in. The family is having dinner."

As he entered the dining room, she said, "We were just talking about you and the land in Michigan. Family, I'd like you to meet Mr. Little. This is my family—Louise, my sister, John, my brother, his wife Pearl and their children, Darlene and Rose. This is Charley Louise, my daughter."

I looked at him as he said, "Nice to meet you."

Mama invited Mr. Little to have a seat at our dinner table. "We saved you a spot right here."

I had seen the extra plate setting on the cabinet in the kitchen and had wondered who it was for, but Mama gave no clues.

She reached for the place setting and asked me, of all people, to move over. I moved, but I didn't like another man sitting between Mama and me unless it was Daddy. Anger started to build up inside me. As he moved toward the middle of Mama and me, I slid my chair next to her.

Mama looked at me and said, "Charley Louise, where are your manners?"

"That's all right. I'll sit right here," Mr. Little said.

As I passed him the mashed potatoes, I asked, "Where did you meet Mama?"

Mama quickly said, "We met at the bus stop on my way to work."

I couldn't figure out how you could meet someone who sells land at a bus stop, so I asked Mr. Little, "How does someone do that … sell land at a bus stop?"

In a stern voice, Mama told me, "Mind your manners and give Mr. Little the same respect as if he was renting one of our rooms."

He wasn't renting, but he was sitting between Mama and me, something no man had done since we left Natchez, Mississippi.

"Mr. Little is a guest in our home," Mama said.

I turned toward him with a stare that meant, "You are not welcome." He returned my stare with a friendly nod and a smile.

After dinner, the kids were asked to go upstairs while Mr. Little and the rest of the family went to the living room to discuss what he was trying to sell.

Darlene and Rose went to their rooms, but I stayed at the top of the stairs, out of sight, so I could hear about Mr. Little.

He told the family, "I'm a traveling man and knowledgeable about selling of land in areas where coloreds are tired of the big city and looking to move to less populated areas."

"Do you have any references and how did you meet my sister, Rose?" Unk asked.

Mr. Little said, "Most times I wait by the bus stops where other coloreds are, talking loudly about plats of land I have for sell. At one of the bus stops is where I met Mrs. Dorsey."

Mama said, "It was the time that the car was in the shop and

I took the bus … two blocks away from our house. Mr. Little was talking loudly, showing pictures, and telling us coloreds about a rural town in the northern part of Michigan.

He told us "For anyone who is tired of the city life, I know the perfect place where you can raise your families. It has beautiful landscapes and plenty of room for growth. The name of the town is Baldwin, Michigan."

Mama said, "The Rosenbergs checked around for me and found nothing ill-willed about him."

"I see, Ma'am." Mr. Little's voice sounded as if he was caught by surprise. "Tell the Rosenberg family thank you for the good recommendation."

"They heard quite a bit about you in your efforts to prosper and help the colored race," Mama said.

When Mr. Little started to describe the land, he showed Mama and everyone else pictures of the town.

"It looks wonderful," Mama said.

"Remember when you said you were tired of the noise and felt that the neighbors were close enough to touch or that you could hear every argument? Now neighbors will be few and in between. The plats are beautiful and large with room for growth. Your whole family could build their own homes right next door. If you want, I could take you to Michigan and you could see for yourself before deciding to buy the land."

"How did you find this town?" Aunt Louise asked.

He paused and said, "Through my travels, I've met a lot of people and have listened to what their needs are. On one particular business outing, I met a couple of gentlemen in the real estate business. They told me that the word was out that I was helping coloreds look for places to live."

He admitted that at first he was concerned, thinking this was something they didn't want to happen. But they had asked to sit down at his table where he was having dinner and had agreed on a business decision.

They told him about the plats of land, and he took them up on their offer to visit the area. When he arrived, he saw that coloreds were already living in the community. He told our family that's how he found out about Michigan and what was there for the picking.

Mr. Little's eyes and mine met at the same time when I was walking downstairs. I wasn't sure if I believed him or not. But I looked toward Mama and could see that her mind was already made up.

When I asked him who lived in this town, Mama asked if I had been standing at the top of the stairs listening to grown-up conversations, again. I said, "No. I remembered Mr. Little talking about the towns at the dinner table."

Mr. Little said, "Yes, Charley Louise, many coloreds and some children your same age live in Baldwin. Just like your family, the families grew tired of the big city life and missed their rural roots. Instead of moving back South, some decided to try the North. I believe that your family will fall in love with the community."

Mama escorted Mr. Little to the door and said, "Thank you for coming. I'll be in touch about the visit to the area and the family's decision."

Like a gentleman, he said, "Thank you for inviting me to your beautiful home. I'll await your telephone call."

Right before walking out the door, he turned around. With a smile and tip of his hat, he said, "Good-bye, Miss Charley Louise Dorsey."

With an unhappy grin on my face, I said, "Good-bye, Mr. Little."

####

Later that week, Darlene, Rose and I were sitting at the top of the stairs. Mama, Aunt Louise, and Unk were in the living room. I heard, "No need to vote."

Aunt Louise and Mama stood up when Unk said, "We're moving to Baldwin, Michigan. That's our vote."

Mama said, "Don't you want to visit the place first before you decide?"

"No need to visit. We're ready to go."

She smiled and hugged them. "I guess we're all moving."

The decision was made. When school let out, the whole family would move.

While the rest of the family clapped and cheered, Mama and I looked right into each other's eyes. She leaned her head to one side and smiled, as if asking for my acceptance.

Her eyes had dark rings around them, and she looked tired. I looked at her and mouthed, "Okay."

I'd have to say good-bye to my friends all over again. This time I wouldn't be coming back or transferring to their school. And, if Daddy wanted to write me, he could without interruptions. Most importantly, he knew about Mama's health.

Day 8, Journal Entry 8 ... Hello Daddy. The family is moving to a town in Michigan. Seems like we have moved more times than I can count, but I'm beginning to adjust to each new venture and home. On Mama's side of the family, we continue to stay together ... Not moving without the whole family.

Mama's health is not the same and all the doctor says is that she needs to rest. I'm not sure if I accept that answer but will have to for now. I love and miss you. Your daughter, Charley Louise

My face in the palms of my hands, I repeatedly looked toward the classroom clock and gazed out the window. Time seemed to be stuck.

"Can't that clock move any faster?" I said. Not because my family was moving, but because I wanted to spend as much time with my friends as possible. Then I heard the bell ding. Another school year was over. I jumped up from my desk.

Feet scampered everywhere and people bumped into each other. Summer was finally here, and along with that, the countdown to moving day.

I reminded Esther, Jill and Mona, my friends from the Damon Street School, our family was moving to Baldwin, Michigan.

"I still don't know where Baldwin, Michigan is," Jill said.

"When I asked my mother about Baldwin, she hadn't heard too much about it except on my Daddy's side of the family," Mona said.

When I looked to my left Susie had dropped her head toward the ground.

"Susie, what's wrong?" I asked.

"My family will be leaving for our summer home earlier this year ... in a few days and I'll miss you."

We hugged and cried, telling each other we'd write.

"I don't know my new address, but I do know where your family will be staying for the summer and I'll write to you," I said.

Susie and I turned in opposite directions and walked away, turning every so often to look back at each other and wave.

After Susie and her family left, the rest of us decided to spend every moment together talking, laughing, and having fun until I had to move.

Chapter Ten

Create your own meal:
Roast beef, swiss steak, bar-b-q ribs, pot roast, or chicken,
au gratin, mashed potatoes ... $5.00

In 1942, that dreaded day came. My family put the final load of furniture in Mr. Little's truck. I was 15 years old, traveling to what Mama said was our new home.

"I'll miss you," I said to my friends.

"We'll miss you too, Charley Louise. Keep in touch, okay?"

I thought to myself Mr. Little's sales pitch and recommendation from Mr. Rosenberg, Mama's employer, is why I was sitting in the back seat of our station wagon waving good-bye to my friends, again.

####

Although there were passenger trains, we traveled by car and packed our station wagon and Mr. Little's truck with our belongings.

We went back into the house where Mr. Little put a map on the living room wall, once again showed us how we'd get to Baldwin, Michigan. I watched his fingers moving up and down on a map made from his many travels through the United States. It showed us where our family would stay for the night and all of the places we could stop for food and bathrooms.

He pointed on the map and said, "Here's where the city streets end and the rural roads begin. The roads will be rough and sometimes not safe to drive at night. Not only because we could be stopped by people who didn't like coloreds, but many of the roads are man-made or two-track.

You could be driving down the road and end up in some bushes or get stuck in a hole. Traveling state-to-state for coloreds wasn't an easy task and the trip could take more than two days."

Mama and Unk looked at each other.

Mr. Little said, "Make sure you packed enough food and water because once we leave the city and main roads, there isn't going to be many places for us to stop and eat."

Unk and Mr. Little looked at each …

"We packed enough food," Mama said.

Mr. Little said, "Until we reach Baldwin, I have made overnight arrangements for you and your family to stay with other colored families. They are very pleasant and familiar with others staying with them while traveling. Are there any other questions?"

I looked around, hoping and praying that Mama would say, "I've changed my mind. This is a mistake and we're going to stay here in Chicago."

My prayers weren't answered. The next thing I heard was, "Since there are no questions, and if everything is loaded into your station wagon and my truck, we should get on our way. We need to use as much daylight as possible."

"Wait a minute. Let me make sure I haven't forgotten something in the house," Mama said.

That gave me a chance to make sure I packed everything from my room.

As we started walking toward the door, I stopped and turned around. I looked up the stairs and around the living room. Mama stood at the top of the stairs.

While walking down the stairs, she said, "Louise, Rose and me will sit in the front seat. Pearl, Charley Louise and Darlene can sit in the back seat. We'll follow Mr. Little's truck."

Unk walked with Mr. Little toward his truck. He said, "Since there isn't room in the station wagon, I'll be riding with you."

"You don't trust me?" Mr. Little asked.

"It isn't that we don't trust you. But, you must understand this is all we own. Everything you see here are our family's belongings and we wanted to make sure it all arrives the same time we do ... you know, just in case we get lost or separated. Besides, where would I ride in the station wagon, on top of the hood with some of the other belongings?"

Darlene and me started fighting about who was going to sit where until Mama yelled, "Charley Louise can sit at one window. Darlene you can sit in the middle. As we travel you can switch seating arrangements. I know this might become uncomfortable, but we'll have to make the best of it."

We hopped into the backseat and Mama pulled away from the curb, following Mr. Little with the other car attached to his truck with more of our household goods.

Mr. Little wanted to start out earlier than before noon, but was running late. I rolled down the window because it was hot and waved good-bye to my friends. Then it hit me—the Chicago smells from the garbage and whatever else mixed into the air.

I looked at each block, watched the girls sitting on the stoop, the boys running around in the street, and the pimps with the big Cadillac.

"Charley Louise, sit back in your seat and roll that window up some."

This is one thing I won't miss—this city's bad smell, I thought. I turned and saw Darlene laughing. Then I looked out the back window at my friends getting further and further away.

The owner of the corner store was sweeping his stoop and shooing away kids who were trying to steal apples and oranges from the crates sitting in front of his store.

I finally turned around and leaned back in my seat, closing my eyes and absorbing all of the sounds I had grown to love.

"Charley Louise, you asleep already?"

"No, Mama. Just remembering," I said as I opened my eyes.

We passed where Mama used to wait for the city bus to take her to the Rosenbergs. On the left and right of us, cars passed.

We passed many large buildings that were becoming a symbol of Chicago and creating its landscape. The "L" was zipping by faster than I could run.

I prayed, *God, please let this place that we're moving to have people. Because as a teenager, I'm giving up a lot, you know?*

Hours later, I had fallen asleep and when I opened my eyes, the city streets had turned into roads.

Shortly after that, Mr. Little stopped his truck. I leaned forward to look out the front window and there was a small town. Mr. Little said, "Use the bathrooms and stay close together. Do what you have to do and come right back out."

We washed our faces, quickly fixed our clothes, and walked back to the station wagon and truck.

When we got back to the car, Unk had sandwiches and Kool-Aid in a jar. I smiled, thanking God that for once we didn't have to eat peanut butter and jelly sandwiches.

Mr. Little said, "We're getting closer to the overnight stay, but the roads will be rough."

"I'm bored," I said.

I felt Mama looking at me. My eyes met hers in the rearview mirror. I swear it was a spying mechanism.

She decided we should play a game—one of the games we had to get rid of the boredom, but most importantly, a bad attitude.

Before she started driving, she said, "Who's our favorite gospel singer?"

"Mahalia Jackson," we mumbled. Then we sang song after song, clapping our hands and make believe tambourines.

It was dusk when Mr. Little's truck came to a stop again. He said, "This is our stop. We'll be staying here overnight."

We were at a small, wooden house painted white. There seemed to be neighbors up the road within yelling distance.

As soon as we rolled down the station wagon windows, the smell of fried chicken, mashed potatoes, gravy, collard greens and corn bread greeted our noses.

There were four kids, two of which looked to be my age. Mr. Little introduced our family and they welcomed us to their home. We sat at the dining room table, talking about everything from where we came from and where we were going.

Mr. Little and the grown-ups were sitting on the front porch discussing something when Mama came into the house and said, "It's time to go to bed. We have to get up early in the morning when the rooster cock-a-doodle-doos."

All of the girls slept together, but we didn't go right to sleep. We talked most of the night about boys, city life, and what to expect living in the country.

It seemed like we had just fallen asleep when Mama came upstairs to wake us up. It was time to wash up, eat breakfast, and pile into the two automobiles.

The night before, Mama and the family had cooked extra food for us because they knew we wouldn't be able to always stop. We had leftover chicken, a fresh jar of Kool-Aid, water, pie, and cake.

When we pulled away, I looked through my window and saw the girls waving from upstairs. I waved and smiled back at them.

I don't remember when I saw the next highway because after we left, there was nothing but roads, bushes, tall trees and every now and then the smell of pigs and cow manure. No more city lights, just rural towns with houses spread far apart.

The buildings seemed thrown together with whatever people

thought would make a house or building. The rest stops weren't as close, either.

Our station wagon followed Mr. Little's truck, swerving around patches of trees in car tracks made by other travelers on pressed down, overgrown grass.

The trip was horrible. At times our belongings that were tied on top of the station wagon fell off, and we had to stop and tie them up again.

With every swift turn and every hole in the road, I heard Mama praying, "Please get us to our next overnight stay before a tire has to be repaired or more rope is needed to tie our things to the station wagon."

We stopped at our second host family's house. They didn't have any kids but were very welcoming. They noticed how tired we looked and told us that we were almost there ... to Michigan.

We left the second host family's house early in the morning, and by noon, I was asleep in the backseat of our station wagon on and off, my butt bouncing up and down.

I was sweating from sunlight shining through the car windows and woke to the clatter of rain.

"What the ...?" My eyes met Mama's. Wrinkles formed in her forehead. Her stare dared me to finish my sentence.

I turned my head and looked out the window. There was nothing but trees, open space, and bump after bump. *Lord, where the hell are we?* I thought.

Our family had been traveling for what seemed like forever, staying at family homes, then driving for miles.

"Is Mr. Little reading the map right?" I asked.

"Charley Louise," Mama said. "We're just about to reach Michigan and are on our way to Baldwin."

To me, it looked like Mr. Little sold us a bunch of grass and trees. He said it would remind us of the South.

####

The first plat of land our family bought from Mr. Little was behind a tall brick building with white pillars that we were told was the courthouse in Baldwin, Michigan.

"Mama, we just got here. Are we going to court already?"

"No, child," she said. "Why are you asking?"

"Because the only time I know a colored person was close to the courthouse was going to court or something."

Mr. Little's truck started to slow down. I rolled down my window to get some air. There were people sitting on their porches, waving at us like we are in a parade or something.

Some of the houses looked like small huts and some were a little bit larger.

People were scattered along the roadside, selling vegetables and produce. They came up to our car, asking if we wanted to buy something.

Unlike Natchez, the coloreds lived inside the town boundaries and weren't clustered outside.

What Mama didn't tell me is that she didn't just buy land from Mr. Little—the land came with a house. It was white, had one entrance, three bedrooms, and three windows, two in the front and one on the side.

Mama and Aunt Louise slept in one bedroom, Unk and Aunt Pearl slept in the second bedroom. Darlene, Rose and me shared the third bedroom.

On the outside of the house there was a pump for water and an outhouse. We were cramped, but together.

While living in Baldwin, our family joined the People's Baptist Church located in White Cloud, a smaller rural community just south of Baldwin. Every other Sunday afternoon, the church would load into our cars following each other up the man-made, two-track, bumpy roads to fellowship with other neighboring churches, one being the Church of God In Christ Church in White Cloud.

There weren't as many coloreds in White Cloud, and the ones we met didn't live inside the town limits. Going to church was the most common way to meet other people and that's where Mama met Mrs. Ollie.

The both of them seemed to get along as soon as they met and became inseparable. She was a chubby colored woman with a round face, welcoming smile and the same height as Mama. Although Mrs. Ollie lived in White Cloud, she was a native of the Chicago area. Mr. Little had helped her family relocate to Michigan, too.

After a church service, Mrs. Ollie invited our family to dinner. But at the time, I didn't know the importance of that dinner until Mrs. Ollie invited Mama to take a walk with her. I tagged along as we started walking along the two-track road where Mrs. Ollie pointed from one side to the other.

"All of these plats you see here belong to me and my husband. If you want, we could sell you some of them. It would be more than enough land for your family to build your own homes right next to each other."

"You're right. If we stayed in Baldwin, our houses would be up the road from each other."

A month after we had arrived in Baldwin. Mama said, "Surprise, we're going to White Cloud."

The ride was tough getting from Baldwin to White Cloud. Right before we got there, Mama told Unk and the rest of the family to turn right on the two-track road Mrs. Ollie had shown us.

It was nothing but more flattened grass made from cars and trucks.

To make it worse, it had rained two nights before and covered up much of the old tracks.

Darlene, Rose and I were sitting in the backseat of the station wagon when it came to a sudden stop.

"Are you sure this is the way?" Unk asked Mama.

"Yes, I'm sure."

Unk asked Mama to get behind the steering wheel. He got in front of the car and started clearing away brush and weeds, putting them underneath the tires until they were able to turn.

The tires sank deeper and deeper into the mud. Unk pulled weed after weed and put them underneath the tires until he got frustrated.

Mama clamped her hands around the steering wheel and rested her head in between them. She looked up at Unk and said, "Maybe we should turn around while there's daylight and try again tomorrow."

There was nothing but tall trees. If our car got stuck, help might not come until daylight.

Unk was standing at the driver's side of the car. He leaned in, looked at us kids and said, "Maybe that's the best thing to do. Next time we'll mark our tracks."

Mama turned around. "I wanted to surprise everyone with the land. It's large enough for all us to live right next to each other."

The surprised outing was ruined. We turned around and went back to Baldwin.

When we got back to the house, Mama asked, "Has anyone seen Mr. Little?"

We knew he'd know how to get to the land in White Cloud, but we were told that he had left town.

That night, the family had a meeting to discuss the route to White Cloud. Unk and Mama sat around the dinner table. I leaned against my bedroom door, trying to hear their plans to get through the rained out two-track road, the tall brush and weeds.

The next day, early in the morning, we headed back to White Cloud, following the map that Mrs. Ollie had given to Mama.

The weather was much better and made it easier to follow the road.

"Oh, my God," Mama said. "There are so many trees."

"Are we there yet?" I asked.

Mama told Unk, "Don't you miss the right turn ... Watch for that bush ... Don't hit that bump."

"Stop! Stop!" Mama turned in her seat, held her left arm straight, and pointing yelling, "This is it. I see Mrs. Ollie's house."

We stared out the left side of the car. It was as if we had found gold. I leaned over. Darlene and Rose were yelling, "Get off us!"

The air smelled of grass and wood, just like in Baldwin, but it had more wilderness and dirt roads. To me, it didn't matter which place we stayed, Baldwin or White Cloud. It all looked the same and had a lot of rural smells.

For the first time since our family left Chicago, the look on Mama's face told it all.

She had been sick, and we moved away from the city for her to settle down, but this was the most excitement I had seen her have in a long time. It was as if she had woken up from a coma.

Mama's right. This is our home.

From a distance, I heard someone yelling. I turned around and saw Mrs. Ollie. She was running, but it was more like a trot, with her swaying from side-to-side. As she moved closer, she yelled, out of breath, "Finally. I have neighbors."

Mama hugged her. "We're just about to bless the land. Come and join hands with us."

The Church believed in blessing everything. It wasn't unusual when Mama asked us to join hands to pray over the land to bring good growth to our crops and build a foundation for the family.

Like in a choir, there was a loud "Amen" after the prayer and clapping. As we lifted our heads, Mama looked at Unk and said, "Now, how are we going to build the houses, and which one should be first?"

We knew that Mr. Little helped a lot of the coloreds get settled, building their homes and maybe he could do the same for our family.

Mrs. Ollie said, "Lumber up here is very expensive for coloreds, but Mr. Little has a Chicago connection. Last my sister wrote she told me that the city is changing and tearing down the old houses and building what they call 'projects.' The wood and windows from the houses will be cheap. To find already cut wood and windows ready to build up here will be a hard task, and we don't have any way to cut your own timber."

Later that day, Mr. Little came to our house and sat on the front porch with Unk, Aunt Louise, and Mama. It was a hot day and the front door was open. As usual, I wanted to know everything, so I leaned close to the screen door.

What I heard was Mr. Little saying, "I'd need someone to go with me to Chicago and help with pulling nails and loading the truck. That's one way you could cut the charges."

I heard chairs creaking. I peeked around the corner. Mr. Little was shaking their hands. Mama told him, "We'll look over the paperwork and contact you tomorrow."

When I leaned closer to the front porch screen door, Mr. Little turned around at the same time. He put his thumbs and pointer fingers together around the rim of his hat as he fitted it on his head and smiled.

"You have a good day, Ms. Charley Louise."

I didn't respond, just stared through the rusty screen door and watched him walk away, wondering why we had to go so far to get wood when there were plenty of trees as far as we could see right here.

I asked, "Why is it that coloreds have to work so much harder for things that seem so simple?"

Mama looked at me. "That's just how it is. We'll be all right."

Later that evening, Mama, Aunt Louise, and Unk decided that he'd travel with Mr. Little to Chicago. But would need an extra hand to help gather the lumber, pull nails, and tear the windows apart.

Unk looked up at Mama and said, "Ted would be perfect. He knows a lot about carpentry and helped most of the coloreds, including our family, get settled with odds and ends."

"Ted … Mr. McKinney? How would we pay for his services?"

"There won't be any charges. I'll explain later. Just sign the papers Mr. Little left."

Mama didn't take kindly to Unk's persistence. She had a pen in her hands and looked back and forth across the dining room table.

With a stern look, she said, "You better be right about this." She signed the papers.

The following weekend, Mr. Little, Unk, and Mr. McKinney made plans to go to Chicago.

They made trips from Chicago to White Cloud, carrying truckloads of wood, windows, and nails to our land until there was enough to build the first house and the plans were set to build.

The family had decided that Mr. McKinney should start on the house and wouldn't travel to Chicago with Mr. Little on his next trip.

It was while we were at our land trying to decide which house to build first when Mr. Little stopped by to see if we needed anything on his next trip. Mama told him the money we have needed to be spread around for food and other items—that we'd work with what we have.

A week later, a honking sound was coming from up the road. We all looked up and saw Mr. Little driving towards our land continuing to honk. Although Mama hadn't asked him to bring more supplies to build with, he did anyway—mostly more wood.

Behind him, I saw another colored family with what seemed like all of their worldly belongings.

Mama welcomed the family and told them to get out of their trucks and stretch their legs. We shared our water and sandwiches and talked before they loaded back into their trucks, going toward Baldwin, looking anxious to see their land.

Waving good-bye, I could see the same questions in the kids' eyes that I had when we moved here thinking, *What'll happen next? Where the hell were we?*

Mama bought a considerable amount of acres of land from Mrs. Ollie, seven miles west of White Cloud.

She divided the plats between herself, her sister Louise, and her brother John. There was another plat of land that was saved for someone, but Mama kept it a secret from everyone.

During the family meetings, everyone noticed that Mr. McKinney was hanging around more and more. When we were deciding which house to build first, Aunt Louise said, "Why not ask Ted to help? He has been working around these parts for some time helping other coloreds build outhouses, fix windows, and everything else."

Unk and Mama turned towards Aunt Louise with confused looks on their faces until Aunt Louise said, "The first house can be ours."

Mama dropped the bucket of water she was holding and Unk choked on the watermelon he was eating.

The secret was out. The 'hillbilly,' as everyone called him, and my Aunt Louise were getting married.

The most our family knew about Mr. McKinney was that he was a tall, slender man with a light-complexion who had once been a hobo, hopping from one train to another until he ended up in Chicago. He then met Mr. Little, and that's how he ended up in Baldwin. He was known in Baldwin for his carpentry work and always had a banana boat smile just like Daddy's.

He mostly stayed to himself, so people mistook him for being a loner. I thought it was because he didn't want every Tom, Dick, and Harry in his business. He was a private man.

Although Mama wasn't sure about Mr. McKinney, she hugged Aunt Louise. Unk shook his hand with his usual grumpy look on his face.

Aunt Louise said, "Ted's a fine man and would be a good provider for any woman."

"We'll see," Unk said as he turned around and walked away.

####

When Mama and the family had decided to move to Michigan, she thought everything was planned. She had saved up enough money to live in Baldwin, but building three houses wasn't part of the plan.

The family decided that the first house to be built would be Aunt Louise's and Uncle Ted's. The rest of the family would live together until the next house was built.

"Uncle Ted, are you a real hobo?" I asked.

"Well, Charley Louise, some people say I am. I just say that I've traveled a lot."

I followed him as he started walking around the land, measuring.

"Are you really going to build a house for the whole family?"

"With the help of others, I will."

"That's a lot of wood, nails, and—"

"Charley Louise," Mama yelled. "Are you bothering people?"

I loved to talk and always asked questions. Mama called them debates. So it wasn't any surprise when she told me, "As soon as school starts, you make sure you're in that debate class."

Uncle Ted went back and forth between Baldwin and White Cloud building our house, leaving before the sun went down. He made sure not to stay later into the evening because the road was hard to follow and who knew where he'd end up.

On one early sunny day, we loaded into the station wagon and headed to our new address: Rural Route 1, White Cloud. As the car got closer to our land, it came to a slow stop.

I jumped out the back door, excited, and then halted. I had expected to see a house, but there was just a wooden shell with holes for windows and doors.

We looked around the outside of the house. Mama asked if a window could be put here or if this or that could be done.

Uncle Ted didn't respond. He took us inside and said, "This is the kitchen area, and over there we could put a table and chairs."

Walking more into the wooden shell, he said, "This is the living room." He pointed and said, "Up there will be a bedroom." From there he walked onto what would be the front porch.

Since there wasn't enough lumber and windows to build a house large enough for everyone, Uncle Ted suggested that some of us stay in Baldwin until the second house could be built.

Mama said, "I don't like that, but it's what we might have to do."

Uncle Ted, Aunt Louise, Mama, and myself would live in White Cloud. Unk and his family would live in Baldwin.

With more lumber and windows we had enough to start building Unk's house a few plats over to the right. A clump of trees separated the land, but that was all right because mine and Mama's house would be built in the middle of both of their houses.

"Just don't touch that plat of land to the left of Ted's house. Remember, I'm saving that plat," Mama said.

She still didn't want to tell us what or who the plats of land was for, and believe me, no one asked.

Near the end of summer, Uncle Ted and Aunt Louise's house was completed.

Mama pulled me to the side for a talk. I wasn't sure what she wanted to talk about, but she looked serious.

She said, "You're coming of age and growing up to be a beautiful young lady, showing a great deal of responsibility."

I looked at her, but her facial expression was sad, not happy. She said, "I'm having a hard time finding work and need to go back to Chicago to work just a little bit longer."

She had worked many years for the Rosenbergs in Chicago and had saved a lot of money, but the purchase of the land and the property in Baldwin was expensive. She didn't have enough to stop work completely, and the move was more costly than expected.

It had been Mama's decision to buy all of the land herself. She had decided to divide it and portion it off to each sibling, only to save one plat. The houses were built, but she wanted to keep hold of the land and wouldn't let her siblings be part-owners. I was mad. Why didn't she include Unk and Aunt Louise?

She said, "If I work just a little longer, I'll have enough to get through the hard times. You'll have to live with Uncle Ted and Aunt Louise while I go back to Chicago to make more money."

I wasn't prepared to hear this. All I could think about was that now I wouldn't be with Daddy or Mama.

Mama put her hand underneath my chin. "I won't be leaving until the end of summer and I'll visit and send money for you to put in the bank."

I cried when she hugged me. She said, "Everything will be all right. Just remember we'll always be a family. Never forget that."

We'd walk around our land, sometimes at night, gazing at the stars, looking at the moon, pretending that the imaginary shape inside was a lady sitting in a chair brushing her hair.

"Every time I look up at the moon I'll be thinking of you ... that you're the lady sitting in the chair," I said.

Mama smiled and said, "I'm marking the plats. This is where our house will be built. In a year, Ted and John will help build our house."

She said, "Under no circumstances should the plats of land next to your Uncle Ted's house be sold. That's for your Daddy." I felt my eyes widen when she showed me the paperwork.

Mama purchased a safe deposit box in the bank and told me, "At all times, the paperwork should be kept and never taken out."

I put the key in a safe place that no one else knew about, especially my nosey cousins.

The plan was to complete Unk's house so that all of the families could be together. Uncle Ted's and Aunt Louise's house needed some final things to finish the house. Some church people, Mrs. Ollie's husband, and others helped. The intent was for the family to be together before the end of January.

There was one thing missing from both houses. I looked around the houses until I walked outside and my eyes saw these buildings with four wooden walls which included a front door that locked only by the turn of a handle. In the middle was a wooden platform with a hole in the middle where a person could sit.

Two outhouses were built: one for Uncle Ted and Aunt Louise's house and one for Unk's house.

My God, I'm supposed to use this? I realized that I'd have to get used to rural living, but an outhouse?

During the middle of a hot day, I stared at the outhouse and then slowly walked closer and closer. I peaked in and there was a large wooden circle waiting for me.

128

I'd make the best use of my time when I was inside these splinter amenities. At first, I'd hurry in and hurry out, but there were times when I had no choice but to stay longer. I'd crack the door open while trying to hold onto the handle so no one would walk in on me. At the smallest noise, I'd jump and then look around and see nothing.

I grew used to the outhouse. Eventually, some of my best conversations to myself and thoughts happened while I was in it. I also used it in emergencies, like running away from the chickens and dog.

Usually, I woke up to loud hammering and sawing sounds, but on this day it was different.

"What are you building now, Uncle Ted?" I asked. "It looks too large for another outhouse and too small for another house."

"We need something for the chickens to live in."

Why they needed a house, I wasn't quite sure.

Uncle Ted said, "When it gets cold in the winter, they need to be somewhere warm or else they won't make it to spring." He told me the chickens give us food like eggs and meat. He told me that the house is also for when I have to fetch the eggs. They didn't want me standing outside.

"Me?" I yelled. "I have to take care of these smelly, cackling animals?"

I ran into the house with the screen door slamming behind me. "Mama, do I have to feed the chic—"

"Calm down. It isn't that bad," she said. "Uncle Ted will show you how to fetch the eggs and how to make sure all the chickens are kept in the coop. If you weren't so young when we lived in Natchez, this would had been your responsibility. And, we didn't have as many chickens."

The first time I was awakened early in the morning and had to fetch the eggs, I wasn't happy.

"Mama," I asked, "Why do I have to take care of the chickens? Is there something else I can do?"

With a stern voice, she said, "For now, young lady, this is your chore and you'll do it. You don't have to like it, but you will do it. Do you understand?"

"Help!" I screamed the next morning after walking outside. "The chickens are getting out."

Uncle Ted and Mama ran toward the chicken coop and tried to help me gather the chickens.

They were scattering everywhere. Their tiny little legs were running so fast. Mama circled in one direction and I went in another direction until the last of them were in the coop. I slammed the door shut.

We fixed a hole that was near the bottom of the coop, but I asked myself, *Did I leave the gate cracked open? I started counting. One, two, three, four, five, six ...*

"Charley Louise, did you double check to make sure the door was closed tight when you left from the chicken coop? If you don't, this will happen again."

"Yes, ma'am, I double checked."

I turned around to the chickens and whispered, "You little things have to stay with your mamas and daddies. You're a family. You can't be leaving like that. Plus, I can't keep running after you." Then it hit me. *Wait a minute. Why am I talking to baby chickens? Have I lost my mind?*

I fell in love with the smelly things and claimed them as my pets. We didn't always get along, like when they chased me into the outhouse. But from then on, I made sure the coop door was closed.

The chickens and I became friends. I talked to them about things I couldn't talk to anyone else about—how I really felt about being taken away from my daddy, the move to Chicago, racism, and moving to Baldwin, Michigan and now to White Cloud. They didn't answer or talk back, but I didn't care.

####

It was almost time for Mama to leave for Chicago. We walked up the dirt road while I kicked rocks from one side to the other, talking about everything.

We talked about the first day of school and to let the teachers teach me and not the other way around, remembering to do my chores and listen to Aunt Louise and Uncle Ted. She gave me a necklace to wear saying this will keep us close together.

She wrapped her arms around me and said, "You'll be in good hands. If nothing else, the cousins are here to worry you to death." Do you still remember the Rosenbergs? The family I worked for in Chicago?"

I looked up at her. "How could I forget? For years you worked for them."

Just when I was about to get excited, Mama said, "I'm not going back to the Rosenbergs. They already hired another lady, but they gave me a good recommendation to work for another family in the same area that has three girls who are in junior high school."

Mama reached into her dress pocket. "Here, this is my address where I'll be staying in Chicago. You can write anytime and I'll get your letter."

I guess it made me feel somewhat better knowing that the Rosenbergs helped Mama to find work. They had always taken care of Mama and me, so I felt sure they wouldn't let anything happen to her.

Three weeks passed before it was time for Mama to leave for Chicago. The whole family went to Uncle Ted and Aunt Louise's house for breakfast.

We had scrambled eggs with ham, fresh biscuits, grits, homemade pancakes, and milk. For any big occasion, the family would make these big meals. This would be the first time that a family member traveled or left without another family member. It was also the first time that Aunt Louise, wouldn't travel with her sister.

The family decided everyone would eat at the same table. We pulled the table apart from each end and inserted the leaf in the middle, making the table much longer. We pushed the kid's table next to it and made one long table where everyone could eat together.

We squeezed around the table, eating, laughing, and remembering the good times and some of the bad times, like when the chickens got out of the coop.

Eventually everyone became quiet except for when chairs rubbed against the floor and dishes clattered while being washed. Smiles turned into sadness.

Mama would travel by train. The ride would be long, but not near as long as it was getting here.

Most of the family said their good-byes at the house. Uncle Ted, Mama, and me got into his truck and headed toward town.

The family didn't like the idea of Mama traveling alone. We knew she wanted to make more money before moving to Baldwin, but what if something happened? The family would be so far away.

She looked at us and said, "Don't worry. I'll be in good hands. The Rosenbergs will look out for me. They promised."

We lived seven miles from town, and outside of us trying to find our land earlier in the summer, to me this was the shortest ride.

I talked to Mama about missing the Rosenberg girls, feeling like it was just yesterday that we played hide-and-seek or tried on clothes from one of their family shopping sprees.

We laughed at homemade jokes, and Mama talked to me about our future until we finally reached the train station. There were a lot of other people with their families, waiting to say the same words, "Good-bye" "Take care," "Write to me."

The train's whistle grew louder and louder. At that moment, I don't know who was moving the slowest, Mama and us or the train coming to a stop.

She hugged and kissed me on the cheek, telling me to behave and to listen to Uncle Ted and Aunt Louise. When the train started moving, Mama leaned out the window and yelled, "And don't forget to take care of the chickens and pigs."

Tears started rolling down my face. I chased the train as far as I could, waving until she disappeared. Then I stood still, staring until all I could see was the sky filled with the train's smoke.

A hand touched my shoulder. "Are you all right?"

It startled me. I wiped the tears from my face, turned around, and saw Uncle Ted. "Yeah. I'm all right."

When Mama had boarded the train and waved good-bye from the window seat until I couldn't see her anymore, I had wanted to take back all the back talking and complaining about feeding the chickens and pigs.

Uncle Ted drove, keeping his eyes on the road. He told me, "Your Mama will be all right and will write you. We'll make sure you receive all of her letters ... unopened."

Hitting bump after bump, the truck wiggled from side to side. Uncle Ted rubbed my head. "Your still with family and everyone will take good care of you until your mama comes back."

Chapter Eleven
Fried chicken, potato salad, relish w/dip,
rolls w/butter, and dessert … $5.00

Mama was back in Chicago so Aunt Louise enrolled me at White Cloud High School in the tenth grade. We drove up to the school on a gravel-filled road that was surrounded by trees and tall grass.

It was a small, three-story brick building located in the center of town and within walking distance for the kids who lived in town, but not for any coloreds.

When we arrived, everyone was staring. Uncle Ted, Aunt Louise and I sat in the truck staring back. Aunt Louise said, "When you get out his truck, hold your shoulders back and walk with confidence."

It was like I could feel their eyes going right through my body. Uncle Ted drove the truck near the front door and Aunt Louise and I got out.

I thought to myself *doesn't the racism every stop?*

"Turn around and keep walking. I told you to hold your shoulders back and walk with confidence. You're new and they don't know you."

I turned around, held my shoulders back until my breasts stuck out, put my nose up in the air, and walked into the principal's office.,

"Hello, Mr. Jackson. My name is Charley Louise Dorsey. I live on Rural Route 1 and have come to enroll in school."

Mr. Jackson welcomed Aunt Louise and me and gave us a tour. He showed me my locker and the classrooms.

He introduced me to my teachers, and they gave me my school books and assigned seat. They had placed me at the back of the room. Aunt Louise spoke up and asked why.

The teacher said, "Most assigned seating ..." He paused and

must have changed his mind. "Would this be a better seat for Charley Louise?"

Aunt Louise looked at the seat and then at the teacher. "That would be just fine."

He asked, "Do you have all of your school supplies?"

Aunt Louise looked at him. "Yes, we do. We take care of our own."

The man sounded polite to me, but Aunt Louise must had thought otherwise because she didn't speak to him kindly.

As we turned to leave, he said, "Mrs. McKinney, have a nice day. I'll see Charley Louise in class next week."

Aunt Louise turned toward the door mumbling something, but I couldn't understand what.

When we got in the truck, I asked Aunt Louise how I was going to get back and forth to school. There were no busses and I lived seven miles from town, too far to walk.

Uncle Ted said, "I'll take you to school and pick you up."

For a year, that's how I got to school. I didn't care because Uncle Ted and I had many conversations, talking about anything, sometimes with laughter. It was almost like when I was a little girl again. Before Daddy left for work, I'd jump on his foot and hang onto his leg. We talked only for a few minutes, but it was so meaningful it seemed like ten minutes. That's the same relationship Uncle Ted and I had, but I'm fifteen and too big to jump onto his foot.

When bus service started a year later, I found myself missing those conversations.

The bus route passed the colored homes and picked up kids who'd be at the end of the route and then picked up the coloreds. At the end of the day, the bus route reversed.

Some kids on the bus were nice and spoke to me, but others thought they were better than me, asking where I shopped for my clothes and why I had a boy's name.

Teasing also happened in class. On the first day when attendance was called, I raised my hand and a boy said, "Isn't that a boy's name?"

I stared at him. In my head, I heard Mama say, "Charley Louise, be good and please behave in school." So I turned around.

He was right. I hated my name, but there wasn't anything I could do about it.

That night at the dinner table, I talked about school and how some of the kids teased me about my name.

Uncle Ted told me, "You have a beautiful name, and it's your name. People may try to take away your pride and tease you, but one thing they can't take away from you is your name. Charley Louise is a beautiful name and will be part of you forever. Be proud of your name and yourself."

He told me his story of choosing to change his life and becoming a hobo. People stared and laughed at him all the time as he hopped from train to train, peddling at each stop for work. He said, "One thing they couldn't take away from me was my pride and dignity. I always knew who I was. Although they may laugh and tease, they can't take away who you are ... and don't you let them."

I nodded.

"Have you made any friends?"

"There are twenty-two kids in my class, but there are only three coloreds—me, Karen, and Gladys. They live on the other side of town, but we're friends."

Every time I was teased, I thought about Uncle Ted and our conversation. I think that's when I changed. My friends and I would tease back. Sometimes I'd just walk away with a banana boat smile on my face.

####

Many nights I laid in bed looking out my bedroom and listened to crickets, frogs, birds, chickens and pigs.

The crickets seemed to have their own conversations. I'd try to mimic their sounds. We had our own choir. It was almost like they were the sisters or brothers I wished I had.

Early one winter morning while getting ready for school, the biggest animal stopped right near my window. I wiped my eyes and said, "Wait a minute, that's a deer." Deer never came this close to our house.

I went downstairs to tell Uncle Ted and Aunt Louise, hoping to get a reaction, but they knew deer came on our land.

Uncle Ted said, "With the woods being all around our land, and many of the deer living there, this isn't uncommon. We prayed that the hunters wouldn't catch them."

Every morning I looked out my window for the deer. It didn't always show up, but it was a beautiful sight when it did, nibbling on the bottom branches of our trees and bushes.

To make extra money, Aunt Louise cooked breakfast for the hunters. I worried that one morning they'd see the deer. I knew Aunt Louise wasn't going to stop because they paid her good money. All I could do was pray they wouldn't see it.

As badly as I wanted to leave food for the deer, I couldn't. If I did, the deer would come to my window all the time, looking for food, and sooner or later, the deer hunters would see it. Whenever it showed up underneath my window, I whispered to it.

One morning while getting ready for school, I glanced out of my bedroom window. I looked once and then twice.

At first I wasn't sure if it was the same deer, but, as I looked over her short brownish colored hair, I noticed the ring of spots that made her stand out from the others.

"The hunters didn't kill you." I smiled. "Where have you been?" Next to her was a smaller deer—a doe. "You have a family," I said.

The house doors closed. Before I could turn my head back to the window, the deer had scampered away.

It seemed like we had a friendship until the deer stopped coming.

I asked Uncle Ted if he had seen the deer, but he hadn't. He thought maybe one of the hunters had caught them.

We heard gun shots all of the time. One of the bullets must have killed the deer. I didn't see them nibbling on the bushes and trees, but that didn't stop me from looking out my bedroom window early in the morning, praying to see one of them. Since living in the rural area of White Cloud, they were one of the most beautiful animals I had ever seen.

####

During the fall, winter, and early spring, Mama would send me letters about every two weeks without delay.

When I wasn't writing Mama letters, I'd write in my diary wondering what she was doing at a certain moment, or if the kids were playing jokes on her again, or what perfume she was wearing.

Before she left for Chicago, we had many conversations underneath the moon. I really missed those conversations, listening to the chickens, pigs, and dogs as we talked. I don't think I can replace the words of wisdom she gave me, especially about girly topics and helping ease my mind about entering another new school. It was as though the separation made us closer than when we lived together.

I settled into the rural way of living. There were only a handful of coloreds, so most of us were friends and stuck together.

Day 9 Journal Entry 9 ... Usually I write to Daddy, but this time I want to write about missing Mama and her being in Chicago has put a void inside me. Both uncle houses are complete. I have concerns about Mama's health, but I'm sure her employer is taking good care of her. I dream of springtime when Mama comes to visit. Charley Louise

####

A year later, one other family moved within walking distance to our land. On Rural Route 1, there were three families.

I heard voices, ran downstairs, and saw the neighbors from up the road.

"Hello, everyone."

Uncle Ted said, "Everyone, this is Charley Louise—"

"We know Rose's daughter."

"How do you know?" Uncle Ted said.

"Our kids talk to her in school."

Before Uncle Ted could say anything else, they started talking. "We noticed you've started the ground work on a house. We want to help. More hands could help build the house sooner than a few."

A big smile came on Uncle Ted's face. "In early spring, we'll start work on the house again." He showed them the layout he had drawn. Uncle Ted told me, "Hopefully the frame would be completed before your mama visits."

"Will we have to go back and forth from Chicago for more wood and windows?" I asked.

"No. I have all the tools and equipment to cut down trees that are right here behind us."

Uncle Ted had built his own small work space behind his house where his tools were stored and he could work year-round. He was also able to help others around the area. I don't think there was anything he couldn't fix or build.

Uncle Ted grew to be my favorite. He was always gentle and kind to everyone. I can't think of a time he said 'no' to anyone.

There were times when he'd let me come into the work shed. He never let me cut anything. I mostly learned about the tools and cleaned up. One day he showed me some of the tools he was going to use for building me and Mama's house.

I would look at the bricks and envision the bedrooms, living room, kitchen, and a bathroom to take the place of the outhouse we used.

Every time I asked a question, Uncle Ted told me to be patient. I put a calendar on my wall and crossed off one day after the other until the snow finally started to melt and spring came.

The chirping of birds and men talking outside woke me up. I went downstairs, looked out the window facing me and Mama's house, and saw men laying down the concrete foundation.

I rushed back upstairs, hopping around, trying to put my legs into my jeans and falling to the floor. I buttoned up my shirt and put on my tennis shoes. I ran out the back door with a piece of toast, yelling, "What can I do?"

"You're up bright and early," Uncle Ted said.

"Yeah. Can I help?"

"Sure. Why don't you hand me that nail."

The men worked on the house most of the week with Uncle Ted if they didn't have their own work to do. Most of his help came on the weekends. That was okay with him because he was determined to finish the house.

At dinnertime, Uncle Ted showed me the layout that he had drawn on paper. He marked off things he had completed. For the most part, our house was just as I had envisioned.

"Uncle Ted," I said. "Where is the bathroom?"

He hesitated before speaking then said, "For now, you and your mama will have to use the outhouse.

I felt my mouth drop as I looked at him.

"We hope to have the house almost completed by the time your mama comes for her next visit in July."

Uncle Ted and the neighbors worked hard into the night. One day I stood and watched them complete the roof. There was no paint, only a brown, tar-like shingle siding that covered the sides of the house. But I didn't care. I had a house ... at least the outside of a house.

It was a hot July summer when the whole family rode into town to pick up mama from the train station.

As we got closer to the house, we asked Mama to close her eyes and to not open them until we said so.

She had no idea what was happening and started to ask questions. I kept saying, "Mama, close your eyes." She wanted to peek, so I covered her face with a handkerchief.

"Not so tight, Charley Louise."

"We're almost there."

The car wheels rolled slowly over the two-track road turning into our driveway. I removed the handkerchief.

"Open your eyes."

"Oh my God," Mama said. "You've been busy. I expected to see a partial building, but not this. It is beautiful."

Uncle Ted told Mama, "It isn't quite finished. The inside of the house needs a lot more work."

"I don't care," Mama said. It's still a beautiful home."

I told Mama, "People moved up the road and came over to help us"

Charley Louise Dorsey house / White Cloud, Michigan

"We'll have to invite them over for supper to thank them."

She stood outside looking around and said, "Now each family's home is built, but the best thing is we're all right next to each other ... a family.

Each home was built on Rural Route 1, seven miles west of the city limits of White Cloud and nine miles east of Hesperia.

About a month after Mama returned from Chicago, we went for a walk inside our house, looking at every room. She asked me how I liked living in White Cloud.

It's all right. It's growing on me and I've made friends."

"There's a chance I'll be coming to live in White Cloud for good."

She said, "I'm making plans with my employer to send the rest of my personal belongings."

"You're staying?"

"Yes."

"Have you told Aunt Louise and Unk?"

"Not yet. I wanted tell you first to get your reaction."

"Uncle Ted will have to hurry and finish our house."

"Until the house is finished, we'll stay with Aunt Louise and Uncle Ted. You and I will share a bedroom."

"Do we have enough money?"

"Yes."

I still felt something must be wrong.

She said, "The Jewish family I worked for will be kind enough to support us for a few months. They want me to keep in touch."

"Mama?"

"Yes, Charley Louise."

"Is everything all right?"

"Don't worry so much. Do you remember what I told you about the plat of land that's next to Uncle Ted and Aunt Louise's house?"

I noticed Mama was walking slower. "Are you all right?" I asked.

"Go and get Aunt Louise."

I ran toward the house screaming, "Aunt Louise. Aunt Louise. Come quick. Something's wrong with Mama."

As Aunt Louise and everyone else ran toward us, Mama fell to the ground.

"What's wrong with her?" I kept asking.

Aunt Louise called the doctor, but by the time the doctor arrived, Mama wasn't moving or breathing.

No matter how he tried to help, it was too late. Mama was dead.

"I'm sorry, Charley Louise," the doctor said. "Your Mama died of a heart attack."

Mama was in her early 50s. At the funeral, I remembered that she worked all her life raising me, making sure I had a roof over my head, the family stayed together, and there was food on the table.

For weeks, I went to our unfinished house, walking from room to room and sitting on the stairs. I stared at the moon, looking for the woman who was brushing her hair, talking to her as though she was Mama.

I was only 16 with no Mama and a Daddy I had been removed from and hadn't seen in years. Many nights, I asked the Lord, "Why? Why did you take away the two most precious people in my life? Why did you leave me alone? And why should I keep believing in you?"

####

One night about a month later, I wiped my eyes and remembered the last conversation that Mama had with me was about the plats of land on the other side of Uncle Ted and Aunt Louise's house. I went to them. "Do you have Daddy's address?" I asked.

"Why?"

"I made a promise to Mama and I intend to keep it. Mama told me that if she died, the plats of land next to us, right over there, would go to Daddy."

The last contact I had with Daddy was when I lived in Chicago, but Mama must have talked to him about her health. He needed to know that she died and that he had land up in White Cloud. After Aunt Louise gave me his address and I wrote him.

Dear Daddy,

How are you doing? I'm writing to let you know that Mama has died. She left you some land in White Cloud, Michigan. It's a small plat of land, with no house on it, but it's yours. Please let me know what your intentions are for this land. Love, Charley Louise

It took about two weeks before Uncle Ted told me that I had mail. Daddy wrote back sooner than I thought he would. I walked over to me and Mama's house, sat on the back steps, and read the letter.

Dear Pumpkin,

I'm sorry to hear that Rose has died. I wasn't aware that her illness was that serious. I want to move up North and settle on the piece of land that you say your Mama left for me.

I also want you to know that I have remarried and will be bringing my wife along with me. I hope that this doesn't make you sad.

As it is late fall and making it difficult to move everything, we will come up next spring.

I miss you and love you. I'll see you very soon.

Love, Daddy

"Remarried," I said. I guess when time passes, something happens to you inside. Emotions change … Time changes.

Although I had plenty of family around me, I felt alone and abandoned. I felt like my soul had left. It seemed like pieces of my life were starting to chip away. But I still looked forward to seeing Daddy again. I didn't feel the same way about his wife.

Chapter Twelve
Menu Addendum ...
Under 10 people, add 50 cents per person
$5.00 delivery charge

The Jewish family that Mama worked for when she went back to Chicago wrote me letters, asking how I was doing, almost as if I had grown up as one their girls.

Even after Mama died, they kept their promise to make sure I was taken care of up until I received the last check. We kept writing to each other, but no more money came with the letters. It was very gracious of them since Mama was no longer working and I wasn't their child.

Some days I'd walk on the two-track road and remember playing hide-and-seek with the Rosenberg children, the first family Mama worked for, in what I thought was the largest home in America.

I think the best part of their home was the foyer. I remember asking Mama where the television and furniture was, and she told me that it wasn't their living room. I remembered when Mama went to Europe and always brought me back one of the snow globes with a girl on skates.

Mama instilled in me an excellent trait for saving money. I had enough money to live off without working for a while, but the account grew smaller.

####

I was sitting in class when someone from the principal's office came into my classroom. When the teacher read the note, she called my name.

"Charley Louise, the principal would like to see you in his office."

I was scared and thought, *I haven't done anything wrong today.*

When I opened the door to the principal's office, he had the biggest smile on his face. "Take a seat," he said.

"You're doing exceptionally well in all of your classes, far ahead of the other students. Because your credits transferred so high, you could possibly graduate a year earlier than the rest of your classmates."

"Why didn't you tell me this sooner, when I first got to this school?"

At first, he had a weird look on his face. Then he said, "The school wanted to make sure. We wanted to see your grades for ourselves."

I looked back at him thinking, *He didn't think I was that smart. He must have thought I cheated somewhere along the way.* I said, "So, I can graduate and be out of school sooner?"

"That's right, but you'll have to take some state exams. We'll send you home with a letter to your parents ... guardians because they'd have to approve of this first."

On a warm Saturday afternoon I heard the chickens clucking and the pigs snorting. The air was cascading with the smell of nothing but ... well, chickens and pigs.

I was sitting on the porch when Uncle Ted came and sat down with me. At first, we just chatted and the subject changed.

"What are your plans?" He asked.

I shifted my eyes left and acted like I hadn't heard him. "Where is Aunt Louise?"

Our heads turned toward each other at the same time. Looking me in the eyes, he said, "Don't try to change the subject. Before your mama died, Aunt Louise promised her she'd take care of you. We have, but it's time for you to contribute something."

The screen door opened, and Unk joined us. I felt trapped. Most times the women talked to the girls, but since I was closer to Uncle Ted, he talked to me.

I didn't mind Uncle Ted, but Unk ... He never smiled or laughed, just gave orders.

"So, Charley Louise, what plans do you have for yourself?" Uncle Ted said.

"I'm—"

"Could you start that sentence again?" Unk said.

"*I am* not sure. I do have some savings."

"How long do you think that will last? You don't want to use it all up and then have to wonder, what next?" Uncle Ted said.

I looked at Unk and then at Uncle Ted. "Why is it that Uncle Ted can say 'don't,' 'can't,' and 'won't' and I have to speak proper?"

They said, "Say no more, child. Do as I say and not as I do."

I didn't dare ask what that meant. Asking questions was considered talking back, and that was definitely not tolerated.

"*I do not* know what my plans are," I said. "I guess I'll have to come up with something."

That is when they told me they had an idea. Uncle Ted and the adults were going to meet with a person who had helped other coloreds find work. After that meeting, they said they'd talk to me.

There are many things to learn about living in the country. One thing I learned is that with gravel roads, you always hear cars coming into the driveway.

About noon, we looked out the window and saw a colored man in a red truck coming to a stop. Before he could get out, Uncle Ted and Unk came out of the house to meet him.

When they went inside the house, we stood outside the

screened door listening. He was talking to the rest of the family about picking crops in the surrounding small towns.

"Pickin' crops?" "What kind of crops?" I asked. Darlene and Rose hurried to cover my mouth.

The man said, "Blueberries, cherries, onions, and others."

Charley Louise whispered to the Darlene and Rose, "I'm not going to pick any blueberries, cherries, or onions."

The screen door opened and slammed. Aunt Louise stood with her hands on her hips, frowning. "What do you mean you're not going to pick any crops?"

"After the family talking so much about education, I'll have to pick crops?"

Aunt Louise said, "And, what suggestion do you have, young lady?"

"I'll ... I'll go to college. That's what Mama wanted." I had never talked back to Aunt Louise, but I felt this was the right time. I had to stand up for myself.

Aunt Louise said, "There's not enough money for you to go to college right now. Until you graduate from school, this is what you'll have to do to earn money toward your college education."

"That's the final decision." I looked at both of them and walked off, stomping to my house.

Aunt Louise yelled, "You're a teenager and too young to make such a decision."

I sat on the steps pouting and counted the ants. I didn't know what to do. Mama was gone. Daddy wasn't here.

I started thinking. This is a long way from the Chicago life we had. By this time, my friends from Chicago and I had stopped writing each other. Especially Susie who after all we went through with the racism became one of my friends.

Watching the pimps and their girls working the street corners at night, and the kids stealing fruit from the corner store barrels and the owner running them out the door, shouting, "I'll get you next time." That would be replaced with dirt, trees, and picking crops.

I sat on the steps for the longest time. Then I looked up and saw Unk standing over me. "You have to do something, and these are the only jobs the family can find. Other families will be picking crops, too. We're trying to look out for your best interests. The money that you have, you want to keep it for a rainy day. So, when school lets out for the summer, all who can will be going to the farmers and picking crops."

"I don't think so. I'm not pickin' any farmer's crops all of my life," I said underneath my breath as he walked away.

That night after supper, I sat near my bedroom window, looking up at the sky, searching for the moon. But there was no moon, no woman brushing her hair. I felt alone with my thoughts until I decided to pray to God.

"Is this all there is for me in the world, God? Please hear my prayer. I don't want to pick crops. Isn't there something else out there for me?"

####

The bell rung and school was out for the summer. We cleaned out our lockers. Since I had a few things, Uncle Ted had told me that he'd pick me up from school.

"Do I really have to pick the farmer's crops this summer, Uncle Ted?"

"Yes, you do. Most of the family will be picking crops."

I looked out the window… *Will I have fun with my friends? No. I'll be picking some farmer's crops for him and his family while his kids have fun in the sun with their friends. I'll be sweating in the sun all day long until the sun goes down.*

A week after school was out Aunt Louise woke me up at 4:30 a.m. to eat breakfast while she packed the lunches. We loaded into the station wagon and headed to Beulah, Michigan to pick cherries.

We went home to eat dinner that Aunt Louise had prepared over the weekend, watched the evening news, and went to bed to be up early in the morning to repeat the same thing.

While at Beulah Uncle Ted was in one of the cherry trees when a man came up to him. He said, "My name is Mr. Jones and I work for the farmers, transporting workers from field to field, and I see that you're driving yourselves to the field. If you ride with me, I could save you money on gas and wear and tear on your car. If you'd like to ride with me, please meet me on Straight Road at 5 a.m."

During lunch, Uncle Ted met some of the other men in the orchard and asked them about riding with this man. A lot of them told Uncle Ted that they rode with him because they didn't have transportation. The others said they didn't want to pay him for bringing them when they could drive themselves.

At the dinner table, Uncle Ted and Aunt Louise discussed riding with the man to the fields. At first, Uncle Ted wasn't sure until Aunt Louise said that she had spoken to some of the workers in the orchard.

It was about a week before the family decided we'd ride with him, but if there were any problems, Uncle Ted said that we'd go back to driving ourselves to the fields.

The next morning I woke up at 4:30 a.m. and ate breakfast while Aunt Louise fixed the lunches.

It was so early the birds weren't even up. I complained the whole time. We were almost at the truck when I said, "The cherries are probably still asleep."

"Good morning, everyone," Mr. Jones said. "Hurry up. We have to get to the orchards. Now, as I said to each of you, I expect to get paid for transportation each day. Is that understood?"

"You mean to tell me that after our hard day's work in the hot sun and after the farmer pays us, we'll have to pay this man?"

Aunt Louise told me to be quiet while the man explained he had two different trucks. To keep families together, we could choose which truck we wanted to ride in.

Mr. Jones said, "It's chilly, so everyone should bring extra clothing and a blanket. If you didn't dress warm enough and get cold, I have blankets available for no cost."

Our family had dressed plenty warm enough and had brought our own blankets.

I slept until bumps in the road kept jiggling my body up and down. I opened my eyes and thought I had gone to a heaven of trees. I had never seen so many red dots.

The morning was misty and cold. As the truck came to a stop, I rubbed my eyes. All I could see were trees, trees, and more trees all lined up, as if to say, "Here comes another group of people to pluck." On them were the biggest, reddest cherries I had ever seen.

I had eaten cherries before but had never seen where they came from or cared.

The man who took us to the orchard introduced the families who had not met the farmers, and his helpers. Each family was then taken to their area of the orchard where they'd work for the day.

"This is where you'll start, and you'll have to pick these trees for the day in order to get your pay," the farmer said. "Here are your holsters and buckets."

Although I had lived in White Cloud for over a year, I still considered myself a city girl. I wasn't used to climbing trees with a ladder that was as tall as the top of the tree and didn't seem sturdy.

We wore pants that fit tight to our legs at the bottom because the bushes we had to walk through from tree to tree were tall and wet from the early morning dew.

The younger kids picked from the bottom of the trees. The older kids and adults picked from the middle to the top.

Our family worked two trees at a time. In order to reach some of the cherries, someone would have to get up on the ladder. I looked around, saw the ladder, and propped it against the tree limbs. Then I asked, "Who's going to climb the ladder to pick the cherries from the top?"

"You are," Aunt Louise said.

Aunt Louise would climb the ladder on the other side of the tree to pick the cherries, and I'd do the same on the other side of the tree with my ladder.

Before climbing onto the ladder, I put a belt around my waist that held the cherry bucket.

I climbed up on the ladder, frowning. "This is not how life was supposed to turn out, and I will not pick cherries the rest of my life," I said.

"Did you say something?" Aunt Louise yelled from the other side of the tree.

I didn't reply. While on the ladder, I prayed the wind wouldn't blow. If it did, I'd fall right to the ground on my butt, cherry bucket and all.

If it seemed like the ladder was wobbly, there would be a designated holder. I yelled, "I need a holder." But no one helped. I tried every idea I could think of such as rocking the ladder against the tree hoping someone else would feel the tree moving, but it didn't work.

Aunt Louise had already filled one bucket and stood at the bottom of my ladder. "When you fill your bucket, pour the cherries into this container over here."

Someone from the next tree told Darlene and Rose to be careful because the limb their ladder was propped against didn't look sturdy.

Aunt Louise ran over to hold the bottom of the ladder until their bucket was filled with cherries and they climbed down.

I saw only two people fall from the ladder when they tried reaching too far for the cherries. They rested and someone else took their buckets and filled them. Then they went back to picking cherries like nothing had happened. What a life.

"This is going to take all day to fill this cherry container," I said.

"Charley Louise, no more complaining. Stop it right now. No one is enjoying this," Aunt Louise said.

The container the cherries were dumped in was a two-sided wooden crate. Each side held a gallon of cherries. It took forever to fill it.

I took my time and started counting each cherry I put in my bucket. "One. Two. Three. Four. Five. Six ..."

Aunt Louise came to the bottom of my ladder. "How many cherries have you picked? If you count a little faster, the bucket will get full quicker. Next time I come over here I want to see a full bucket of cherries, you hear me?"

After she left, I started picking a little faster, thinking to myself that if Mama hadn't died and Daddy was here, I wouldn't have to be here early in the morning picking these darn cherries.

Mama and Daddy, this is your fault. You left me alone and now look what happened. I'm picking cherries for a living. Lord, why did you have to take both of my parents away from me? Why?

Riding back in the truck, I sat in the corner by myself, not saying a word. Aunt Louise asked, "How were your first two weeks, Charley Louise?"

"I hated it, but I pray that we find regular work soon."

"Well, for now this is it. Let's go home and try it again tomorrow."

Mr. Jones, the man who drove us to the orchard dropped us off at our cars and trucks.

"You children go and sit in the car and wait." I stood still while the others walked over to our car. Aunt Louise said, "You too, Charley Louise."

Uncle Ted and Unk met us at the truck stop. I looked out of the car window and saw them paying the man part of our daily wages.

"See all of you tomorrow bright and early?" Mr. Jones said.

At the dinner table that night, Uncle Ted and Aunt Louise talked about how much money was made and how much money we paid the man for taking us to the orchard.

"Why are we paying this man to drive us to the orchards?" I said. "Why don't ...We can't drive ourselves?"

"This man knows all of the farmers. Once we get a chance to know the farmers, we can make our own deal with them.

"But Aunt—"

"Let it be," Aunt Louise said. "Clean the dishes from the table while I talk with your uncle."

They went into the living room, which is right next to the kitchen.

I heard Aunt Louise ask Uncle Ted how much we paid the man with the truck and found out we had paid him a lot of our wages. We were making quite a bit of money picking cherries, usually getting twenty-five or fifty cents per bucket.

After that, Uncle Ted and Unk spoke to some of the other families, trying to figure out if there was a way to remember the orchards and fields we were taken to by Mr. Jones.

Within a week, they found other places to pick crops. The only problem was that we were not close to home and would have to stay away for a week or two. And Aunt Louise and Aunt Pearl would have to stay home to watch the houses.

I was surprised when the family decided to go up North for a week at a time only to come home on the weekends.

We lived in tents. Then the younger adults decided that if we were going to pick crops all summer and be away from home, why not have *some type* of fun?

We formed baseball teams. The team names were from the various orchards or fields that we worked. Our family didn't win too many times, but we had fun.

I met a boy, but that didn't last too long because Uncle Ted and Unk found out and reminded me of why we were up North and away from our families ... and it wasn't to meet boys.

We worked the northern cherry orchards for about a month, came home, and went straight to the muck fields to top onions.

The good thing about working the muck fields was that they were close to home and we were able to sleep in our own beds. We were paid ten cents a crate if the onions were big and twenty-five cents a crate if they were small. I didn't think that was enough money. The hot sun shined down on us like it was mad at the world. There was no shade and we worked up and down long rows full of black, thick muck, pulling onions out of the ground.

We chopped the green stems with gigantic sheers and put them into a brown burlap bag. Once the bag was full, we dumped the onions into a wooden crate. When the crate was full, Uncle Ted or Unk stacked them. I worked two rows at a time. Each night the crates were counted and we got paid.

I picked crops from spring until school started. Some families picked crops until late fall. I was happy to start school so I wouldn't have to pick another crop.

####

On our way home one night from the muck fields, I said, "Unk, I can't go to school on Monday smelling like a bushel of onions. How can I get rid of this smell?"

He said, "You won't smell like the muck when school starts."

But I did.

I watched the bus come around the bend and stop in front of my house, flashing red lights. The door opened and I hesitated. The bus driver asked, "Are you getting on the bus."

"Yes," I whispered, taking baby steps.

"Hurry up," he said. "Or I'll have to shut the door."

I walked to the back of the bus with my shoulders held back, saying to myself, *I'm Charley Louise Dorsey, and I have pride.*

"What's that smell?" Someone yelled.

"Oh, it's the muck girls," another person answered.

"Ha. Ha." I frowned. "Is the onion smell that bad?" I asked Karen and Gladys.

"It's pretty bad ... No, it's horrible," Karen said.

"I wish I didn't have to pick any crops, just like some of the white kids on this bus ... the ones you see at the beach in town."

"I know, Charley Louise. Maybe one day that'll happen, but for now this is reality," Gladys said.

We were humiliated. That black muck dirt stained our hands and fingernails. Our family always worked the onion fields and I started school with the same smell. It was embarrassing watching the kids walk past me holding their noses.

"I don't ever want to top another onion in my life," I said.

"I agree. But for now we'll have to put up with the kids laughing and talking about us. Just don't get into any fights over it. Okay?" Karen said.

"I promise there wouldn't be any fights ... today."

My friends asked, "If you don't work the muck fields or orchards, how are you supposed to make enough money for college?"

"I don't know, but I'll have to find another way. Besides, I do have some money saved up in the bank from Mama. All I know is that after graduation, I'm not going to pick another cherry, blueberry, string bean, top onions or pluck another apple unless I'm eating it."

Charley Louise Dorsey high school graduation picture

White Cloud Public Schools

White Cloud, Michigan

This Certifies That

Charley Louise Dorsey

has completed the Course of Study prescribed by the

Board of Education for the High School

and therefore merits this

Diploma

Given this twenty-third day of May, 1945.

S. K. Ridler
President of Board of Education

William J. Beach
Superintendent

Margaret M. Larson
Secretary of Board of Education

Marguerite Champion
Principal

Charley Louise Dorsey high school graduation diploma

Chapter Thirteen

Baked chicken, green beans, salad,
rolls w/butter, dessert ... $5.00

Although the credits from the Chicago public school transferred extremely high, I still had to prove myself by taking state exams. I passed it and graduated a year early on May 23rd with the White Cloud High School Class of 1945.

We were lined up in the hallway single file, talking and laughing, when Pomp and Circumstance began to play. During that time of the year, every school and college played it.

I was the sixth person in line, right behind Dolz, who was one of the handsomest boys in the school. We never spoke much. The senior class marched in two lines with the girls on one side and the boys on the other.

As we turned the corner, a person directed us to a row of empty chairs. It was rumored that in a previous graduation, a girl switched rows and sat next to her boyfriend. When the people in that row had to stand up to go on stage, she crossed over to where she was supposed to sit.

I kept walking in step to the beat, looking for my family. It wasn't too hard to find them because all of the coloreds sat in the back rows.

I smiled at them and mouthed, "Can you believe it?"

Sitting in my seat and waiting through the boring speeches and ready for my name to be called, I began thinking back on my school years.

I remembered saying the word "Senior" for the first time. I

told my friends to pinch me so that I knew this was real. "I'm really a Junior but no, I'm a senior graduating."

In Newaygo County, I couldn't think of one other colored person who had accomplished this. There were only 23 people in my senior class, three of whom were colored. After Robert, the valedictorian finished his speech, the principal came to the podium and said, "Everyone in the front row whose last name starts with letters A to E, please stand."

I stood and walked as the principal started calling names. Then he said, "Charley Louise Dorsey." I had thought of this day all summer but couldn't do anything but stand still.

"Charley Louise Dorsey," he repeated. Someone nudged me. I was sweating like I was working out in the muck fields. I walked onto the stage. He handed me my diploma and said, "Congratulations, Ms. Dorsey. You have graduated from White Cloud High School. Good luck in your future endeavors."

I walked with my shoulders back and smiled again at my family. I whispered, "I know you're here, Mama. I'll make you proud." Daddy wasn't at my graduation. I'm not sure what happened and never forgot that day.

Right after graduation, the People's Baptist Church held an ice cream and cake reception for the graduates of the church. On the car ride to the church, I gazed out of the window, thinking, *What does the future hold for me and how soon can I go to college?*

While at my graduation party I looked around at Aunt Louise, Uncle Ted, Unk, Aunt Pearl, Darlene, Rose, and Mrs. Ollie. No matter what, we're family and helped each other through the good and the bad. I realized how strong our family is. Mama taught me to hold my shoulders back, keep my head high and to have pride in myself. Never let anything or anybody bring me down, work hard, and to keep the Lord in front of my path.

Aunt Louise startled me out of my thoughts. "Come on, Charley Louise, and open your presents," she yelled.

"Yes, ma'am," I said. "Here I come."

The next morning, it was back to usual.

I got up groaning, put on my clothes, and went to the coop.

"Is everyone ready for breakfast?" I opened the coop and the chickens scurried to the front of the door. "Come on, you can't be starving."

As I watched them eat, I said, "I graduated yesterday. What do you think I should do this summer? Should I pick crops or go to college? There's some money, but I'm not sure if it's enough." As though they had answered me, I said, "I agree. Let's go and tell the family my decision."

I moved backward toward the door, continuing to talk to them, and threw some of the chicken food toward the back of the coop. When they ran for the food, I hurried out of the coop and locked the door.

I walked over to Unk's house and then to Aunt Louise and Uncle Ted's house, asking each of them to meet me at the back steps of my house. The house wasn't complete, but I visited it from time to time.

Standing in front of the family, I was a little nervous. "I have an announcement," I said.

I could feel the tension filling the air. Uncle Ted nodded and I put a smile on my face.

"First, I want to say that I love you all ... even you Darlene and Rose."

"Get on with it, Charley Louise," They said.

"I have decided to go back to Chicago."

"Chicago?" They said. "How will you live? Where will you stay? What will you do?"

Looking from one person to the next, everyone talking at the same time, I yelled, "Wait a minute. I have a small savings that will help me and I have been in contact with a few of my old friends. Although they have one year left in school, one of the families has agreed to let me stay with them."

I stopped talking and looked around at some of the saddest faces.

Darlene said, "Are you sure?"

Staring into her eyes, I said, "Yes, I'm sure." I hugged her and then told everyone, "All I could see in my future here in White Cloud is picking crops and having babies ... being poor. That's not want I want to do for the rest of my life. Why can't I at least try something else? Isn't that what you all have preached over the years—to work hard and make choices to improve your life? Well, I have decided to go back to Chicago and try it there."

"But Charley Louise—"

"No" came out of my mouth louder than it was supposed to. "I've made up my mind, Aunt Louise. What else can I do up here in these woods? What else? I have decided to go to cosmetology school ... Madam C. J. Walker College of Beauty and Culture. I'll be leaving soon and have made my train reservations."

I knew that if I wanted to learn how to do colored people's hair professionally the Madam C. J. Walker College of Beauty and Culture is where I should study.

But, the only person who seemed to understand and accept my decision was Uncle Ted. He said, "Follow your dreams. If you want to come back home, you'll always have a home to come back to."

"If Mama and Daddy were here things might be different, but they're not. I'm just going for school and will be back to visit in the summer. After all, I'll have a new home to come back to."

That night, Aunt Louise planned my good-bye dinner. They didn't like my decision, but we talked, remembering and laughing at the dinner table before everyone said their good nights.

I laid in my bed, staring out the window. "Mama, your little girl has grown up and made a grown-up decision. I know you'll be with me while I'm in Chicago and will take good care of me."

I loved Chicago. Although White Cloud was a nice, small rural community, the change was hard for me. My family was here, but I made the decision to leave and to come back with a degree from the Madam C. J. Walker College of Beauty and Culture.

####

It was a warm, summer morning. The air smelled like perfume and straw. While walking to the chicken coop for the last time, I heard clucking and snorting from the pigs. But today it sounded different. It was as though they knew this was our good-bye. I opened the coop door. Like magnets, all of the chickens scampered toward me.

"You guys take care of everything for me, you hear?"

The clucking sound grew louder and louder, as though they were talking to me.

Before I closed the door to the chicken coop, a few of the baby chicks tried to follow me. I stopped all but one from getting through.

After corralling it into a corner at the steps of the house, I cuddled the chick near my chest, rubbing it softly. "I'll be back. And when I do come back, you'll be all grown up and have chicks of your own. For now you'll have to go with the others." I put the chick in the coop and walked away.

I went to my house, imagining what the rooms would look like when completed. Sitting on the back steps, I looked at Uncle Ted and Aunt Louise's house and through the scattered trees looked at Unk and Aunt Pearl's house. Our family had built these houses with our own hands. For a moment I almost changed my mind about leaving White Cloud.

A cool breeze passed my face, carrying a rancid smell. I looked toward the outhouse. "No. My mind is made up. I'm going back to Chicago."

That night the whole family came over for supper and Mrs. Ollie and her husband who helped our family to move to White Cloud. We feasted on homemade corn bread, collard greens, corn on the cob, fried chicken, ham, potato salad, homemade apple pie, and cake. We also had grape Kool-aid.

Some of the neighbors came and wished me well, too. Aunt Louise offered them something to eat, but they said they had already eaten.

"Chicago is a big city. Take care of yourself," The neighbors said.

"I will. I'll make everyone proud."

"You have already made us proud without going to Chicago," another neighbor said.

I looked around at each one of them. It was as though they were family, too. I would miss them all.

"Charley Louise, are your suitcases packed?" Aunt Louise said.

"Most of them," I said.

"What you doing up there ... daydreaming again? I'll be up in a minute and want to see suitcases snapped closed."

Three years had passed since I had left Chicago and moved to White Cloud. During those three years, my wardrobe had changed, and making a decision on what to take and what not to take was hard.

While looking inside my closet, I heard a clumping sound coming up the stairs, and I jumped. *It could only be Aunt Louise,* I thought. She was heavyset, and each time her foot touched a stair, I heard a rickety sound.

I peeked around the corner of my closet and didn't see her, but her voice made it sound like she was near the top stair. "How's the packing coming along?"

"Well ..."

"I hope you're taking the right clothes. You'll be gone a long time."

I did need more clothing, but I wasn't going to take my countrified clothes to Chicago and have my friends laugh at me.

I thought, *If I'm going to change anything, there are only seconds to do it because Aunt Louise is on her way around the corner.* I pulled the pencil skirt from the hanger and picked up the high heeled shoes from the back of my closet and the nylons with the seam down the middle, which were the hardest things to keep centered in the middle of my legs.

As I saw Aunt Louise appear closer around the corner on the stairs, I shoved the city clothes in the bottom and closed the suitcases. I turned around before she could ask me any questions and said, "I have decided not to take certain things and only what I moved here with ... the things that came with me from Chicago."

I hoped the wrinkles wouldn't form in her forehead. She said in a soft voice, "Do they fit?"

I breathed a sigh of relief. "Some of them do and some don't but, I'll be all right."

Aunt Louise wasn't a very affectionate person and was a strong disciplinarian, so when she sat next to me on my bed and put her arms around me, I was shocked. She said, "I understand that the country way of dressing isn't the same as the city girls. Don't forget that I lived in Chicago, too."

She got up, started walked downstairs, and then stopped. "Don't stay up too late packing. We'll have to get up early to take you to the train."

"I won't. Just have a few more things."

It was as if she knew I took that pencil skirt and the nylons with the seam down the middle. I looked around my closet and thought, *She's right. I'll take a few of the sweaters and dresses just in case.*

After snapping the last suitcase shut, I laid on my bed, looking out the window. The moon was big, but I didn't see the lady combing her hair. I don't know how long I stared at that moon wanting to see her.

Aunt Louise shook me, saying, "Charley Louise. Charley Louise, wake up. It's time to get ready. Everyone will be here soon for breakfast. I'm going downstairs to set the table. Now get up!"

It was a hot morning and I wiped the sweat from my face. Opening the bedroom window, I heard chickens and pigs.

Today was one glorious day. No more cherry picking and pulling big burlap bags up and down the black dirt.

I looked in the mirror at myself, making sure my suit fit just right and smoothing out the wrinkles. I brushed my hair and put bobby pins in to make sure no strands were out of place.

Then I made sure my hat sat perfectly, tilted on the side on my head. Aunt Louise had lent me one of her hat stick pins. Sliding the pin into the hat, I had to be careful to not stick my scalp.

On the weekend, we usually had pancakes and eggs. But for this occasion, we also had bacon, oatmeal, grits, fresh hash browns, and juice.

The grown-up table included the younger adults and stretched clear across the kitchen area.

"Now, don't you go off and meet some fella while you're in Chicago," Rose said.

"And don't hang out at the juke houses playing all of that worldly music," Mrs. Ollie said.

Aunt Louise and Unk peered at me with stern eyes as if to say, "You better not."

I said, "Let me go upstairs and make sure I have everything. Thank you for coming to my breakfast."

Darlene and Rose asked to be excused from the table and followed me upstairs, chuckling. Then we hugged each other and cried. At that moment it seemed like we had bonded forever in a different way.

I said, "We're growing up into young women, and the world is wide open. Don't get stuck in White Cloud. Find your dream and pursue it because you can always come back home."

That's when I heard, "We're going to be late, Charley Louise. Come on down here."

We tried to walk downstairs with our arms around each other, but the stairwell wasn't wide enough, so we held hands.

"Take care of the chickens for me, okay?"

Rose said she'd feed the chickens but not the other animals. Darlene didn't want any part of feeding and taking care of chickens or pigs ... she had her own chores to do.

Uncle Ted loaded my suitcases into the station wagon. As we pulled out of the driveway, I heard the tires rolling over rocks, a sound I wouldn't hear for a long time. I looked at my house and whispered, "I'll be back." Then I turned around and straightened my skirt.

When Uncle Ted's eyes met mine in the rearview mirror, he smiled a banana boat smile. He said, "We'll take care of your house. Don't worry." He winked.

"Tend to your studies and come back home with that degree. Without it, the cherry, onion, and apple fields would be waiting, saying, *Charley Louise, we've missed you. Where have you been?*" Aunt Louise said.

Chapter Fourteen

Croissant filled w/ham, turkey or beef, relish
& fruit tray w/dip, dessert

*Day 10, Journal Entry 10 ... I'm all grown up and on my way
back to Chicago, Illinois to the Madam C. J. Walker College of Beauty
and Culture. I'll come back creating hair designs all over Newaygo
County ... making money without having to pick another cherry, apple,
or onion, no longer having the smell of fields and no longer being
laughed at because I pick crops. I'll name my business the Dorsey
Hair Designs.*

I sat in the back seat of the station wagon thinking, This seems
like the longest seven miles. Uncle Ted was driving and I leaned the
side of my head near the window.

"We'll ship some chickens to you so you don't forget them,
okay?" Uncle Ted chuckled.

"Yeah," I said. We all laughed ... even Aunt Louise.

The rest of the family followed us into town in Unk's station
wagon. When they arrived at the train station, Unk took the camera
out. "Let's take some pictures."

He told us where to stand and asked a person waiting on the
train platform if they could take a picture of our family: Unk, Aunt
Pearl, Uncle Ted, Aunt Louise, Darlene, Rose, and me.

I heard a "whoo, whoo" and yelled, "The train is coming! How
many more pictures do we have to take?"

"One more," Unk said.

As the train turned the corner, the smoke filled the sky.

Each section of the train, full of passengers, passed us. I

thought, *I should have taken the train during the weekday with less people traveling.*

We had only a short time to say our good-byes before the conductor said, "All those headed to Chicago, Illinois, the train will be leaving in five minutes. All aboard."

The whole family hugged, kissed, and cried, telling me to take care of myself and to write. It reminded me of when Mama was going back to Chicago, except this time I was leaving.

I hurried to my assigned window seat. I opened the window and leaned out as far as I could, waving and yelling, "I love you." My family stood in the same spot, waving until I couldn't see them any longer.

Slowly, I sat back in the seat. It was as if Mama was there telling me, "Remember, you're a Dorsey." I whispered, "Yes, Mama, I'll remember."

Another girl was sitting with me and we introduced ourselves. I told her that I was going to Chicago to the Madam C. J. Walker College of Beauty and Culture. She was going to Grand Rapids to visit family.

We were startled by a man's voice. When we looked up, there stood a tall colored man. He was wearing a black hat with a suit, similar to what Daddy wore when he went to work.

The man said, "Where are you headed?"

"Chicago," I said.

In a strong, deep voice, he said, "Ticket please."

I fumbled through my purse and couldn't find it. I looked in every compartment.

"Do you have a ticket, young lady?"

"I have it, but I can't find it."

With a stern voice, he said, "If you don't have a ticket, the train will stop and you'll be asked to leave."

"Wait. It might be in my blouse pocket." Sweat started rolling down my face as I felt inside of my pockets. "Here it is, sir."

"Destination Chicago" the conductor said.

"Chicago, here I come," I said.

I talked with the girl next to me all the way to Grand Rapids until it was time for her to depart from the train.

The conductor shouted, "Next stop: Chicago. Next stop: Chicago."

During the trip, I fell asleep. I don't know how because I was too excited. I dreamt I was in Chicago talking and laughing with all of my old friends and then walking into the Madam C.J. Walker College of Beauty and Culture, all eyes on me.

In my dream, I was sitting at the design stall and heard a loud voice getting closer and closer, saying, "Chicago. Chicago."

I had just opened my eyes when someone tapped my shoulder.

"Young lady?" I sat up and rubbed my eyes. "Is this your stop? We're in Chicago."

I looked out the window and turned around. "Yes sir."

The train stopped and a sense of excitement started running through my veins. No more picking cherries or topping onions, waking up to the sound of chickens and that darned rooster every morning.

With the biggest smile on my face, I jumped out of my seat and reached above my head where my luggage was. I hurried, saying to the other passengers, "Excuse me, please."

After I had taken two steps off the train, I dropped my luggage and said loudly, "Chicago, I'm back." The people in front of me turned around, looking at me like I had lost my mind, but I didn't care. I was back to civilization.

No matter which way I walked, people bumped into me left and right, telling me, "Move out of the way" and "Watch where you're going" until finally I stood against the closest wall of the building. Not the side, but in front. I watched people hurrying one way or the other.

Someone yelled, "Charley Louise." I looked around but didn't see anyone. "Charley Louise," the person repeated.

I turned around. There was Esther, my best friend, and her family. We ran toward each other, screaming and yelling, hugging as tight as we could, talking over each other's sentences, saying, "How have you been?"

Mrs. Johnson said, "Let her catch a breath of air, Esther. Charley Louise, you sure have grown since the last time I saw you. The country air must have had something to do with it."

Mrs. Johnson was such a beautiful colored woman. She was tall and light skinned with long hair that she wore in a bun. When I'd spend the night at the Johnson's house, her hair smelled like fresh flowers. She must have bought perfume from every department store in Chicago. She wore nylons with the line down the middle of her legs, just like Mama did when she went to church.

Next to Mama, I thought Mrs. Johnson was a true woman. She walked with a lot of grace and elegance. She carried a clutch purse … the ones that fit underneath your arm pit, pointing her pinky finger outward.

She said, "We heard about your mom's passing. Please accept our condolences."

"Thank you," I said. "Are you sure I can stay with your family while I attend school?"

"Don't be silly. I'm quite sure if Esther needed a place to stay, your family would do the same. You're always welcome in our home. Stay as long as you need to. Besides, it'll be nice to have another face and voice in the house. Perhaps some of your good manners will rub off on …"

Esther looked at her mother in a stern manner, something I'd never do in my family, but she's a spoiled girl. Mrs. Johnson said,

"You see, that's what I mean."

Soon the conversation switched to how I had graduated so early. Esther and I were sitting in the back seat. When I talked about my grades transferring, Esther sunk into her seat and started looking out the window. I sensed that she felt left behind.

I scooted closer and put my arm around her. I said, "It wasn't easy adjusting to the rural area or lifestyle. Imagine seeing nothing but trees and no neighbors for miles. You'll graduate this year and we'll both be out of school, going to college and starting a family one day."

She said, "Who would have thought that moving from the big city and becoming a country girl would help someone get out of school quicker? Maybe I should've come with you."

"You wouldn't have lasted in the country picking cherries or working in the muck fields topping onions. You're a city girl and nothing else. Besides, how could you work in the fields and keep your fingernails pretty?

Instead of going straight to their home near Damon Street, we passed the old neighborhood where I lived. Driving up to the house, it didn't look that much different except there were more pimps, more girls on the corners, and new neighbors. Someone had moved into our old house.

Mrs. Johnson looked back at me and noticed a sadness come on my face and said, "Are we ready to go home?"

The Johnsons lived in a neighborhood far different than West 14th Street. Their curtains matched throughout the house except the bedrooms. The houses were painted and fresh cut lawns.

Esther's mother told us we would share a room. She went to the attic and brought the foldaway bed for me to sleep on. Esther and I would share the closet and dressers.

The house smelled just like home with freshly cooked collard greens. Mrs. Johnson said, "While you're putting your clothes away, you can catch up on girl talk, but don't be long because I'll need your help setting the table."

####

We sat at certain places around the table. Mr. and Mrs. Johnson sat at both ends of the table and Esther and I sat across from each other. The baby sat next to Mrs. Johnson.

We talked about the days when our families lived next to each other and the big move to Baldwin, Michigan and then White Cloud.

I said, "The roads were made from small rock and bumpy. We built our own family houses, but they're still working on Mama's and my house. It seemed like when Mama died, things just stopped. She bought extra land ... enough for Daddy to build on, if he chose to.

After she died I let him know about the land, and he said his plan was to come to White Cloud to take a look at it before he decided to move up North. That's the last time I talked to him."

I was interrupted by Mrs. Johnson. She changed the subject, asking, "What are your plans for school?"

"Tomorrow my plan is to enroll in the Madam C. J. Walker College of Beauty and Culture and look for a part-time job so I can save up enough money to get my own place."

Mrs. Johnson said, "That's a good plan, but there's no hurry. You can stay with us as long as I want."

Mrs. Johnson had a church meeting, so she told me and Esther that we'd have to clean up the kitchen, which meant putting away the food and washing the dishes. Esther didn't like this because her mama usually cleaned the kitchen.

Mrs. Johnson said, "Do you see Charley Louise complaining?" I thought to myself, *I wish she would stop using me as a role model. I didn't want to hurt my friendship with Esther.*

While we were cleaning, I said, "This isn't that bad. Imagine having to take care of chickens, grabbing their eggs, feeding pigs, and picking farmers' crops."

Esther said, "I'd never do something like that. I'd run away from home."

We finished the dishes and went upstairs. The windows were open, but it was dark out and almost time to go to bed so we decided to close them. As I went to the window, I saw the Susie getting out of a car and going into her family's house. I paused, but didn't say anything.

Although we worked the fields and I had to take care of the animals, I was proud of my family for instilling in me to get an education and to take care of myself and to not make a living by selling my body … like the women on West 14th Street.

Esther asked, "What are your staring at?"

"Nothing."

We turned out the lights and went to bed.

Our alarm clocks went off about the same time. It was strange. I was used to getting up to the sound of the rooster and feeding the chickens, collecting the eggs, and feeding the pigs.

This morning all I had to do was clean up and make sure I caught the bus. Esther and I walked together for two blocks. Then she turned one way and I turned the other. Just before I saw the bus coming, I reached into my pocket and grabbed three coins. I didn't need to transfer because this bus stopped a few blocks from the college.

When I arrived at the college, I stood for a minute looking up at the sign. My eyes read each letter. Madam C. J. Walker passed away before I could attend her college, but her pictures were on the walls. She was a chubby woman with a lot of hair that was pulled back.

The rooms were filled with girls and boys from freshmen to seniors learning how to process, press, and style colored people's hair.

On the first day of classes, I dropped the curling iron more times than I could count. One time when I bent down to pick it up, I felt someone looking over me. "Have you ever held a curling iron before, young lady?"

My eyes followed the shape of the person talking to me from her feet until I was face-to-face with the instructor who had a similar resemblance to Madam C. J. Walker … I froze. I felt a big lump in my throat and embarrassed noticing other students looking at me.

With a quivering voice I said, "Not much, ma'am."

"You forgot to pick up your comb."

"Yes, ma'am."

"The instructor said, "Hand me the curling iron and watch how I move my fingers and the hair at the same time." She placed the curling iron into my hands and said, "Here, you try it."

My hands were shaking. She told me to relax. But I couldn't.

She said, "I overheard you talking about twirling the baton for the band at school. Imagine twirling that baton and wrap the hair around it. There is an art form to placing the curling iron between your fingers and wrapping the hair around the iron at the same time, but with practice you'll be able to do it."

My fingers, curling iron and hair were fighting against each other. I moved my eyes to the side of my head to see how she was looking at me.

"No. No. Like this," She said.

I watched her twirl the hair in between the curling iron like it was magic. My eyes couldn't keep up with her fingers clasping the curling iron and passing hair through them.

She handed the irons back to me. "Try it again and be gentle this time, not yanking on the hair."

I took the curling irons and tried my best to repeat what she had done. My fingers still got twisted around the iron handles. The hair was sort of curled.

"Keep practicing," she said as she walked away, checking on other students, but I sensed her glancing back and forth at me to see how I was doing.

All the students had to buy their own set of curling irons and a model head. I practiced every day at home on the model head and on Esther when she'd let me.

One week after arriving in Chicago, I got a job at a mail order company, which made my days even longer, but I loved it. I'd go to school, come home, and practice until it was time to go to work. It beat picking some farmer's crops. I wouldn't trade it for anything.

####

On the bus, standing right next to me, was a tall, dark, handsome, good-smelling colored man reading a newspaper. I couldn't help but stare at him.

Each day we rode the Chicago public transportation bus together, not saying a word until one day when he was sitting right behind me. I was nervous and my hands were sweating. As the bus emptied, two stops before I was to leave, I felt a tap on my shoulder. I turned around and the man had a big smile, as though he was waiting for a response.

I asked, "Can I help you?"

"What's your name, Madam?"

"Char ... Charley Louise Dorsey."

"Why did you hesitate to tell me your name?"

"Because Charley is a boy's name."

He looked at me and said, "Charley Louise Dorsey is a

beautiful name. Don't be ashamed of it. That's who you are. I'm Melvin Hammond."

From that day forward, we grew to know each other more and more. We went from sitting near each other to sitting with each other. Each day I'd make sure I caught the right bus at the right time and would hope Melvin would be riding it.

One morning we started talking about our families.

Melvin said, "I come from a family of eleven brothers and sisters who all live in Chicago, mostly working in the manufacturing industry."

I said, "I'm an only child and my family used to live in Chicago but moved to Michigan and that I'm here for college ... the Madam C. J. Walker College of Beauty and Culture."

"Beauty and Culture," He said with a smile. "Would you like to have dinner with my family this weekend?" Melvin asked.

"Let me think about it," I said.

I talked with Mrs. Johnson and Esther about it and when I met Melvin on the bus on Monday morning, I invited him to the Johnson's house instead.

He said, "If one of my sisters wanted to meet a man's family, the proper thing to do is for the man to meet her family first." He paused. "When do you want me to come over for dinner?"

A week later, Mrs. Johnson put together the dinner menu. We all helped in the kitchen. The seating arrangements were as usual. I sat on the right side next to Mrs. Johnson and Melvin sat on the right corner side next to Mr. Johnson.

We talked about his family, where they lived in the city, and what they did for a living. It seemed more like an interrogation. I felt sorry for him, but no matter how I tried to change the conversation, Mr. Johnson wouldn't stop. Melvin took everything in stride. From time to time, he'd sneak a smile at me, meaning everything was all right. After dinner, Mr. and Mrs. Johnson gave me their blessings to meet his family.

Three weeks later, I met his family. After they all said "hello" and "nice to meet you," grace was given, food was passed around the table, and voices came from everywhere. It was much different from our house where it seemed like most things had a protocol.

At the Hammond dinner table, I remember sitting very quietly, listening to all of them talking at once. Somehow they answered each other, but I couldn't tell you who was talking to whom. It was one simultaneous conversation.

At the end of the evening, Melvin drove me home in his father's car. He was a perfect gentleman and walked me to the front door. We drew closer to each other and, although I wanted to kiss him, I left with a hug.

The Johnsons were still up, waiting, I believe, until I came home safe. It wasn't late, but while I was in Chicago, it was their responsibility to keep me safe. That's what they had promised my family.

I ran up the stairs and talked to Esther all night, telling her how at one point in the night I felt like I had sisters.

There were times when Melvin asked me about my family in White Cloud. I told him that White Cloud was a very small, rural community with few coloreds. The houses were far apart from each other.

I told him how I had picked farmers' crops all summer until school started. It was during those years living in White Cloud and picking crops wasn't something I wanted to do for a living. That's when I decided to fulfill Mama's wishes to attend college and make something of myself. I told him that's why I'm here in Chicago.

Two and a half years later, I had passed all of my exams from college and was about to graduate. It was a happy day, but also sad. I didn't know what would become of Melvin and me. I'd have to start thinking of my future.

Sitting on the top stair of the Johnson's home, I read a letter from Aunt Louise and the rest of the family:

Dear Charley Louise,

We received your letter informing us that you are to graduate from college and inviting us to come to the graduation ceremony. We will be at the graduation, but are you planning to come back home?

Your house here in White Cloud looks good. We made sure to keep a close eye on it. Love, the family

I folded the letter and put it back inside the envelope. I was uncertain about my future plans.

Aunt Louise and the rest of the family had come to visit me a few times. Every time we said our good-byes, I'd watch the same station wagon that I rode in to White Cloud with my mama and my family. It brought back memories.

Esther rushed out of the house, slamming the screen door. "Are you excited about graduation?"

I didn't know how I felt. I looked at her with hesitation, thinking about Melvin wanting me to stay in Chicago. At the same time, my family was asking if I was coming back home.

Mrs. Johnson called for us to come in the house and help prepare the dinner table. I could hardly eat when she asked me the same questions that everyone else did, "Are you moving back to White Cloud? Has your dad moved there?"

I answered, "Daddy hasn't moved there yet. Last I talked to

him he said he and his wife are coming there this summer. When I chose to go to college he changed his mind about permanently moving there until I'd be there. Daddy and my family aren't exactly close."

I changed the subject telling Mrs. Johnson how delicious the yams and ham tasted. Everyone looked up at me because they knew her food was just okay, not delicious.

Days passed and I had to make a decision. Aunt Louise and the rest of my family would be coming to my graduation and everyone wanted an answer.

They gathered at my graduation, watching the class walk down the middle aisle, girls on one side and boys on the other. Tassels were swaying back and forth with every step. I looked over at the family and smiled, waiting until after the ceremony to tell them my decision.

As soon as everyone had left the reception, I went upstairs with Esther and told her first. "I'm moving back to White Cloud to stay in the house built for me and Mama."

She looked stunned. "What about Melvin?"

"I'm not sure what to tell him, but I'm moving. It might sound crazy, but I've thought hard about it. You know that Mama left all of the land for Daddy and me. If I move back he told me that he'll be coming this summer and I've decided to join him. I'll have my family back. I hope you understand."

Esther looked sad. "We'll miss you, but I understand."

I let her know that I'd be moving in four weeks. Aunt Louise helped me make all of the arrangements.

After supper, Esther and I cleaned the dinner table and washed the dishes. Again she asked, "What about Melvin? Have you told him?"

I paused for a moment. "Kind of." With a frustrated tone I said, "Just let me handle it. Okay?"

It is a moonlit night. Melvin and I were headed to our favorite club—Mr. Fred's Night Club, where all of the Madam C.J. Walker students hung out. We laughed, had some drinks, and danced until the club closed. When Melvin walked me to the top steps at my home, I decided to tell him.

"Melvin, what do you think of me moving back home to White Cloud?"

He looked at me smiling and said, "Are you joking?"

"No, it's not a joke."

The smile disappeared from his face and there was silence. My family is very religious and strict, inviting Melvin to come with me would be against everything they stood for.

I could see in his eyes that he wanted me to invite him, but he's a city man and I didn't think he would adjust to the country lifestyle.

We were both sitting on the top stoop looking straight ahead. I blurted out, "Would you like to come with me?"

"I don't know if that's a good idea, Charley Louise. Where would I stay? I can't stay with you." He had met my family and knew how strict they were.

After more silence, we decided that he could come and visit so that my family could get to know him better. By coming, he might find a place to live and work. He didn't understand why my family had such control over my life, especially since I was a grown woman, and why I had to get their permission to do everything.

His family was more open and carefree. That was good, but it was not how I was raised, and some of the strictness was instilled inside of me.

Melvin and I decided to spend as much time as we could with each other.

Right after work he'd go home, clean up, and meet me

somewhere or pick me up.

On the night before I was to leave, we had a large dinner and invited Melvin. After dinner, Melvin and I sat outside, laughing and talking. It was like unleashing every thought in our mind from the differences in his part of Chicago where he lived to the Damon Street neighborhood. Then we hugged. I started crying. This was another sad moment in my life, but my decision had been made.

The next morning, Esther helped me carry my bags to the car and the whole family took me to the train station.

When I arrived at the station, there was Melvin waiting with that smile. He said, "I'll miss you, Charley Louise Dorsey."

"I'll miss you too, Melvin Hammond."

We all hugged and cried until I had to step onto the train. I hurried to my seat and opened the window, waving until I couldn't see anyone.

I sat back in the seat and said, "Ready or not, here I come White Cloud. I hope you're ready for me."

The trip back to White Cloud was long. I was awakened by a loud, deep voice yelling, "White Cloud. White Cloud."

I leaned up and grabbed my bags from the top compartment. It seemed like the whole town was at the train station. I knew they didn't come to see me, but I wasn't sure why they were there.

Aunt Louise and the family come running up to me and said, "Welcome home, Charley Louise."

After all the hugs and kisses, I asked Darlene and Rose, "What's going on?"

She said, "It's the town's celebration ... the day White Cloud was founded. If you go further into town and down to the beach, there's a carnival that has a ferris wheel, an animal petting area, games, people selling cotton candy, and caramel apples."

As we started getting closer to my house, Aunt Louise said, "Put your hands over your eyes." I heard the tires rolling over gravel as we drove into the driveway when she said, "Okay. Take your hands down."

I put both hands against my cheeks. I don't know how wide my mouth got, but I was never so happy. I hadn't seen my house and Mama's for almost three years. There were the chickens and the pigs. It seemed like the chicken coup had gotten bigger.

There was a pump for water right outside the back door. In front of the house was a small porch addition with windows on both sides and a door leading to a mailbox across the road.

"Without a mailbox your mail won't be left and you'd have to go all the way into town to get it at the post office," Aunt Louise said.

I wanted to know about the bathroom. I was so excited about a pump for water that I forgot to look behind the big tree in the backyard. There it was, a big, ugly, four-walled, wooden structure. I felt like it was staring right back at me smiling, saying, "How was school? I've been waiting."

Someone tapped my shoulder, surprising me.

Uncle Ted said, "Here's your key. Welcome home." As soon as I took the keys, the dogs leaped up onto my shoulders, licking me in the face.

I pushed the dogs away from me.

Uncle Ted said, "Your Mama wanted this house built for the both of you, and we're sorry that you can't share it together in person, but you can in spirit."

I knew that Mama was looking down from heaven right then and was very proud of all of the hard work it took to build our home.

Uncle Ted said, "Well, go in. Take a look at your new home,

Charley Louise."

I opened the door slowly and glanced inside.

Rose shoved me saying, "Just go in. It's only a house."

It was more than that to me. To me, it was a sense of growing up, of entering into womanhood.

I walked slowly, taking in everything. When the Darlene, Rose and I made eye contact, we counted to three and then started running, peeking into each room.

There was a dining room, a kitchen, and a living room that had a wood stove. Off to the side of the living room was one bedroom. I paused.

"Is this—"

"Yes, you and your mama were going to share this room, but now it's all yours."

There was a door inside the bedroom that had a few dusty stairs that seemed to lead to nothing, just open space to what they called an attic. I asked what the space was for.

"You can store things up there," Uncle Ted said.

It wasn't a big space, but I could use it for storing things like suitcases. I loved my home, but I wasn't sure that I wanted to live all by myself.

Uncle Ted and Aunt Louise said, "You can stay with us during the nighttime. Your old bedroom is still upstairs."

In the meantime, Darlene, Rose and I stayed in my house and sat around. We imagined furniture in one corner and thought about where to put the television. We decided to put it in the corner away from the windows. If a storm came, our family thought that the house could burn up with a television sitting in the front window.

When we went into the bedroom, we heard chickens cackling. "God, please," I said. "Somebody go and shoot those things."

"Charley Louise. You can't use God's name in vain."

"What do you mean?"

"That's using God's name in vain. Take it back."

"Okay, but somebody please do something about those chickens.

Don't they get tired of cackling all the time?"

I was standing inside the back porch of my house when I heard

Darlene and Rose fighting over my clothes and what they were going to wear. "This is beautiful. Can I wear it sometimes?"

I peeked into the room, leaning against the door frame, not saying a word. I could understand why they were feeling this way. All their clothes were hand-made or bought from the thrift store.

"Enjoy it because this is the closest you'll get to them," I said.

"Well, can I wear—"

"No. Don't let me catch either of you wearing my clothes, you hear me? Keep wearing those countrified things you have on."

They told me not to be so selfish and mocked me because I went to college.

After that argument we went and sat on the back steps to talk. I leaned over and whispered, "I met a man. His name is Melvin."

Darlene looked at me. "What did you just say?"

Louder, I said, "I met a man in Chicago. His name is Melvin Hammond. He comes from a family of 13 brothers and sisters, and the plan is for him to come to White Cloud and meet the family."

They looked at me with shock and awe. Then Rose said, "He's a city man. How will he get along with the chickens, pigs, and country living?"

The other one said, "Forget that. How will he fit with our family? We go to church all the time and pray over everything."

"Melvin wants to come and visit me, and I was hoping you'd back me when I tell the rest of the family."

"Hell will freeze over before our daddy and Aunt Louise let

that happen. Where will he stay? Not here in the house with you."

I told them Melvin could stay in a motel somewhere. That's when Rose and Darlene said, that's a hurdle I'd have to conquer, but they would support me.

My thoughts went to how I would make a living … most certainly not picking cherries, topping onions, or do anything like that. I wanted to do hair and start my own business.

Every time I talked to Darlene and Rose about it, they'd laugh and say, "Girl, you must be crazy. There are no colored hair salons up here."

Both of them stared at me, waiting for me to respond. With a stern voice, I said, "I'll find work. There has got to be more than picking crops."

Darlene and Rose chuckled and said, "You'll see."

They left the house yelling, "Be ready at 4:30 in the morning. See you later at Aunt Louise's house."

I yelled, "I'll talk to Aunt Louise tomorrow to see if she's heard about any coloreds wanting their hair fixed or if there are houses that need cleaning. But I'm not going to pick anybody's crops."

"Good luck, Charley Louise. You always had big dreams."

Why not dream big? I thought. I wanted to do bigger and better things.

I stayed at my house for a while, sitting on the window sill. I started wondering about my friends Karen and Gladys. When I had left for Chicago, we had promised to write. We did for a while but lost track of each other. I was in college, working and dating Melvin. Darlene and Rose told me that they both got married and one had a kid.

I decided that tomorrow I'd ask Uncle Ted to use his truck to go and visit them. Since we last saw each other, they had moved. I wanted to ask Darlene or Rose to go with me, but forgot. I wasn't as familiar with some of the roads and new ones seemed to had been created.

190

####

That darned rooster woke Darlene and me up. While we were whispering and laughing the stairs made a rickety sound … when someone was walking on them coming closer and closer.

"Aunt Louise must be coming," I said.

"How do you know Aunt Louise is coming up the stairs?" She asked leaning on her elbows.

We whispered, "Go back to sleep ... or act like it."

"No. How do you know?"

When she asked again, I said, "Who else would be coming up the stairs."

"Are you girls awake up here?" Aunt Louise asked.

We didn't answer.

"Do you girls hear me?"

We pretended we were asleep. Seconds later, I felt a hand touching me, wiggling my body.

I rolled over and rubbed my eyes, acting like I had just awoken. "Aunt Louise?"

I glanced at Darlene and Rose. We leapt from our beds, surprising her, and said, "Good morning."

"Well, all of you are certainly in a good mood. Especially you, Charley Louise, for someone who has no future plans."

I looked at her and with a soft voice said, "Oh, Aunt Louise don't ruin the moment."

She has no sense of humor. I think that's a trait that was missed on Mama's side of the family. They are always so serious and seemed to have no fun.

She looked at me and said, "It's too early in the morning to scare people. We have a lot of work to do around here."

"Oh. Sorry. I won't say those dreadful words again." I laughed.

Aunt Louise turned half around and said, "It's not funny, young lady. You girls come on downstairs and help me with breakfast."

There was always one smiling face to greet me in the morning, Uncle Ted.

"Morning, girls," he said. "How was your night? Did you sleep good?"

We all said at once, "Good morning, Uncle Ted. The sleepover was great. We talked most of the night."

I started to cook some bacon when Uncle Ted asked, "When and where I did learn how to cook?"

Everyone knew that wasn't my favorite pastime, and if I could get out of it by bribing or changing chores, I would.

I said, "I might not have cooked much before I left for Chicago, but you do remember that Mama and Aunt Louise were cooks and would cleaned a house like a tornado went through it? Maybe I picked up some of those traits, too."

"Since you picked up some of their traits, what are you going to do about the working trait ... getting a job?"

Aunt Louise and Aunt Pearl cleaned houses, mostly in Fremont for rich folks who wanted their summer homes cleaned before their arrival.

"Could I help you and Aunt Pearl until I get hair customers?"

Aunt Louise stopped eating before her spoon touched her tongue and looked at me. At first she didn't say anything. "As a matter of fact, we have two houses in Fremont to clean, and we could use some help. You, Darlene and Rose can come with us this morning. If you're good, these types of jobs are available all summer long."

Darlene and Rose crossed their arms and looked in my direction.

I whispered, "This is better than picking crops."

Aunt Louise and Aunt Pearl told me they started looking for other ways to make money besides picking crops because they certainly didn't want to climb those cherry tries much longer either.

"Where are the jobs located?" I asked.

Aunt Pearl said, "Many rich folks like lawyers, doctors, and businessmen built houses around the lakes. The men come back and forth, but the women and kids stay all summer long."

####

The directions that Aunt Louise and Aunt Pearl had for the houses took us winding up a long one-track road.

The first one I cleaned wasn't as big as the house in Chicago that Mama used to clean, but for a place where the families stayed only for the summer months, it was a good size house. There were large living rooms and dining room, but not as large of a kitchen ... three bedrooms, one and a half bathrooms. What caught my attention the most was the large windows in every room with a spectacular view of the area wide lakes that continued upstream and connected to the house.

The living room had a fireplace. Although the house had been unoccupied until summertime, the wooden floors seemed spotless. I could slide across them in my socks without getting splinters.

After myself, Darlene, and Rose had a tour of the house, Aunt Louise handed me the dusting and cleaning supplies. She told us that we could start in the upstairs bedroom ... the girl's room, first then the boy's room.

I was walking upstairs when I heard Aunt Louise yell, "Remember to change and straighten the linen on both beds. When you're finished with the girl's bedroom, let me know because the floors have to be mopped."

I opened the bedroom door slowly, wanting to be surprised, and saw the most beautiful room. Everything was in place.

There was a delicate looking box on one of the dressers. I

made sure to handle it with care. When I opened it up, it chimed and a ballerina twirled around.

Then I heard, "Try not to touch anything except what you're supposed to touch and that includes no fingerprints on the walls."

How did she know? I wondered. She was way at the bottom of the stairs in the living room. The music box wasn't that loud. "Yes ma'am," I hollered.

The girl's room was painted yellow. Both beds had matching bedspreads. Both girls had her own vanity table with triple mirrors, just like the one Mama had at our home in Chicago. At the window sat a large wooden chest, full of stuffed animals.

I looked out of the window. Hidden behind a scattered group of trees was the most beautiful lake. I unlatched one of the windows and heard water maneuvering around scattered rocks and tree branches.

I told myself, *"One day, I'll have something like this."*

I could definitely tell the difference between the year-round houses and the summer houses. The summer houses were decorated with bright colors. The year-round houses seemed lived in. The wall colors were not as colorful. There were winter coats, boots and wood for the stove.

"Charley Louise?"

I jumped. "Yes, ma'am?"

"Have you finished the girl's room?"

I yelled, "Yes, ma'am" although I hadn't. "Darlene and Rose are going to clean the boy's room."

When she asked me to come and help finish the downstairs, from upstairs I yelled that I'd help Darlene and Rose clean the boy's room and be right down. I ran over to the boy's room, dusted, and hit my hands against the bed.

With the biggest fake smile I could muster, I ran downstairs and said, "All done with the children's bedrooms."

When Aunt Louise checked the girl's room, I started sweating. She rubbed her fingers against the dressers and looked at me.

She then went to the boy's room. She fluffed the pillows and made sure the windows were cleaned. I thought, *Oh my God, I'm in trouble,* but she said nothing.

Aunt Louise said, "You did okay for the first job, but next time the windows needed to be cleaned better."

We went up the road and cleaned another house.

At the end of the day, Aunt Louise asked, "How do you like cleaning houses?"

"It's all right. More work than I thought, but I'd rather do this than pick crops."

"Maybe after working with me and Aunt Pearl for a while, you'll be able to pick up work on your own."

She told me that most people who wanted cleaning help posted notes on the grocery store, hardware store, or laundry mat bulletin boards.

I listened to her and said, "My goal is to do hair. That's what I went to school for. Maybe I could do this on the side, but not making a living out of it."

She stared into the rearview mirror and with a stern tone said, "There's nothing wrong with following your dreams, but until then, you need work."

For a minute, our eyes seemed to be cemented. She gave me the sternest look I had ever seen from her. I turned my head to look out the car window. Was she right? Are my dreams deterred? Cleaning houses was easy money and one of the things our family knew best. Maybe I could do hair on the side and make more money cleaning houses. Maybe Aunt Louise was right.

Chapter Fifteen

Chicken salad, relish & fruit tray
w/dip, muffins, & cookies ... $5.00

The rural town of White Cloud, Michigan seemed like a million miles from the big city lights of Chicago, Illinois, and every night I missed Melvin more and more. There was nothing to do but go to work and church.

The most enjoyable moment was checking the mailbox to see if Melvin had written me. I thanked God every day for whoever invented pencil and paper.

Every day except for Sunday, I had to beat Aunt Louise to my mailbox. It wasn't a task that easily accomplished. We cleaned houses and got home at the same time. Aunt Louise changed her clothes after work, and that was the perfect opportunity for me to go next door to my house and wait.

I'd stand inside the small porch with my eyes glued on the road for the mailman and peeked out the porch window where I could see Aunt Louise resting in her favorite chair. When the mailman came, I'd walk fast so Aunt Louise wouldn't catch me.

The extra mail I left. I waited on my front porch, hiding in the corner, peeking out the window as she walked over to my mailbox. I couldn't help but laugh as she lowered her head, looking inside for the mail. Before she would straighten up and look toward my porch window, I moved away. I waited until she walked back to her house to open Melvin's letter.

Aunt Louise didn't care for Melvin because of two reason: *1# he wasn't a Christian man and #2 from time-to-time he visited the nightclubs.* She felt that anyone who worked all week and spent time doing anything but serving the Lord on Sundays wasn't good enough for me.

The house wasn't finished, but Darlene, Rose and I went inside often. We wrote on the floors in the rooms, giving them names—dining room, kitchen, living room, etc. We made comments like "a table right here" and "a china cabinet over there." Walking to the bedroom giggling, Rose said, "And you can put a big bed right here."

Sitting in the corner of what was marked the front bedroom, I read a letter from Melvin. I was in the middle of the first page when I heard footsteps. Darlene and Rose were calling my name.

I didn't answer. I kept reading until they found me. "Can't I have any privacy?" I asked.

"That's a letter from Melvin, isn't it? Can you read it out loud?"

I didn't look up. "No. He wrote this letter to me, not you."

"Please? Please?"

"Okay, but just a little."

They hovered next to me in the corner on the floor until I read "Love, Melvin."

After that day, I'd go to the house, sit in the make-believe bed, and read my letters over and over until I could recite them by heart. Sometimes I'd read them to my cousins, but most times I read them alone.

Darlene, Rose and I stayed at the house until it started getting dark. I locked the house and we said good-night. They went home and I went to Aunt Louise and Uncle Ted's house.

Every day Uncle Ted asked, "Charley Louise, how does the house look?"

I don't know why he always asked. There was nothing new

happening, so sometimes I'd make up stuff by saying, "Today we put in a sofa" or "Today we put the bed up in the back bedroom."

He'd laugh and say, "Your house will be finished soon enough. Be patient."

Each night I brought over some letters to read. Tonight I decided I wanted to read some of the other letters and made a plan to go get them.

I tiptoed and touched the first step with what seemed like the loudest rickety sound. I quickly moved my foot off the step. I stopped and listened, wondering if Aunt Louise had heard me.

I quickly went back to my bed and sat with my arms crossed, frustrated, wondering how I was going to get over to my house and gather the letters. Aunt Louise believed that after dusk, everyone should be in the house. Uncle Ted locked the doors and closed the windows.

I told myself, *try it again.* So, I tiptoed down the ten wooden stairs, praying each time I stepped on one that it wouldn't creak. I reached Aunt Louise and Uncle Ted's bedroom and debated whether to go out the back door or the front porch, hoping neither door squeaked to wake up everyone, including the bullfrogs.

Afraid of getting caught, I gave up on my plan. I decided to keep the letters I did have with me in a secret hiding spot upstairs in my bedroom, just in case Aunt Louise took it upon herself to clean my room.

The bedroom is large enough to fit one twin size bed and a dresser for my clothes with a small cut out area that is my closet. I laid in my bed fanning myself, looking out the window. It was a bright moonlit night with the sky completely filled with stars.

When I opened the window, a breeze brushed across my face and blew the curtains back and forth. I decided to write in my diary.

Day 11, Journal Entry 11 ... Today I read through Melvin's letters. Some of them are at Aunt Louise and Uncle Ted's house, and some are at my house next door. I tried to figure out a way to get all of the letters here with me so I could read them at night before I go to bed. That plan didn't work out. I miss his touch, smell, sense of charm, and humor. Charley Louise

I closed my eyes and cuddled with my pillow, smiling. Aunt Louise yelled, "Charley Louise, turn off those lights up there. We have to get up early in the morning."

"Damn," I said. "If anyone needs someone to mess up a beautiful dream, call my auntie. She will not fail you." I turned off the lights.

My house was between my uncles and aunts' houses. When I first came back, I had agreed not to stay at my house alone at night, but now I was frustrated with going to my house in the daytime and staying away at night.

I felt it was time for me to live at my house without family pressure. I knew unless I was married to a Christian man, the family wouldn't allow it, and I think that's why they were taking so long to finish my house. As a grown woman, I didn't know why I had allowed the family to have such control over my life. I should be able to speak for myself.

Every day I'd stay at my house as much as I could. Today after I got a letter from Melvin, I stayed at my house into the night. I found a corner in what is to be the living room to read his letter over and over, wondering what to do.

He asked me if I had spoken to my family about his visit to White Cloud. This was something Melvin and I had talked about many times in our letters, but not to my family. I decided that tomorrow would be as good as any to talk to them.

The next afternoon sitting at the table eating lunch wasn't our family's typical announcement time. Instead of homemade baked yams, fried chicken, mashed potatoes, etc. there was only sandwiches from the left over chicken we had for last night's dinner.

It was during lunchtime that Uncle Ted asked, "Charley Louise, are you sick or something? You're not your talkative self."

"No. I'm not sick. Just tired, I guess."

After Darlene, Rose and I cleaned the kitchen and put away the dishes, we went to the front porch. Uncle Ted sat in his favorite lawn chair and Aunt Louise sat in the swing slowly rocking back and forth. I sat on the top step, leaning against the wood railing, and turned toward both of them.

I took a deep breath. "Remember the friend I told you about? The one I met in Chicago while attending college?"

"Yes," they said.

"Well, I was wondering ..." I paused for a moment, looking toward the road. "I was wondering if that friend could come and visit this summer."

They asked me to tell them more about this friend. They had met several of my new friends and didn't know if I was talking about Melvin.

I said, "This person comes from a good family, a large family of 13 kids, and both parents live in the home." I figured that would be important. "Their name is ..." a lump was growing in my throat. I swallowed and said, "Mel ..."

I looked at Aunt Louise's eyes starting to roll to the back of her head at the same time I was about to say his name.

"His name is Mr. Melvin Hammond," I blurted.

"What, a man?" Aunt Louise shouted. "And where do you

think this Mr. Melvin Hammond will stay during his visits?"

Before I was able to say he could stay at one of the motels, Aunt Louise asked if he attended church and if this was the man who had been writing me letters.

"How did you know?" I asked.

"One day I saw the mailman putting mail in your mailbox. You weren't living in the house, so I checked the mail and saw it was from a Mr. Melvin Hammond."

"Why didn't you say anything?" I asked.

"You left here to attend college, not to meet men."

"I did attend college and graduated, but on the way I met a special person by the name of Melvin Hammond."

Uncle Ted spoke up and said, "Wait a minute. I'd rather meet this young man than have Charley Louise sneak around. He'll probably come anyway."

I saw fire in Aunt Louise's eyes. This was the first time I had heard them disagree since I had decided to leave White Cloud to go to college.

A few days later, they sat me down in the living room and said, "He can stay with your Uncle John and Aunt Pearl next door. And believe us, young lady, we'll be watching your every move."

I was told there were three rules: the whole family would meet him, he'd go to church, and he'd never be in my house.

I wanted to smile, but I thought that might make them change their minds. "Thank you." The thought of Melvin visiting rushed through my mind. That's when I hurried over to my house and wrote a letter to Melvin.

Dear Melvin,

Today I talked to my aunt and uncle about you visiting us here in White Cloud this summer. At first it didn't look good, but then they both agreed that you could come and visit.

I must remind you, though, that my family is sanctified, filled with the Holy Ghost, Bible-carrying, and churchgoing people. They do not drink or go to clubs, so please try to be on your best behavior. I miss you. Kisses, Charley Louise

I checked my mailbox every day for Melvin's letter, but nothing came until three weeks later.

Dear Charley Louise,

I received your letter telling me about my visit to White Cloud. Sorry it took me so long to write you back.

My bus ticket is already paid for and I'll arrive in three weeks. I'll be on my best behavior with all of the family rules.

I miss you and can't wait to hold your body against mine. Love, Melvin Hammond

Until his arrival, I continued to clean houses around the lakes with Aunt Louise and Aunt Pearl.

One day when I went to White Cloud to pick up some can goods and other items for the house, I saw a lady post a note. She was looking for someone to do cleaning. I turned around to find her, but she was walking out of the store. "Ma'am," I yelled. Once I caught up to her, I tapped her on the shoulder and asked, "What type of cleaning do you need?"

"Just general cleaning—sweeping, dusting, and mopping, those type of things."

I asked her how long she needed somebody, and she said every weekend for two months. That's when most family and friends visited over the summer. I told her I did house cleaning.

"I see. You seem mighty young to do house cleaning."

"It all started with my mama cleaning houses years ago, but since then, I've been cleaning houses with my aunts—summer homes around the lake."

She wrote down an address and told me to bring her some references. I went to the address the next day. To be on the safe side, I asked Darlene and Rose to ride with me.

Uncle Ted let me use the truck. While driving, all I heard was, "Slow down, Charley Louise. You're driving too fast. We'll miss the turn.

You know how these country roads are."

"Stop worrying and read the directions so I don't pass the road."

Rose yelled, "Stop! Stop! There's the road. Turn here."

I stepped on the brakes and turned onto a small two-track road surrounded by trees. It had three mailboxes, but we still didn't see the address we were looking for.

"Charley Louise, are you sure we turned down the right road?"

"Yes, I'm sure ... I guess."

Rose asked, "Are we lost in these woods?"

I kept driving until I saw a big, white house on a hill all by itself.

Two kids were playing in the yard. I stopped the car and walked up to them, introducing myself. I asked, "Does a Miss Lee live here?"

The kids ran away terrified, like I was going to attack them.

Darlene leaned out the car window. "Haven't they seen a colored person before?"

"Hush," I said, walking toward the front door.

I knocked three times until someone yelled, "Coming."

When Miss Lee opened the door, she had a wide-eyed, surprised look on her face. With confidence, I said, "Good afternoon. I brought the references."

She had a wired porch that stretched across the whole front of her house. We sat outside while she read my references. "Your family has worked for some prominent people, she said. "Do you mind if I make telephone calls to a few of them right now?"

"Please feel free to call any of them. I'm sure they'll give nothing but good comments."

I couldn't hear what she was saying, but I could see that she was shaking her head up and down. Now, I didn't know what that meant, but I was confident.

When she returned to the porch, she asked, "Are you and your family able to start in two weeks and work a couple days during the week for a month?"

I hesitated to answer because her note in the store said *cleaning help needed during the weekend days in three weeks,* which would allow me to spend time with Melvin before I had to start working the weekends.

"Do you want the job or not?"

Without thinking, I said, "Yes. We'll take it."

"Good. Come back on June 8th at 9:00 a.m. ... and don't be late."

I walked to the car.

"Did you get it?" Darlene and Rose asked.

After closing the door and putting my head on the steering wheel teasing Darlene and Rose for a moment, I then shouted, "Yes. We got the job."

I went home and told Aunt Louise and Aunt Pearl about the job. They were excited until I told them the job started in two weeks, but it didn't work with their schedules.

They told me that I had been cleaning enough to take on the job but that it would be challenging to work alone.

"We'll help," Darlene and Rose said.

"Most of the time, but not every day," Rose said.

I decided to take the job and figure out what to do with Melvin later.

All summer I cleaned houses, realizing how many people had summer homes and how tiring domestic work is.

I hadn't realized how difficult it would be to accomplish my dream of opening my own hair salon or to at least do hair in someone else's salon.

After a long talk with Aunt Louise, I began to see my fate. In White Cloud, there weren't too many people who needed their hair done because they had learned to do it themselves. They also knew where to buy curling irons and pressing combs. White people went to their own salons, and those hair salons weren't going to hire a colored girl.

I was upstairs in the bedroom, writing in my diary about work. Aunt Louise yelled from downstairs, "What time does Mr. Hammond's bus arrive?"

Oh Lord, she doesn't sound happy at all. Please don't let her embarrass me at the bus station, I thought. Standing at the top step, I said, "In one hour."

During the car ride, I could hardly hold my excitement. Every now and then, Uncle Ted looked at me in the rearview mirror and smiled. He was relaxed about Melvin's visit, but Aunt Louise … I just hoped she wouldn't tie Melvin to a tree and beat all of his sins out of him.

The family pulled up to the bus station. At first I didn't see Melvin. I glanced at my watch.

"Boo."

I jumped. It was him. With a friendly jab to his shoulder, I said, "Melvin, you scared me."

I straightened my dress. "Let me introduce you to some of my family. This is Uncle Ted and Aunt Louise."

Melvin extended his hand to Uncle Ted and said, "Good to meet you, sir." Uncle Ted shook his hand, but Aunt Louise …

We all got into the car. Aunt Louise sat in the backseat with me and Melvin sat in the front seat.

When we got to our driveway, I saw Melvin's head moving from one side to the other. I couldn't wait to know what was going through his mind—a big city man coming to the northern part of Michigan for the first time.

At the dinner table, the whole family finally got to meet Melvin. Aunt Louise felt it very important to have a seating arrangement and she made sure he sat next to her.

It didn't take long before the questions came, "Melvin, how do you like the dinner? Charley Louise tells us that you come from a large family."

Aunt Louise asked questions about his faith and if he attended church, and if so, what church his family attended.

I said, "He just got here. Can he at least settle down before all of the interrogation questions?"

It got quiet around the table. "What do you think so far of our rural area?" Uncle Ted asked.

"There are so many trees, land, and …"

Everyone was watching him. He changed his mind and said, "It seems to be a quiet town, for families." He ate a spoonful of potatoes. "What type of work does everyone do?"

Unk said, "Ted and I work in the factory."

"I work in a factory, too," Melvin said.

Aunt Louise said, "The women clean houses … domestic work."

"What about you, Charley Louise? What were your aspirations after graduating from college?" Melvin asked.

I saw my family's looks growing worse by the minute, so I changed the topic. "My mother made good money doing domestic work. That's how she supported the family."

"But, what about your schooling? You know, doing hair," Melvin said.

I wiped the sweat from my forehead. "That seems to have fallen to the wayside for now, but I do have a few customers."

Aunt Louise's eyes met mine. *How do I get out of this mess?* I thought. Then I remembered the dessert. "Let me get that delicious homemade ice cream."

As usual, the females cleaned the kitchen while the men sat on the front porch talking. I wished I could be out there with Melvin.

Once the kitchen was cleaned, Melvin and I spent time together. Aunt Louise and Uncle Ted let us sit on the front porch, but the whole family sat in the living room that was right next to the porch.

We talked and laughed for an hour. Then I heard, "Charley Louise, it's time for you to come in. Mr. Hammond can walk with your uncle and aunt over to their house," Aunt Louise said.

Melvin tipped his hat and said, "Until tomorrow, Ms. Charley Louise Dorsey."

"Are you going to wear that hat all summer long?" I asked. "If you do, it might get a little hot and sweaty."

He turned and walked away with smile.

In White Cloud, there was nothing much to do. It was mostly the same way for whites, but they were more accepted at the beach in White Cloud and at resort areas that surrounded our town. The nearest thing the coloreds had to a beach was some lake area inside of the woods.

We would make up games and race from one tree to another, up and down the gravel road, and up the top of a hill. If we weren't racing, we played baseball across the road in the tall grass with either a wooden bat or anything that resembled one, like a stick, and pieces of cardboard for the bases. This was our rural way of living, and I wasn't sure how Melvin felt about it.

On my days off, I introduced Melvin to the same rural games. To my amazement, Melvin fell in love with them. But it was only his first week visiting, and he was going to be staying for four weeks.

Eventually, I knew he'd want to go to a bar. That's what he did most weekends in Chicago. In White Cloud there was one bar, but coloreds weren't welcome there. The only other bar I knew about was in Baldwin.

Every day when Darlene, Rose and I pulled into the driveway after cleaning houses, Melvin sat in the wooden swing at Aunt Louise's house waiting, greeting us with that big smile.

I'd hurry out of the car and sit next to him on the swing. Aunt Louise would say, "I'm watching you, Charley Louise."

I smiled at Melvin and asked, "What did you do all day?"

He always gave the same answer, *"A little bit of this and a little bit of that."* What that meant, I didn't know, but he was happy and that's all that mattered.

One day he said, "I learned how to fish."

"What?"

"Uncle John and Uncle Ted took me."

I couldn't picture Melvin grabbing worms and putting them on the hook, let alone getting into a narrow boat that seemed to hold only one person, waiting until who knew how long to catch one fish.

"How did you like it?"

"It was all right, but not my favorite thing to do. I for sure wasn't going to gut any of them."

Melvin Hammond and Charley Louise Dorsey wedding picture

I laughed. "It's not all that bad once you get used to it."

He smiled and said, "I think I'll leave that to your uncles, but I'll enjoy eating some of the fish."

White Cloud celebrated its anniversary every summer by having a parade and carnival. Every night Melvin and I went on as many rides as we could. Other times we walked through the carnival doing nothing. It was one of the few times we could spend alone together. We would also sneak walks down the road by the house to hold hands.

It really surprised me that he didn't say anything about going to a bar and drinking. I didn't know if he drank while we were at work or if he didn't drink at all. I never smelled it on his breath. If Aunt Louise did, she would have said something.

Melvin and I sat on the steps at my house. We talked about the future and what I wanted to do with my life and what he wanted to do with his life.

His visit was about to end in a couple of days. I was praying he'd want to stay and figured he was going to tell me that he was thinking about moving here. His eyes seemed softer and there was a different gentleness to his hug.

"Are you all right?" I asked.

"What do you mean?"

"I don't know. You just seem different."

"Charley Louise, look at me." I moved a little closer and looked into his eyes. "Will you marry me?" He asked.

I froze.

"Will you marry me?" He asked again.

"I don't know," I said.

With a high pitched voice, he said, "What do you mean you

don't know?"

"What would you do up here?"

"I'll find something."

I knew my family would have a fit. Aunt Louise would jump out of her skin and Unk would probably take him out to the woods for a hunting lesson.

"We should talk to my family about this first."

"Why? We're adults."

"I know, but ...—"

"Okay, if I ask your family and they say yes, will you marry me?"

"Let's ask them first. You know how they feel about you?"

In an upset tone, Melvin said, "We're grownups, and you're no longer that little girl. You're a grown woman who can make her own decisions. Charley Louise Dorsey, will you marry me?"

I paused, not because I didn't want to marry him. I just knew the family wasn't going to approve. I looked at the ground and then into his eyes. "Yes, Mr. Melvin Hammond, I'll marry you."

He leapt from the steps and hugged and kissed me. I looked over his shoulders to see if Aunt Louise was peeking out of her house.

He wanted to tell the family right away, but I thought it would be best to wait. We walked through the grass path to Unk's house and I turned around and walked to Aunt Louise's house. When I got to the back porch, I watched the man who would be my future husband walk down the path, hoping I had made the right decision. I began to sweat thinking about how everyone would react.

Every girl thinks about when she'll get married, but I wasn't expecting Melvin to pop the question. After he did, I went up to my bedroom and repeatedly said, "Mrs. Hammond."

I laid in bed feeling very happy, but also sad because Mama and Daddy weren't here. I'd have to go to Aunt Louise and Unk and wasn't looking forward to that.

I heard footsteps coming up the stairs. They sounded heavier than normal, as if Aunt Louise was mad.

"Had she found out that Melvin asked me to marry him? I hadn't messed up any house cleaning, had done all of my chores yesterday, and hadn't gone inside my house with just Melvin. Why else would she be walking so hard?

She called my name, but I laid motionless like I didn't hear her. "Charley Louise," she repeated, "wake up."

She stood over my bed and asked, "Why isn't Melvin packing his clothes to go back to Chicago?"

I rubbed my eyes like I had just woken up. "What do you mean?"

"Your aunt said that he wasn't packing."

I wondered if I should keep playing dumb or just let her know that Melvin and I were getting married. Before I could decide, someone knocked at the front door.

Uncle Ted opened the door. There stood Melvin.

"Come in," Uncle Ted said. "What time does your train leave?"

Aunt Louise came down the stairs. Before Melvin could answer, She said, "He hasn't packed his clothes. Melvin, is something wrong?"

He stood motionless and then asked, "Could I sit down for a minute? I want to talk to the family."

It was already hot outside, and it seemed even hotter inside the house while we waited for Unk and Aunt Pearl. When they arrived, everyone turned around and looked at me in surprise. Rose said, "You're about to get in trouble."

Melvin and I looked around the room at the family. My throat was getting drier by the second. "I'm going to use the restroom. Melvin, can I get you a glass of water?"

Before I could take two steps, Aunt Louise said, "No. Get on with it."

Melvin had started sweating. He reached into his shirt pocket and pulled out his handkerchief. I thought he was going to faint. I blurted out, "Melvin and I are going to get married."

The room was so silent you could have heard a chicken lay an egg. Melvin and I looked at each other with fear. Darlene was chewing gum and choked on it. Rose' mouth opened large enough to fit a golf ball inside.

Everyone started talking at once. "What? How will you support her? What about church? You're not a churchgoing man."

All I could think was, *I have to get Melvin out of here, and fast.*

Aunt Louise leapt from the sofa. "Did he force you to say yes?"

"Melvin asked me to marry him two nights ago. He doesn't have a job yet, but he will find one." I asked both of my uncles that maybe they could help him get a job at the factory.

Uncle Ted, the one who I thought would like the idea, asked, "Are you sure about this?"

I looked at him and said, "I've never been so sure of anything. Melvin and I are in love and want to spend our lives together. He's a good man."

Aunt Louise said, "Well, that's still to be proven."

When Melvin and I left to go over to my house, he told me he had decided to find somewhere else to stay … a motel in Baldwin.

We started to make plans for the wedding. Darlene and Rose came over and said they'd help. Even if the family didn't care for the marriage, with the two of them coming over made me feel a little better.

During that summer, I continued to clean houses. Although it was an easy way to make money, I began to wonder if there was anything else I could do. So far, my college degree hadn't worked out in White Cloud. The goal I set for myself was to bring new ideas and change to a community. I began to wonder if moving back to Michigan was the right thing to do or if Melvin and I should both go back to Chicago so I could pursue my dream.

Whenever I started feeling glum, I thought of Melvin and his smile and the same smile came on my face.

One afternoon when I drove home, there sat Melvin on the front steps of my house.

Aunt Louise and Uncle Ted invited Melvin and me over for dinner.

For some reason he seemed different. I don't know what was happening but at dinner is when the big surprise came out.

The dinner started out pretty quiet. Then Melvin started smiling. I looked at him and asked, "Are you all right? Do you need a glass of water?"

"No. Everything is just fine."

"Are you sure everything is still just fine?" Aunt Louise said sarcastically.

"Everyone, I have gotten a job."

We all looked up from the dinner table. "Why didn't you tell me?" I asked.

"I wanted to surprise everyone," Melvin said.

"That's great, Mr. Hammond. What will you do?"

"Well, I'd like to thank Mr. McKinney."

"What does Ted have to do with your getting a job?"

"He made a call to one of the construction companies around town. After I met with them, they hired me."

"Melvin, you're a city man. What do you know about construction?" I said.

"I'll be fine. I like to venture out in the world and learn new things," Melvin said.

Aunt Louise grunted.

"Leave him alone. He found a job, and that was one of your complaints about him," Uncle Ted said.

Aunt Louise grunted again. "We'll see how long this lasts."

"I'll make it work, ma'am. You'll see."

Chapter Sixteen

Meat loaf, vegetables, potato,
rolls w/butter, dessert ... $4.95

It was a hot Saturday afternoon when Melvin and I married. He moved from Baldwin to my house in White Cloud. We got married at the People's Baptist Church. Melvin's entire family came, including his aunts, uncles, and cousins from Chicago.

Melvin wore a standard suit and tie with his brothers standing by his side. I wore a beautiful lace dress. With a few alterations, it fit my small waist perfectly. Darlene and Rose stood by my side.

Since Daddy hadn't moved up North yet, I asked Uncle Ted to give me away. He looked so dapper in his suit.

Melvin and I spent all our time together, walking up and down the dirt road and eating dinner together. But almost three years into our marriage, we started to drift apart. I attended church every Sunday, but Melvin never went. Aunt Louise and Unk weren't pleased and began to nag him, telling him he needed to go to church and that he was starting to hang out at the bars in Idlewild and Baldwin too much.

People were starting to gossip, and my family pressured Melvin even more. The worse thing about it was that since I lived next to nosey Aunt Louise, she saw his car pull into our driveway on Sunday morning right as we were all going to church.

She fussed during the whole car ride to church, and there was nothing I could do but listen. This wasn't the marriage I expected and I was upset. The wedding vows we both took were "for better or for worse." I asked myself is this the worse part?

The church didn't believe in marrying outside of the church, and they also didn't believe in divorce.

What happened to the wonderful days of walking and enjoying each other's company? I thought. I was trying to understand how they had gotten replaced by arguments, yelling so loud the animals in the woods could hear us. It seemed like the house wasn't large enough for us and our family.

A year into our marriage we started having children. The first child, Mike was born January 1948, the second child, Edward was born April 1949 and the third child, Maggie was born 1952.

I needed more consistent work and started working at the White Cloud Manufacturing Company along with a few friends and had to let go of some of the houses I was cleaning.

Mrs. Ollie, the woman who helped Mama and our family by selling us plats of land, lived just four houses up the road and helped me out by baby-sitting. She always had a smile on her face with one gold tooth on the side. I wondered if it was real gold but never questioned her about it.

Behind Mrs. Ollie's house was a gully called Cold Creek that the kids loved to play in. There were snakes and quicksand in the gully, and she told me that she repeatedly stopped the kids from playing in it, afraid they might get hurt, but that one child persisted, Edward. She told me that he was spanked the most.

When I drove down the road and my children saw my car turn into the driveway, Edward and Mike ran like a snake was chasing them. Maggie wasn't far behind. They didn't know that before they could tell me their version of the story, Mrs. Ollie had called me at work and told me the real story.

"What are you boys running from?" I asked.

"We were in the woods and something scared us," Edward said.

"What woods?"

"Back there." Edward and Mike pointed.

I noticed that their shoes were covered with mud. "Is that mud on your shoes?"

They looked down and then the Edward and Mike looked at Maggie.

"It's from playing with water outside. It got our shoes muddy," Maggie said.

"Haven't I told you not to go back behind Mrs. Ollie's house in the quicksand and snake-ridden woods? Since you like the woods so much, I believe the woods behind our house need some tending to." I told the boys to go and get a rake and start cleaning the back area around our crops.

I didn't punish my daughter to rake the woods because she rarely went in the woods behind Mrs. Ollie's house and was probably following her brothers. But, I did make her clean the house. She liked to follow her brothers but was afraid of bugs, so I knew she hadn't gone in the gully.

Mrs. Ollie and I were talking in the house when we heard, "Help! Help!"

I only had three children, but they kept me running like I had more. Their daddy wasn't around much because he worked long hours.

At times it seemed like Mrs. Ollie had the kids more than I did, so it wasn't unusual that we both yelled, "What's wrong out there? Are you boys fighting with sticks again?"

We hurried out the door and saw Edward stuck up in a tree. "Hold on tight to the branch," I said. "I told you boys to stop climbing these big trees." I ran over to Uncle Ted's house and looked for the ladder.

When I got back I asked, "Whose suggestion was it to climb the trees?"

They both blamed each other.

"I don't care who suggested it. Both of you go to the house, get

218

cleaned up, and sit on the couch until I say you can get up."

I turned around to walk into the bedroom. Mike asked, "What if we have to go to the bathroom?"

Without turning around, I said, "I'll decide that when the time comes."

Melvin was still working in construction while Aunt Louise and Aunt Pearl moved on from cleaning houses full-time and found a job cleaning at the Fremont Hospital, the biggest employer in the area. I was laid off from working at the factory in White Cloud.

One day while cleaning the floors, Aunt Louise collapsed at the Fremont Hospital and told me she'd need heart surgery. Her supervisor had asked if she knew of anyone who could take her place and she had recommended me.

Aunt Louise told her that I was laid off from my factory job, was in my 20s, and very educated.

It took two days before her boss and I met to talk about the job. The next day Aunt Louise told me that I should receive a telephone call letting me know that they were going to hire me, but I couldn't mess up or they'd find someone else.

When Aunt Louise's supervisor called, she told me that she was trusting in Aunt Louise's word that I was a good worker and could do the job. She then asked me if I could start next week.

I paused because since I was laid off I didn't need Mrs. Ollie to watch the children as much except while I was looking for work. Melvin couldn't because his work schedule changed from week-to-week.

When I got off of the telephone with the supervisor, Melvin told me that Aunt Louise wanted to see me.

I opened the screen door and it slammed behind me. She yelled from the living room, "Please stop slamming that screen door. Can't you walk in the house without slamming it?"

I entered the living room. "Did my supervisor call you?" She asked.

"She did. I'm starting next week, working second shift but not making the same money you did."

Aunt Louise felt that if I had a chance to improve my finances by working, I should. She believed that I needed to start saving my own money and look out for myself and the kids. She was surprised when I told her that Melvin approved of me working at the hospital. I told her that I'd have to make arrangements with Mrs. Ollie to see if she could watch the children because Melvin had to work and Aunt Louise will be too sick to take care of them.

I was tired of my family butting into my life and not accepting Melvin. He wasn't perfect, but he was still my husband and the father of our children. He worked and put food on the table for our family. I had to remind them that I had married him for better or for worse, and if I chose to talk to him about family matters, that was our business.

The hospital was the largest area employer, but didn't pay much. The hours were conflicting with cleaning houses. I was faced with making a decision of letting my summer job go ... again.

"Charley Louise, remember this is a step up from cleaning houses," Aunt Louise said.

"Maybe I could make arrangements with the houses I cleaned to work on the weekends. I wouldn't be able to keep all of them, but possibly a few. The job at the hospital would only last until you got healthy again," I said. "Melvin and I would discuss the baby-sitting arrangements along with the work schedule and I'll be ready next week."

As I was walking out, she said, "Don't slam that screen door. And don't mess up this job. It's a great opportunity."

220

####

While working at the construction company, Melvin was told about a job working on the railroad that paid much better, but would require him to travel. By this time we had three more children. I started questioning myself, wondering if I had them in an effort to keep my marriage together.

Melvin was coming home less and less. Our arguments got worse *over what time he will come home and his work schedule ... hours.* I tried to keep up with working part-time at the hospital and clean houses.

In 1957 he moved out to a house within walking distance, close enough that the kids could visit him.

Mrs. Ollie watched the children during the morning and Aunt Louise watched them in the afternoon until close to dinner time when I came home from work. Melvin watched the six children, Mike, Edward, Maggie, Thomas, Joe and Mary who are twins, when time permitted and he was home.

The time Melvin spent with his children didn't sit well with my family nor me, but nothing more than what he was about to tell me.

Chapter Seventeen

Lunch menu: casseroles, dessert selection
create your own meal ... $5.00

It was a Saturday morning and for once I didn't have to clean at the hospital or at anyone's house. I was sitting on the front porch and heard kids' voices. I turned around and looked out the window. Melvin was walking toward the house with the kids, who were yelling and kicking at each other.

When he got close to the house, he said, "Louise, I'd like to talk to you."

I wondered what he wanted to talk about and started to think perhaps he wanted to get back together, hoping we could work out the problems in our marriage.

"Kids," I said, "why don't you go out in the backyard and play? And please don't chase the chickens and pigs around."

Melvin and I moved to the back porch to watch the kids. He clasped his hands together and held his head down.

"Did you go and go ...?"

"No. It's not that." He paused.

The way he was acting didn't make me feel happy inside and I didn't see a bouquet of roses.

"I'm thinking of moving back to Chicago ... near my family."

I kept waiting to hear, "I want you and the kids to come with me," but he didn't say that.

"Melvin, we have six children. What am I supposed to do?" I started to swing my hand, at his face, but he caught it and held it in his hand.

"Rural life isn't for me. And your fam ..."

"And you think it's for me, alone with six children? How can you just leave me?"

He stood up and said, "I'm sorry." He walked away without turning back.

That week I cried. I woke up one morning and told myself, *Times will probably be tough, but I need to do whatever I can to make sure my family has food on the table and a roof over their heads.*

At this time, Daddy had moved to White Cloud with his wife. We were renewing our relationship and I found many days walking to his house to talk.

When Melvin left I ran to his house crying, asking, "What will I do?"

After looking out the window at the children I told myself, *You'll have a good cry, get up out of your bed that you'll find yourself laying in and raise those children. They'll need you more than ever now.*

My temporary job at the Fremont Hospital was coming to an end because Aunt Louise was healed enough to go back to work. Although I still had a few houses to clean, I knew it wasn't going to be enough. I had to go back to what our family first did when we moved to White Cloud ... working the fields.

Me and the six children had to learn how to grow together as a family without their daddy. He was no longer up the road. He was in another state, not where I could drive the children up the road for a visit.

This meant we all had to help and bring money into the house. I had never thought this day would come. Memories of my youth overtook my mind. I kept telling myself, *I went to college and earned a degree.* I never thought the day would come when me and the children would be going to the cherry and onion fields together.

Every morning the children and I woke up to join the darkness. We piled into Mr. Tucker's truck with other families and headed to the cherry fields, getting dropped off at home in the late afternoon.

I told the kids, "Go inside and run the bath water. Dinner will be ready soon."

The benefit of being around a family that liked cooking was that there was always food. Sometimes Aunt Louise made extra dinners. Otherwise, I cooked the children's dinner earlier in the week and we ate that. This night, we walked across the yard to Aunt Louise's house.

I was so tired that as soon as the kids were sitting at the table and eating, I flopped down on the sofa. I said, "Aunt Louise, what has happened to my life? Why do I seem to always be going backwards?"

"You're not going backwards. Life is helping you grow up."

"What does that mean?"

"Use this to your advantage. You remember when we picked crops?"

"Yes."

"See if the farmer will barter with you for some of the cherries or onions or whatever you are picking. This could help you with your food. With the cherries, you can make pies. You can use the onions for seasoning. Whatever else you and the children pick, think of it as a meal."

The first time I tried to barter was when we picked cherries. We had worked for the farmer before, so he knew our family. I told him, "I have six children and want to know if I could barter a certain amount of cherries to make pies."

He rubbed his chin for a minute and agreed.

I was able to make four cherry pies and still had some cherries left over. I couldn't wait to tell Aunt Louise.

####

My uncles and aunts helped me and the children a lot. Uncle Ted, Mike and Edward built an addition to our house, a bathroom, which was the demise of the outhouse. He taught Mike, Edward and Thomas how to saw wood and lay down the floor.

An additional room was built at the back of the house. A door was added that became the back entrance to the house, although the room was never completed. We used it mostly for storage.

I bought a large freezer while Uncle Ted, Mike and Edward built a shelving area next to the freezer and in the kitchen. As the family needs grew, so did the house.

We learned how to can collard greens, tomatoes, string beans, peaches, and other food to help get us through the winter months. We used Ball jars, which the kids hated to clean because of the rust that would collect around the top. Maggie, the third oldest, especially hated cleaning the Ball jars or doing anything related to cooking.

I was sitting on the back steps watching the children play and looking at our own chicken coop and pig farm. Maggie was sitting next to me when I said, "Who would had thought I'd be showing you kids how to collect the eggs from the chicken coop and feed pigs?"

"What are you talking about, Mama?" Maggie said.

"It doesn't seem long ago that I was doing the same thing you kids are doing, collecting chicken eggs, raising pigs for the slaughter, and planting our own seeds for greens, carrots, corn, strawberries, and anything else we wanted to eat."

It was starting to get dark, so I told the children to go into the house and get cleaned up for bed. I stayed outside. It was as though I was glued to the top step.

Maggie laid her head against my shoulder when I said, "I remember this moment like it's the first time I set foot on this ground ... when I moved from Chicago to White Cloud as a teenager."

I pointed toward Uncle Ted's house. "They had a chicken coop right over there behind that big tree. That's where I learned how to take care of the chickens. I never boiled them, plucked them, or rung their necks, but I sure ate a lot of them."

Times had started to get tough for my family. The children were growing and needed clothes. It seemed like every day I looked inside my purse there wasn't enough money.

Martha Harris lived up the road from our family. One day she came to visit me and we started talking about how Melvin had left me and the children and moved back to Chicago. "How are you doing financially?" she asked.

"Money is tight. It's a struggle."

She looked at me and said, "What about getting some help?"

"What kind of help?"

"I was assigned a social worker who came out to my house, and she helped me register for government assistance. Once a month I go into town and get boxes of food."

"Maybe I'll talk to Aunt Louise." I frowned. Our family didn't accept assistance. We always helped each other.

"You'd better do more than talk about it. You have six children to clothe and feed. The government assistance program is here to help families like ours. You better apply for the assistance or you might not make it."

Our family is very religious and believes in God. We are hard workers and helped each other survive, but financially, this was more than everyone could help me with. I entered into a world I wasn't familiar with called government assistance—welfare.

When I called to make an appointment with a social worker, a woman with a sharp voice answered. She said, "Meet me at the office at 10:00 a.m. and don't be late."

Uncle Ted agreed to watch Mike, Edward, Maggie, Thomas,

Joe and Mary until we came back. We drove into town to the welfare office.

We sat down at a woman's desk and shook hands. She said, "Hello. My name is Miss Parker and I'll be your social worker."

I wanted to get up and walk out. This seemed so humiliating sitting down talking to a stranger telling them you are poor. I told myself, *This can't be real. I can't be here asking for help like I'm poor, although I am.*

She started asking me personal questions. "How many children do you have? Do you work? How much money do you have? Where is your husband?"

I felt insulted, but knew I needed help feeding my kids. When she asked me to sign the paperwork to receive government surplus food, I took my time.

Aunt Louise looked at me and said, "Charley Louise, you have to do something. We can only provide so much help. You need to sign these papers."

I picked up the pen and held the paper down with one hand and I signed on the dotted line. This made it official. I thought to myself, *I'm going to be standing in a line stared at by everyone.*

The government provided our family with coal for the winter months. We piled it up outside of the house next to the back door underneath the tree. The social worker also took the children to get winter boots, hats, scarves, coats, and gloves.

Once a month, Uncle Ted drove me and Mike, who was about 12 years old, to the VFW Hall in town. We stood in a line with other poor families to pick up boxes of food. Some families I knew.

We walked into the VFW Hall we saw tables with boxes of food. Each table had letters of the alphabet. We walked to the table marked with an "H."

Inside of the boxes labeled "Hammond Family" was cheese,

chopped meat, shredded beef, powdered eggs, powdered milk, and a box of dried flaked potatoes.

We put the boxes into Uncle Ted's truck and drove off. I looked back at the line of people. There were so many who needed government assistance … welfare.

"Charley Louise, are you all right?" Uncle Ted said.

"I'll be okay, but it will take a while to adjust to what just happened."

"Just think of it as free food. You're a good cook. You'll figure out how to make it work with the other food."

When Uncle Ted, Mike and me got home Aunt Louise told us that the pig area had to be fixed. It took me back to the time that I had to catch those chickens because I didn't close the gate. "If it's not one thing it's another," I told myself.

I asked Mike, "Have you ever tried to catch a pig? I remember the time I was real close. I leaped to catch it and got covered in mud."

Mike laughed. "I wish I could have seen that."

"Chickens are harder to catch because they lift off the ground, and this coop is much larger."

I called the other children to come and get the food out of the truck while Uncle Ted showed Mike and Edward how to fix a chicken coop and pig pen. I sat on the back steps watching them. A small pig tried to escape. I must admit that it was kind of hilarious watching them. When they caught it, it squealed so loud that is sounded like they were trying to kill the poor thing. I didn't know who was more muddy—the piglet or the boys.

Miss Parker, our social worker, said that part of her job was to visit our house to check our living conditions.

I was forewarned by Martha that most times the visits would be a surprise. "Make sure no man is in the house except for relatives," she said. "Hide anything that looks new or be ready to explain."

"Thanks for the tip," I said. "I'll make sure that the house is spotless and the kids are clean." I wasn't too worried because I always kept my house clean and the kids clean, too.

The welfare system was strict and the little money I was getting wasn't enough to buy necessities, like clothing, for the kids. Aunt Louise and Aunt Pearl taught me how to sew skirts and pants.

In the summer, I occasionally visited the garbage dumps in wooded areas. During that time there wasn't a Goodwill or Salvation Army. It is a common area where a lot of people, especially well-to-do families, threw away their pots and pans. One day I saw brown bags filled with shirts, blue jeans, dresses, and skirts.

The clothes folded neatly like someone was supposed to put it in their dresser drawer and closet.

My first thought was to cut the clothes to fit the children. Maggie was with me, so I held a dress and skirt up to her. With a little altering, the dress would fit her. The jeans would be the hardest to alter because of the seams. I had to learn how to double stitch.

When I finished the dresses and shirts, they looked brand new. Since Maggie knew where I was getting some of the clothing, I told her not to tell the others.

The social worker visited our home, making sure Melvin or no other man was helping. She thought someone helped purchase the clothing. I told her that my family had helped me buy a used sewing machine.

"Where did you get the pots and pans from?" she asked.

"They were picked up from a dump back in the woods," I said. "I can take you there if you want."

She looked at me with a frown.

If there was anything new or different in the house, there needed to be an explanation. It was humiliating when she questioned how we got these things.

"Uncle Ted is good at building things from wood. He has a wood shop in the back yard behind his house. If something was broken he'd fix it. If we needed cabinets he taught Mike and Edward how to build them," I told her.

This was the way our family lived, getting government assistance and picking crops. I got occasional jobs cleaning houses.

I was hanging clothes in the backyard when Aunt Louise drove into the driveway. She got out of her car and said, "Come over. I have something to tell you. The hospital is looking for another person to clean rooms. I told them about you. They thought it would work out because you've worked there before. They asked me if you wanted the job."

"Are you serious? When can I start?"

Aunt Louise said, "You'll be working with me and should use my name as a reference. The job will start soon, so you'll have to go to the Human Resource Department of the hospital. They'll give you a start date."

I wouldn't make as much money as Aunt Louise and Aunt Pearl, but I wasn't going to complain.

####

Our dog Tuffy started barking then someone knocked at my door. The rest of my family was at work, the children were in school and I wasn't expecting anyone. I peeked out the window and recognized the car. Even though I knew who it was I still asked, "Who is it?"

"Your Social Worker, Miss Parker."

"What is she doing here," I whispered to myself. I opened the door. "Come in and have a seat," I said.

Her eyes scanned the house as she walked through the dining room to the living room. There wasn't anything different in the house than when she came to visit about a month ago.

"Has anything changed your circumstances?" she asked.

"What do you mean?"

"'Money," Mrs. Hammond

I tried to look surprised. I was going to tell her about my job, but at our next visit, which wasn't for another three weeks.

She looked at me and didn't even blink when I said, "The Fremont Hospital hired me. I had the interview only three days ago."

"Why didn't you call and let me know?" she asked.

I looked back to her. "I was going to tell you at our next visit. I wasn't hiding anything."

For a moment, there was so much silence except for the chicken cackling, hog grunting, and dog barking sounded louder than ever.

She wrote in her notebook. "Well, Mrs. Hammond, since you have employment, your welfare will have to change."

"How?"

Still writing in her notebook, her head down, she said, "You won't be able to receive any more money from the government, but you will keep receiving food assistance and clothing for your children."

She got up from the couch. "This will be effective upon your first check from the Fremont Hospital. I'll contact the hospital to make sure that our dates match their dates."

After she left, I closed the door and peeked out the window to watch her. Then thanked the Lord because this was a start to getting off welfare.

Our family still had to pick crops for extra money, but like Aunt Louise and the family had said, "Look at it as free food because you can always barter with the farmers, and your social worker doesn't have to know."

We worked the fields all summer long. When school was in session, we worked the fields only on Saturdays.

Soon a position opened in the Newaygo County Nursing Facility, just up the road from the Fremont Hospital. Mama had always taught me to be ready for opportunity, and this was a better opportunity. I got the job and did laundry for some of the patients.

In the kitchen area, open hospital positions were posted. Six months after I started, there was a position open in the kitchen area—stacking and cleaning food trays. The only stacking I had done was with the dishes at my house, but I applied anyway.

While doing one of the patients' laundry, the supervisor in the kitchen department came over to me. She said, "Mrs. Hammond, you can stop doing that and follow me."

We walked into the kitchen. When we reached the trays, she said, "Here are the trays that you'll have to clean and stack in the proper order. Have you done this before?"

I hesitated. Instead of answering her question, I said, "Oh my God. I've never seen so many trays."

It wasn't a hard job, but it was strenuous. After a while I got a rhythm going, and each day became less stressful. I was on my feet all day with two fifteen-minute breaks and a half-hour lunch.

After work I was so tired. Thankfully, Mike, my oldest son watched the kids when they came home from school. He made sure their homework was done and their clothes and lunches were ready for the next school day. He complained only when the children weren't doing what they were supposed to.

Word got out that a second nursing home was going to be built in Fremont and would be looking for workers. The head cook from the Fremont Hospital and I both applied for jobs and were hired.

One day she came to work and didn't look the same. Her face was white as a ghost. "Are you okay?" I asked.

"No. I need to have surgery. I'm hoping that will fix everything. Will you take my place until I get back?"

I thought, *This couldn't be true. A white lady is asking a colored person to take her place and make up a menu for the whole facility. She must have lost her mind. What'll the new administrator think?* Alice had shown me how to make menus, but I have never put a menu together.

"It's not hard, Charley Louise. How many times have you shown me the menus for your kids that you made up for an entire week?"

"But that's for my family."

"Just think of how you had to create menus to stretch your family food, because if you can cook for six children, you can do this."

We sat in her office and studied every chance we could. Then she'd give me a pop quiz and time my preparation first and then creating a menu. Most menus that would come from the State of Michigan, we prepped.

The first day I had to not only prep a menu but create a menu for the facility, I was both nervous and excited. Cooking seemed to come naturally for me. The more I studied, prepared and created the menus, the easier they became to write.

I was proud of myself. The longer I kept this job and continued to work at the facility, the closer I was to getting my family off government assistance. My next goal was to stop picking crops.

The children told me how embarrassing it was to be paraded out of school by the social worker to get clothes. Then the day came when my social worker said, "Based on your income and work ethic, you will no longer be eligible for clothing allowances from the government."

I jumped for joy, praising the Lord. I think the kids praised the Lord more than I did.

The only thing left was to stop getting food assistance. I did everything I could to take advantage of opportunities at the second Fremont Nursing facility.

They hired a new administrator, Mr. Marshall, who usually worked late. He asked me to prepare him a late night plate of food. I did this for him for about a year. We talked about anything and everything. To my surprise, he was nice and seemed genuine, unlike the other administrator who was cold and didn't speak to many people.

"Mrs. Hammond," he asked, "how long have you been on partial welfare?"

"Too long for me, sir."

"How would you like to get completely off government assistance ... completely?"

"This is why I've been working so hard. I'd like to study more about food service and management, but the main thing stopping me is that I don't have the money."

"I'm thinking of retiring in a year or two. If you want to attend school to study this field of work, you better do it before I retire."

I stopped what I was doing. *Did I hear what I just thought I heard? Was a white man encouraging a colored woman to get educated?*

I turned around and looked across the table at him.

"Since the other head cook took ill, you have been cooking at the facility for some time, now. With that and a recommendation from me, the course should take six months instead of possibly two years to attend the Michigan State Hospital Food Service Supervisors Course."

I started imagining all of the advancements this could bring to my family. We could get off welfare completely.

That Saturday, I was out in the backyard hanging clothes when Martha, my friend came from up the road to visit.

I told her, "Mr. Marshall, the Fremont Facility administrator, spoke to me about going to college to get a supervisory degree. It could help me and the kids get off welfare and—"

"Charley Louise," she interrupted. "Why go to work when the government will take care of you?"

The clothes pin that was between my fingers dropped. I put one hand on my hip and pointed with the other hand. "The government doesn't give me enough money to feed and clothe these kids. Our family wasn't raised to sit on our butts all day doing nothing. I never intended to stay on government assistance, waiting in line to get their food."

"Okay. You don't have to get feisty like you're better than everyone else."

"I didn't mean to snap at you."

Mama had worked hard all her life to make ends meet. Why couldn't I do the same? The only difference was that I was a single mother of six children and couldn't afford to stop working.

Michigan State is located in a community called East Lansing. And, to get there I had to drive on mostly a two-track, rough, and rural route that made it a long ways from White Cloud.

During the next family meeting, I'd bring up the subject of me going back to college. We met on a monthly basis, usually on a Saturday before dinner. At these meetings we talked about everything from how the youngest person in the family was doing to how to fix a roof, cars, potbelly stoves used for burning coal and wood for the winter to what family games we'd play this weekend .

This evening in White Cloud on Rural Route 1 was where I decided to add a little more to my family called "What's happening."

My babysitter, Mrs. Ollie, and her husband were invited to most of our family dinners, since a lot of the times it would include them … mostly babysitting arrangements for me. This night was no exception.

"Charley Louise, do you have anything else to add?" Aunt Louise asked.

Looking around the table, I focused on Uncle Ted. Then I stared out of the window behind him. "There are some classes I'd like to take."

Everyone except for Darlene and Rose dropped their spoons. All eyes looked at me.

"The classes would help me and my family financially, and Mr. Marshall, the administrator at the Fremont Nursing facility told me he would make a recommendation."

The questions started flowing. "Where are these classes? How long would it take? What about the kids?"

"The classes would take six months … approximately, because of the experience I have in creating menus and cooking at the Fremont Nursing facility" I paused. "I'm wondering if the family and Mrs. Ollie could help me by watching the children."

Darlene asked, "Where would your classes be?"

"In East Lansing at—"

"Michigan State," Rose yelled.

"Yes," I said. "Michigan State, in East Lansing."

"How will you get there?" Uncle Ted asked from inside the porch screen door.

The car I have isn't great but drivable. I said, "I'll drive every week and come back home on Friday."

There were stares and silence. Then everyone started talking at once.

I became frustrated and threw the napkin on my lap up into the air. "Don't you want me to do better?" I asked. "I need to make more money than what I'm making. Mr. Marshall is helping me to find the money to go back to school and earn a degree that will surely help my family. There will always be hospitals and kitchens that need help."

After a few moments of silence, the family said, "It isn't that we don't want you to do better for yourself. Lansing is a long ways to drive for a single woman ... a single colored woman."

I started cleaning the kitchen table. Darlene and Rose came in to help me. The rest of the family went into the living room to talk about my decision.

Mrs. Ollie and a few others said that they could watch the kids. Uncle Ted and Unk said they'd make sure the car would get me there and back ... checking it every time I'd return home from Michigan State. Aunt Louise and Aunt Pearl said that they'd help me make dinners every week.

Two weeks later, I told the kids that I was going back to college. They looked at me with the kind of look that says, *She's too old to go to college.* Mike would be in 12th grade, Edward in the 11th grade, and Maggie in the 10th grade, Thomas in the 9th grade and Joe and Mary going into the 1st grade.

Going back to college meant I'd have to quit my job. I wondered, *how was I going to explain this to Miss Parker, the social worker.* I made an appointment for her to meet me at the house. Sitting in the living room, I heard tires on our gravel driveway and a car door close. Tuffy, our dog was barking. I began to get nervous and told myself, Get it together. This is everything you've been waiting for.

I welcomed her into my home and asked her to have a seat. Her back was facing the kids. They peeked around the curtain from the boys' room.

She looked at me and said, "I hear you need the government's help."

"Only for a short time because I'm going back to college."

She looked surprised and tilted her head to the side and asked, "What college and for how long?"

"Michigan State University, for six months," I answered.

"How are you going to graduate in six months? It might take a few months longer, but I will," I said. "Until then, will my family qualify for government assistance … food stamps, winter supplies and money?"

"I'll get back with you in a week to let you know."

In the meantime, while I waited for her answer, I had a family meeting with my children, Aunt Louise, Uncle Ted, Unk, Aunt Pearl, and Mrs. Ollie.

I told them that the Mike would make sure everyone was up early enough to have breakfast and ready for school. Mrs. Ollie would meet the bus and watch Thomas, Joe and Mary. Mike, Edward and Maggie were involved in sports or afterschool programs.

The telephone rang before I could finish talking to the kids. It was Miss. Parker, the social worker. She said, "Your family will be receiving full government assistance again. You must be doing something good at the Fremont Nursing facility because Mr. Marshall gave you a remarkable review. You should receive your first check once we see that you have started college."

I hung up the telephone and sat in a chair. Everyone asked me if I was all right. I stood and jumped up and down, yelling, "I can go back to college. They've granted my application to receive government assistance."

Everyone was happy except for the kids. I reassured them that everything was going to work out fine and they'd be safe. I told them that we live between family and friends who would let nothing happen to them. Uncle Ted and Unk said they could work out a schedule to spend nights with the kids.

One day Mr. Marshall asked, "Mrs. Hammond, did you turn in your application to the supervisory program? I haven't seen it on my desk."

"I gave the paperwork to my supervisor a few weeks ago."

Charley Louise Dorsey setting up cake decorated

One of Charley Louise Dorsey's cakes

"Come to my office and I'll give you another application. When you complete the application, turn it into me and me only. Place it on my desk."

Three weeks later, I received word that I was accepted into the Michigan State Hospital Food Service Supervisory Program. I screamed while in Mr. Marshall's office.

"Are you all right, Mrs. Hammond?" He asked.

Mr. Marshall handed me paperwork and showed me my financial aid acceptance. Tears rolled down my face. I never found out who paid for my education.

I was confident, ready to take on the world, holding the acceptance paperwork tightly in my hand.

As I sat at my dining room table figuring out the weekly menus for the kids, my mind started wandering about what to pack for college and driving directions, the struggles I was up against.

By this time, our family was attending the White Cloud Church of God In Christ, where there was an early Sunday prayer for me and the children. The church services let out after Sunday School so that the whole congregation could have lunch in the kitchen. Church members packed food I could carry with me on the road.

Before leaving, I hugged everyone, telling the children to be good and to mind Aunt Louise, Aunt Pearl, and Mrs. Ollie. I sat the lunch on the passenger seat and pulled out from the church property. In the rearview mirror, I saw Maggie running out to the road waving.

I prayed for the Lord to keep them safe from harm's way until I returned on Friday.

The roads weren't the greatest and I had to stop for gas in a little town nearby East Lansing. I don't know exactly how long the trip took, but it was long enough.

When I arrived at Michigan State, there was a group of women waiting in front of the building. I stood at the back of the crowd. A person yelled, "My name is Joycelynn and I'm your dorm leader. All those who are here to attend the Hospital Food Service Supervisory course, please follow me."

Joycelynn took us to our room assignments. I was in a room with one other colored girl, Joan and two white girls, Judy and Linda.

The rooms had two sets of bunk beds on each side of the room. They stayed on their side of the room and we stayed on our side. This went on for about one month before I decided to say something.

"We have about six more months to live together, and we all come from different backgrounds. Maybe we should try to help each other out."

They didn't like that I had experience. I heard their whispers.

I was sitting with Joan, not saying a word, when someone tapped my shoulder. I turned around and saw Linda.

"Charley Louise," she said, "I think you're doing good, but I can't say that in front of the other girls. I just wanted you to know that."

I stood still. We looked at each other. "This would be our little secret," I whispered.

Mike, Edward, Maggie, Thomas, Joe and Mary, my six children were constantly on my mind. The only telephone in the dorm was downstairs in the front office. Wednesday evenings I'd call home to see how they were doing.

Aunt Pearl said, "Melvin and Edward were fighting and Aunt Louise had to go to school and talk to the teacher because Edward was fighting. Maggie has a stomachache. Mrs. Ollie had no problems with Thomas, Joe or Mary."

"Hello, Mike and Edward. Let me remind you that you two are the oldest and should set examples for the younger children. No more fighting in school."

"Maggie, how are you feeling? Aunt Pearl told me you are sick."

"My stomach hurts," She said.

"Aunt Pearl will write a note and sign my name to excuse you from school tomorrow."

"When are you coming home?" Maggie asked.

"I'll be home on Friday, only two more days."

I then asked Thomas, Joe and Mary how they were doing and they said they were doing okay.

We never hung up without saying our prayers and "I love you." So, I asked Aunt Pearl to hold the telephone so that all of the children could hear me and we blurted out together, *"I love you" and hung up.*

I came home every Friday early enough to meet the children when they got off the school bus and picked up the twins from Mrs. Ollie's house.

"How are you doing, Charley Louise?" Mrs. Ollie asked.

"It's harder than I thought, but I'll pass the course. It's hard being away from the children. I hope they don't feel like I've let them down."

"Your kids don't think that. They love you more than you know."

Over the weekend, I posted the house chores on the refrigerator and prepared school lunches. I baked and cooked all day Saturday and labeled the food with the days of the week. I also made sure the kids had clean clothes to wear to school. They did their homework on Saturday afternoon. My oldest son and I checked it.

I think one of the roughest weekends was when Aunt Louise called to tell me that the water pipe had frozen. The kids had to carry buckets of water from her house to ours during the week.

So, when I got home first I checked out the water pipe problem. Aunt Louise told me that Uncle Ted was working to fix the pipes.

The kids and I headed to the laundromat in White Cloud. We used almost a whole row of washers and dryers.

While driving through town toward home is when I saw Uncle Ted's truck at the hardware store. He told me that he was getting a few parts to finish fixing the water pipes.

What a relief to have Uncle Ted around. Without him and the rest of the rest of the family I don't know what I would have done.

But, for every Sunday for six months, I had the same routine. We had dinner and prayed. Then I'd kiss the children and left for Michigan State, telling myself, *this will pay off. It has to. The children are going through a lot without a mother for a whole week and the rest of the family and neighbors helping.*

Aunt Louise had a good view of our house. She sat in her big chair, watching out the window, making sure the children caught the bus on time.

In 1968, I graduated from the Michigan State Hospital Food Service Supervisory Program. There were approximately 33 in my graduating class and eight coloreds. I stood in the front row for the picture.

Sunday dinner at Aunt Pearl and Unk's house, it didn't take long before the family asked me where I was going to look for work. I told them in the Grand Rapids area, but my first stop was going to be the unemployment office.

I went to the unemployment office on Monday morning, waiting in the car for about a half hour until they opened. I was first in line and sat in one of the hardest chairs until a woman called my number. She asked me to give her three different positions I'd like to work.

I got a call from the unemployment office on Thursday, informing me of an opening at a major hospital in Grand Rapids. If I wanted to apply, I needed to go to the hospital as soon as possible.

It was the largest medical facility that I had ever applied to work at. I met with the Head of Dietary. "Why do you think I should give you a job?" she asked.

I pulled my chair closer to her desk so she could hear me. I looked at her and said in a soft voice, "Any woman with six children who would go back to college so that she could advance and make a better life for her family deserves this job. And I know what I'm doing."

After a few more questions, she said, "I'll have to think about it."

Looking at her I said, "I'll go back home to White Cloud and await your call."

Sitting in my driveway after leaving that interview, I prayed with tears rolling down my face. Mike came outside and knocked on the window yelling, "Mama, a lady is on the telephone from a hospital, asking for you."

When I answered the telephone, it was the Head of Dietary asking, "Could you come in to work tomorrow, Friday?"

"I could be there on Monday," I said.

She told me that would be okay and welcomed me to the staff as the Assistant Dietary Supervisor. I was one of the first, if not first, colored person they had hired in this position.

Although working at Butterworth Hospital was a great start, it was where a parent's worst nightmare happened—losing a child. It was one of the worse times of my life. Mary, one of the twins was only 15.

There were so many diagnoses the doctor gave me, but a major factor was cancer. The lump in her throat became as big as a baseball. I went to Butterworth Hospital and sat next to her bed every day.

The time came when the doctors said, "Your daughter has lived a long and good life, but the only thing keeping her alive are the tubes and medical equipment. You should think about pulling the plug."

This was against my Christian belief. I prayed until the day I had to make that decision—the hardest decision I ever had to make. After Mary's death, I moved out of the family house on Delaware Street in Grand Rapids, Michigan and moved to a two-bedroom apartment clear across town on Plainfield.

My oldest daughter visited from college and my son's were scattered across the United States and spoke to me often.

While working at Butterworth Hospital I heard about an opening at a major nursing home in Grand Rapids, Springbrook Manor. I didn't think the interview went well, but a week later, the administrator called and offered me a job as the kitchen Supervisor.

After working at Springbrook Manor I resigned and started my own business called Louisa's Catering. Unsure which direction the business would go, I prayed every night to bring the right clients to my doorstep.

The first client was for a wedding and making the wedding dresses. From there Louisa's Catering blossomed adding a lunch and dinner menu.

Years later, I retired from Louisa's Catering feeling good, but at the same time a void. I had accomplished a lot in my life, including working with the Michigan State University Extension program. I assisted families on welfare, showing them how to manage a home, prepare food, and make sure their children had good hygiene.

But, now my feet are worn and tired from the years of walking on concrete floors. I moan from the pain. I can no longer make the numerous trips to the various food warehouses at 5:00 a.m., lifting heavy boxes of food. My hands no longer have the strength they used to when I decorated thousands of cakes and cooked hundreds of catering meals over the years.

I asked myself, *what will I do with the rest of my life? What will fill the day's void when all I have known to do all of my life is work? I guess I'm just a poor country girl.*

####

Our mother was not only a hard working woman, raising six children, she was a very devout woman who worshiped the Lord, accepting Christ at an early age. She served on the Missionary's Circle, Mother's Board, and was President of the Sewing Circle. Other accomplishments: The Hospital Institution/Educational Food Service Society, International Bible Institute and Seminary Bible Teacher's Diploma, International Bible Institute and Seminary Diploma of Practical Theology, and received her Evanglist Missionary's license from the Church of God In Christ. Later, she was appointed Assistant Church Mother.

After, our mother passed away, our family found an old handwritten book with some of her favorite recipes. The book has a leather cover, protecting the pages that have turned yellow over time. Some of the recipes included directions and some just gave the ingredients. The recipes have not been tried by the family, but are included with this book.

The Recipes

The church always gave the young people who married a little reception and I started making the cakes for the reception. The very first wedding cake that I made was a three tier cake. Each tier had two layers.

I baked the cake, let it cool, started putting the cake together I broke every layer. I thought I was going to have to throw the cake away. There was a lady who lived in White Cloud, a friend of mine, who came over and showed me how to seal or what we called "glue" each layer back together with thin icing and then froze the layers.

After I froze each layer, I took two layers out at a time to begin icing each layer. That's when I found out that it was better to freeze each layer before you begin to put the frosting onto the cake. This made the icing go on smooth and made the cake moist.

I didn't know how to make flowers so what I did was took marshmallows and rolled them real thin to make my roses and leaves. All the flowers were made from marshmallows. I didn't know how to make flowers any other way. Someone told me that if I used marshmallows that was a good way to make the flowers. I rolled the marshmallows out in the color sugar I made and that made the color that I wanted the flowers to be.

The Pound Cake

We always had a lot of butter, so I continued to make more cakes and one of my favorites was the pound cake. My pound cakes consisted of one pound of butter, 10 eggs, three cups of sugar and three cups of flour.

Whip the butter until it gets really light and creamy. Whip sugar into the butter until it has almost dissolved real good. Put one egg in at a time and whip it. After each egg you whip again real good. Add flour a little at a time and whip real good. There is a lot of whipping or it will not be light, it will be a heavy cake.

Next, put it into a tube pan that is greased, and flour. Shake all of the excess flour out, but remember to not leave any extra flour in the tube. Bake the cake in oven on 325-330, but no higher than that. Put the cake in the middle of the middle rack, if baking one cake. If baking two put the cake in the oven evenly on the middle rack. Take the rack above out of the oven so if it rises it will not touch the top rack.

248

This was my first fruit cake:

Fruit Cake
4 ½ cups flour
1 cup sugar
2 cups raisins
2 cups figs
2 cups almonds or nut meat
2 teaspoons spices
2 tablespoons honey
1 teaspoon salt
6 eggs
½ cup sweet milk
2 teaspoons baking powder

Oven 275 degrees and bake for two hours.

Cocktail Short Cake (9x9 pan)
1 cup flour
1 cup sugar
1 teaspoon baking soda

Sift the above, add one beaten egg, add 1 #2 can cocktail with juice, sprinkle light brown sugar, add nut meat. Oven 350 degrees and bake for 45 minutes.

Sauce for Cocktail Desert
Scant cup of sugar
¾ cup water (hot)
1 tablespoon cornstarch

Cook two minutes. Add two tablespoons butter and vanilla.

German Chocolate (Sweet) Cake
½ package German Chocolate
½ cup boiling water
½ cup butter or margarine
2 egg yolks, unbeaten
2 egg whites
1 ½ cup sifted flour
½ cup buttermilk
1 cup sugar
½ teaspoon baking soda
¼ teaspoon salt

Melt chocolate in boiling water. Cool. Cream butter and sugar until fluffy. Add egg yolks, one at a time, and beat well after each. Add melted chocolate and vanilla. Mix well. Sift together salt, soda and flour. Add alternately with buttermilk to chocolate mixture beating well. Beat until smooth. Fold in beaten egg white. Pour in cake mix. Bake in moderate oven 350, 30 – 40 minutes.

Frosting for Chocolate Cake

Combine ½ cup evaporated milk   1/8 pound margarine
½ cup sugar   ½ teaspoon vanilla
1 egg yolk

Cook and stir over medium heat until thickened about 12 minutes. Add ¾ cup coconut and ½ cup nuts.

Tip: If you bake a cake too high a bump will come up in the middle. That's what creates the bump in the middle of cakes.

After everything was said and done my favorite thing to make was frosting for the cakes. This is the recipe that I used.

Frosting

First I would assemble all of my ingredients. Two pounds of powder sugar, one cup of vegetable shortening, half cup of butter, two third cups of water, half cup of flour, half teaspoon of salt and half teaspoon of lemon, vanilla or almond flavor.

The directions for making the frosting is simple, first you whip the butter until it gets real creamy. Add a third cup of water and continue to whip. Add one pound of powder sugar, half cup of flour, another third cup of water, another pound of powder sugar, continue to whip until it's creamy. This makes enough frosting for an 8 inch and 10 inch cake, two layers each.

Crisco White Icing Recipe

2 cups confectioner sugar   ¼ teaspoon salt
2 tablespoons Crisco   1 teaspoon almond
3 tablespoons milk   or lemon extract
1 teaspoon vanilla

Crisco Cocoa Icing

¼ cup Crisco
1 egg white
¼ cup cocoa

2 cups confectioner sugar
2 tablespoons boiling water
¼ teaspoon salt

I was sitting in church and the preacher was in the pulpit delivering the sermon for the day is when I came up with a cake called the *Scripture Cake.* It wasn't meant to be eaten but these were ome of the scriptures that would be a perfect cake.

Scripture Cake

4 ½ cups 1st Kings Chapter 4 verse 22; 2 cups Jeremiah Chapter 6 verse 20; 2 cups 1st Samuel Chapter 30 verse 12; 2 cups Nehemiah Chapter 3 verse 12; 2 cups Numbers Chapter 17 verse 8; 2 tablespoon 1st Samuel Chapter 14 verse 25; 1 teaspoon Leviticus Chapter 2 verse 13; 6 teaspoons Jeremiah Chapter 17 verse 11; ½ cup Judge Chapter 4 verse 19; 2 steaspoons Amos Chapter 4 verse 5; 2 teaspoons II Chronicles Chapter 9 verse 9

But, this Scripture Cake below is meant to be eaten.

Scripture Cake

2 ¼ or (4 ½) cups flour
½ cup butter
3 eggs
¼ cups sweet milk
1 teaspoon baking powder
1 teaspoon spices

1 tablespoon honey
½ teaspoon salt
1 cup sugar
1 cup raisins
1 cup figs
1 cup almond or nut meat

Bake slowly in moderate oven 275 degrees bake two hours.

Nut Cake

1 cup sugar
2/3 cups butter
3 eggs
2 ½ cups sifted flour
½ teaspoon salt

2 teaspoons baking powder
1 cup milk
¼ cup cocoa
1 cup nut meat

Cream the sugar and butter. Add eggs whole (one at a time) and beat each one into the batter until smooth and light. Add flour sifted with salt and baking powder alternately with milk. Beat in cocoa and nuts chopped coarse and slightly flouned. Bake in shallow tin and frost with cocoa frosting.

Fudge

2 cups of sugar
2/3 cups of milk
3 2/3 cups cocoa

2/3 tablespoons butter
2/3 teaspoons vanilla

Put milk, sugar, cocoa in saucepan, stir and boil until it forms soft ball in cold water. Take from fire, cool, add butter, vanilla and stir until creamy.

Cake wasn't the only thing that I baked. There was also regular food such as:

Scallop Potatoes

For the Scallop potatoes you will need 10 white potatoessliced, one cup and a half of celery sliced real thin, one cup of green peppers sliced real thin and one cup of onions sliced real thin.

After I prepared the potatoes I then gathered the ingredients for the white sauce that would be put over the potatoes.

You would need four cups of evaporated milk, two tablespoons of butter, half teaspoon of salt, half teaspoon of pepper, two to three cups of bread crumbs, (bread crumbs can be made simply by putting some slices of bread in the oven and when they're hard take them out and crumble them up with your hand or a jar), teaspoon of corn starch, and one teaspoon of flour.

White Sauce Directions

Mix the evaporated milk, flour, butter, salt, pepper, and corn starch all together. Whip these ingredients as you cook on top of the stove. Lower the heat until slightly thickened.

Now going back to the sliced potato, layer them, sprinkle some of the onions, green peppers, and celery over the potatoes. Now, when adding each layer put some of the white sauce onto them. Repeat each layer the same way. At the end, sprinkle the bread crumbs on top of the potatoes. Bake them in the oven at 375 for 45 minutes.

Cold Slaw

4 cups shredded cabbage
1 cup shredded carrots
½ cup chopped green pepper

½ cup chopped celery
1 cup Miracle Whip
  dressing

Mix together

Fruit Apple Pie with Dates and Lemon

½ package dates (more if a larger pie)
Grated grind of one lemon

Juice of one lemon
remove pits and slice in
two

Mix with sugar and apples. Continue making as usual apple pie.

Canned Beans

1 pack beans
1 gallon water
½ cup vinegar

½ cup sugar
½ cup salt (to taste)

Boil beans to rolling boil 7 to 10 minutes. Can and seal. When eating put in cold water for a while and then warm up and eat.

THE END